*A fierce hunger that was more than lust
seized him as his bride walked toward him
with slow deliberate steps, her head high,
a smile on her luscious lips, her shining,
bright blue eyes holding his.*

Roland scarcely breathed throughout the entire
ceremony until the priest spoke of sealing their
vows, then looked at him expectantly.

The kiss.

He took Mavis in his arms and kissed her to show
them all—including Mavis—that he knew how
to love a woman. She slid her arms around him
and parted her lips. Thrilled, excited, he forgot
everything except her. When he drew back, he saw
that although Mavis blushed with suitable maidenly
modesty, a little smile played about her lips. It made
him wish they could be alone.

And in the bridal bed.

* * *

Bride for a Knight
Harlequin® Historical #1218—January 2015

Moore

—

Bride for a Knight

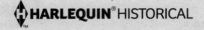

Recycling programs
for this product may
not exist in your area.

ISBN-13: 978-0-373-29818-1

Bride for a Knight

Copyright © 2015 by Margaret Wilkins

Printed in U.S.A.

www.Harlequin.com

Available from Harlequin® Historical and MARGARET MOORE

**Other works include
Harlequin Historical
Undone! ebooks**

The Welsh Lord's Mistress

Harlequin Books

Harlequin HQN

**Did you know that these novels
are also available as ebooks?
Visit www.Harlequin.com.**

For my parents, Donna and Clint Warren,
who've been married for over 65 years.

MARGARET MOORE

Award-winning author Margaret Moore actually began her career at the age of eight, when she and a friend concocted stories featuring a lovely, spirited damsel and a handsome, misunderstood thief. Years later and unknowingly pursuing her destiny, Margaret graduated with distinction from the University of Toronto with a bachelor of arts degree in English literature.

Margaret began writing while she was a stay-at-home mom and sold her first historical romance to Harlequin® Historical in 1991. Since then she's written over forty historical romance novels and novellas for Harlequin® and Avon Books, as well as a young adult historical romance for HarperCollins Children's Books. Her books have been published in France, Italy, Germany, Great Britain, Australia, Belgium, Switzerland, Brazil, Korea, Japan, Sweden, the Netherlands, Russia, Poland and India.

Margaret currently lives in Toronto with her husband and two cats. She also has a cottage on the north shore of Lake Erie in an area that first became home to her great-great-grandfather.

Chapter One

England, 1214

Surrounded by wooden chests packed with dower goods, two young women faced each other in the chamber they once shared. One was dark-haired and dressed in soft, doe-brown wool. The other, fair and lovely, wore her finest gown of green silk, for this was her wedding day.

"You don't have to marry him, Mavis," Tamsin said to her beloved cousin. "Whatever your father's told you, or however he's threatened you, you have the right to refuse. Neither he, nor the church, nor the law can force you to marry against your will. Rheged and I will be happy to offer you sanctuary or take you anywhere—"

"No, please, that won't be necessary," Mavis interrupted, smiling as she shook her head. Tamsin hadn't been in the solar when her father had proposed the marriage between his daughter and Sir Roland of Dunborough. Because *she* had, Mavis spoke with confidence. "I gave my consent to marry freely, Tamsin, and was pleased to do so. I think you're wrong about Sir Roland.

I know what his father and brother were like, but he's not the same."

"How can you be certain?" Tamsin asked. "You've only just met him."

"When we were in the solar with my father, Sir Roland *asked* me if I would marry him. He gave me the choice, Tamsin, and I'm certain he would have released me from any agreement my father had made if I had requested it. More than that, he wasn't looking at me like a merchant wondering if he'd made a good bargain, or with triumph, as if he'd won a prize. He was almost...wistful."

"Wistful?" Tamsin repeated warily. "Sir Roland?"

"Whatever one chooses to call it, I saw something that makes me certain he's not like any other man I've ever met, and that we can be happy. Oh, Tamsin, I realize that to most people he appears hard and cold and arrogant, but when we were in Father's solar, he wasn't arrogant or vain. He was kind, even gentle—very different from the way he is in the hall and vastly different from his father and brother."

"Have you ever been alone with him?"

Mavis couldn't meet her cousin's unwavering gaze. "No, we've never been alone."

That wasn't precisely true, but the one time she had been alone with Roland, he hadn't seen her. He'd been in the stable, talking to his horse in a low, soothing voice, and she'd been hiding.

She had never told anyone about that early morning when she'd been preparing to flee rather than marry at her father's command. That memory was a sweet thing, a secret only she knew, and she didn't want to share it. Nor, did she think, would Sir Roland be pleased if he learned that she'd told anyone he talked to his horse.

Tamsin took her cousin's hands in hers and held them tight as her gaze searched Mavis's face. "You met Roland's father twice and elder brother only once, and here, where they were on what passed for their best behavior. My husband's spent time at their castle. He knows them better, Mavis, and he told me how cruel Sir Blane was to everyone, including his sons. He laughed when Broderick and Gerrard mocked Roland, and called Roland a host of terrible names when he wouldn't strike back."

"But he didn't strike back."

"That's why Rheged considers him the best of the family. But he can fight, too. Rheged saw him in a melee, and while his twin brother fought boldly, almost joyfully, Roland fights to win."

"Surely there's nothing wrong with that."

"Not in battle, I suppose. Yet there is more to consider. Sir Blane openly encouraged the rivalries between his sons, and their animosity. He wouldn't even say which one of the twins, Roland or Gerrard, was born first. That way they would never know who would have the right to inherit should something happen to Broderick." Tamsin looked down a moment before continuing, obviously still dismayed by what she'd done, even though she'd acted to save the man she loved. "As it did."

"Someone must have known, though," Mavis protested, and hopefully, turning her cousin's thoughts from Broderick's death. "A secret like that couldn't be kept in a large household."

"In that one it could, for their mother died in childbirth and the midwife slipped on the steps after attending to her. She died of a broken neck. Some say Sir Blane killed her just to keep the secret, and there are plenty who believe it. Even if it was an accident, if people can believe such a rumor, what does that tell you about the family?"

Mavis pulled her hands free. "There are always rumors about noblemen, and I'm well aware that Sir Blane could be cruel."

"Cruel and lustful. You saw for yourself how Sir Blane and Broderick treated women. What if Roland is the same?"

Mavis flushed, for she'd more than seen how Sir Blane and Broderick treated women. The memory of Broderick's lewd, leering threats were fresh, and the mention of his name alone was enough to fill her with disgust. Nevertheless, she held to her first impression of his brother Roland. "I'm sure Roland's a better man than his father and brothers. You fell in love with your husband quickly, didn't you? Just as you thought you could be happy with Rheged shortly after meeting him, I believe I can be happy with Roland. Otherwise, I would have refused the betrothal, no matter what my father ordered, or any threats he made."

"Then I suppose I must trust your judgment," Tamsin said with a wry, yet sorrowful, little smile, "but if—"

A furious pounding rattled the chamber door. "My lady!" young Charlie called on the other side. "They're waiting for you in the chapel!"

"We're coming!" Tamsin replied before she hurriedly embraced her cousin. "Promise me that if you're wrong about Roland, if he makes you unhappy or hurts you in any way, you'll come to us at Cwm Bron. There'll be no recriminations, no censure, from me or anyone else."

"I will," Mavis vowed, telling herself she was right about Sir Roland of Dunborough, so there would be no need.

* * *

Sir Roland stood straight as a lance as he awaited his bride in the chapel of Castle DeLac. He kept his expression stoic and impassive, although he had never been so anxious in his life. He could all too easily believe that the bride might not appear. He was, after all, his father's son, and that alone would be enough to scare a woman away, even if she'd agreed when the marriage had first been proposed.

Indeed, he'd more than half expected her to refuse. Yet she'd readily accepted, and, even more surprising, had looked at him not as if considering only his title and his wealth, but as if she'd like to be his friend.

Never in all his life had anyone, male or female, sought his friendship. Nor had he sought anyone else's, not since he was a small boy. He had learned early that to seek affection from any creature was to make himself open to loss and pain, and might cause suffering for the object of his affection. He had found and nursed a sick black-and-white kitten back to health, keeping it hidden in the barn, until Broderick had found it and tormented the poor thing. He had pleaded with his older brother to stop, to leave Shadow alone. Broderick had responded by beating Roland until his nose bled and his eye was swollen shut. Shadow had fled the barn and never been again.

After that, he had never outwardly and publicly shown any affection for any person or animal. He hadn't even spoken to the lads of the village, or the sons of the servants, lest they suffer, too.

Gerrard's teasing and mockery hurt far worse than any beating and lingered longer. "Is the little baby going to cry?" he'd said then, and many times after. "Is Rolly going to sob like a girl? Better fetch him a dress!"

And there had been more. "No woman of any worth will ever want a cold stick like you. No woman will ever love you unless she's paid. You have no wit, no charm, nothing to recommend you to anybody except our father's wealth and title."

Now he nearly smiled, envisioning Gerrard's surprise when he returned to Dunborough with his beautiful bride, especially if a woman of such worth wanted him for more than wealth or power. That would truly be a triumph and the fulfillment of a dream he'd scarcely allowed himself to harbor.

"What's keeping the wench?" Lord DeLac muttered, leaning his bulky body against Roland and reeking of wine. Not even his expensive, long blue tunic and gold-linked belt sitting below his belly, or the equally thick gold chain about his neck, could hide the man's coarse nature.

No doubt the lady would be glad to be out of her father's household and it was tempting to think of himself as a hero from a ballad who had come to save a lovely damsel from a monster.

"Women!" DeLac grumbled, a frown creasing his wide, bearded face. "Nuisances, the lot of them."

"Even your own daughter, my lord?"

"Well, she's a woman, isn't she?"

Yes, she was very much a woman, Roland thought as he scanned the chapel without moving his head. Although hastily assembled, given that it had been less than a sennight since he'd arrived and the marriage agreed upon, there was the usual assortment of guests one could expect at the union of two powerful families, including the nobles and hangers-on who'd come to any feast. Also among them would be those who wanted to be noticed and those who would be noticed regardless of their station, like Sir Rheged of Cwm Bron, the husband of his bride's cousin. Few men were as tall as Roland, but he was. Fewer men wore their hair to their shoulders, as they both did. Even fewer were Welshmen, or had that aura of power and command Rheged possessed. Such a man could be a valuable ally, or a dangerous enemy.

No one from Roland's family or household was there, of course. Even if he had wanted his twin brother in attendance, there hadn't been enough time.

His gaze drifted to Sir Rheged again.

He well recalled Sir Rheged's prowess in tournaments. Nobody had been more delighted than he when Rheged defeated his boastful braggart of an older brother, and nobody was more grateful that Rheged's wife, that slender slip of a woman, had rid the world of Broderick. After Broderick had disgracefully attacked and killed an old man, he had then fought and nearly killed Rheged, even though the man was so sick he could barely stand. Tamsin had killed him in the struggle to save her wounded husband.

Rheged had surely spoken of him to Mavis. Perhaps he also owed Rheged for her good opinion.

"If I have to send someone to fetch her again," her father muttered, "she'll regret it!"

"If someone needs to fetch her, I will go," Roland said. And if he found she'd changed her mind, he would leave DeLac at once.

Fortunately, and to his vast relief, the sound of the crowd of villagers, soldiers and servants gathered outside in the courtyard began to grow louder, like the dull roar of ocean waves in the distance. Everyone in the chapel turned expectantly toward the opening doors— and there was Mavis, her white veil not quite covering her golden hair that shimmered in the autumn sunlight, a smile on her beautiful face.

A fierce hunger that was more than lust seized him as his bride walked toward him with slow deliberate steps, her head high, a smile on her luscious lips, her shining, bright blue eyes holding his. Friendship, much as he desired it, suddenly seemed a weak and feeble thing compared to what her smile promised.

"Thank God," Lord DeLac said under his breath.

Roland didn't reply. His happiness had diminished, for he saw that despite her smile, his bride's lips trembled, making him fear she wasn't as confident and happy as she was trying to appear.

That was probably so of every bride, he told himself, and given his family, some trepidation should surely be expected. Once they were wed, though, he would do all he could to make her see that he was not like the rest of his family. He was the dutiful, honorable son of Sir Blane of Dunborough, not the cruel, greedy Broderick or a wastrel like Gerrard.

Joining them at the altar, Mavis stood between Roland and her father as Father Bryan appeared from the sacristy and began to bless their union.

Roland scarcely breathed throughout the entire ceremony. He dreaded someone suddenly objecting or Gerrard bursting through the doors. Mercifully nothing untoward occurred before he put the ring on the bride's finger and the priest spoke of sealing their vows, then looked at him expectantly.

The kiss. He was supposed to kiss his bride.

No woman of any worth will ever want a cold stick like you.

Roland was no novice, no lad about to kiss a lass for the first time. He had been with women, albeit only when natural urges threatened to distract him from his duties, and even then, the coupling had been a simple transaction, money for service provided.

This was his wife. His beautiful, desirable wife, who could make the gods jealous, let alone Gerrard, and—best of all—who had agreed to the marriage.

He took Mavis in his arms and kissed her, and it was no perfunctory, public kiss. It was a kiss to show them all—including Mavis—that he knew how to love a woman.

Until she slid her arms around him and parted her lips. Thrilled, excited, he forgot everything except her and deepened the kiss. He would have kept kissing her had not Lord DeLac loudly cleared his throat and muttered that he was starving.

Roland drew back and was even more delighted when he saw that although Mavis, blushing with suitable maidenly modesty, looked down at the floor, there was a little smile playing about her lips that made him wish the wedding feast was over, so they could be alone.

And in the bridal bed.

Mavis could hardly look anybody in the eye as she left the chapel, not even Tamsin. She had known that there would be a kiss at the end of the ceremony, nor had Roland's been her first. A few bold young nobles had cornered her in the shadows at feasts and put their lips over hers.

Those kisses had been almost childish, like playacting. Roland's kiss was completely, wonderfully different. She had never felt anything like the rush of burning need that seemed to leap from his lips to hers, not even in her daydreams. She'd been completely unprepared for the reality of Roland's embrace and her own passionate response, or the way desire lingered after he let her go.

Until her father pushed past them to lead the way to the hall.

Together she and Roland entered the larger chamber decorated with white linen on the tables, fresh rushes on the floors and new candles in the stands and on the tables. Garlands of evergreen hung from the sconces—Tamsin's doing, no doubt. Their scent filled the air, along with that of the food coming from the kitchen.

"Where's the wine?" her father demanded,

A servant hurried forward with a goblet, and her father couldn't even wait for Father Bryan to say grace before downing the contents in a gulp. His amen was more of a belch.

The rest of the guests, clearly not troubled by any thoughts other than the food, the company and the entertainment to come, ate and drank with gusto, tossing bones and bits of meat to the hounds wandering among the tables. The servants were kept busy bringing more ale and wine, along with soups, roasted meat, pottages and bread, pastries and sweetmeats. As miserly as her father could be, he spared no expense when it came to food and drink, or her dowry, either, to ensure the alliance he craved.

Sitting beside her as stiff as a soldier on parade, Roland ate sparingly and drank less. He barely touched the dainties she'd prepared with her own hands. Thankfully, his manners were impeccable—a pleasant surprise, for his father and older brother had been distinctly lacking in that regard.

Unfortunately, Roland rarely spoke. She had already learned he wasn't a talkative man, but she wished he would say something more in response to her comments and queries than a simple yes or no, especially with Tamsin and Rheged looking on.

Because they were, and because other guests also occasionally glanced their way, she made no sign that she was at all disturbed. She kept up a string of observations about the guests, the harvest, trade, the weather—anything she could think of. She took comfort from the fact that if Roland didn't answer, at least he didn't silence her.

Her father paid no heed to her at all, his attention focused on the food, and especially the wine.

At last the meal was finished. At about the same time her father began to nod off in his chair, in spite of the presence of the guests and his new son-in-law. She glanced at her husband, but if he noticed her father's state, he mercifully made no sign.

She surreptitiously gestured for Denly, one of the senior household servants, to draw near. "Have two of the men assist my father to his bedchamber," she said quietly. "And it's time for the entertainment, so the tables should be cleared and removed."

Denly nodded and hurried to summon Arnhelm and Verdan, two soldiers who'd served in the household in one way or another since boyhood, while a minstrel with curly hair and a weak chin struck up a merry tune. Once an open space was cleared for dancing, several couples moved to take their places facing one another.

Mavis turned expectantly to her husband. "Will you dance with me, Roland?"

"I regret, my lady, that I do not dance," he gravely replied, his expression inscrutable. "You may dance if you wish."

"No, it's all right," she assured him, although her toe began to tap in time to the music. She had always enjoyed dancing, but she was a married woman now, with a husband to please, and please him she would, for if the feelings inspired by that kiss were anything to judge by, he would please her, too. "Perhaps you would rather retire, my lord?"

He turned to her with an expression in his dark eyes that made her heart race. "I would indeed," he said as he rose and held out his hand to help her to her feet. The moment she grasped it, she could feel his strength. Excitement and anticipation began to surge within her.

Every head swiveled in their direction. Suddenly, without warning, without a word, he swept her into his arms and started toward the stairs as if she were one of the Sabines and he an ancient Roman warrior claiming her for his own.

Gasps, whispers and a few chuckles followed her, but she didn't care. Nor was she afraid. She had seen the gentle man residing beneath that stern warrior's visage, and all that she could think of was the night to come and the promise of the bedchamber.

So she wrapped her arms about his neck and laid her head upon his shoulder. Neither spoke, not even when he took the stairs two at a time, or shouldered open her chamber door and carried her across the threshold into the room dimly lit with a candle. He set her slowly down amid the boxes and chests ready for their journey tomorrow.

Still without speaking, he drew her into his arms and kissed her as if he'd waited long years to hold her in his arms and his ardor could no longer be restrained.

Her body seemed to melt with need and, leaning into him, she gave herself up to the yearning coursing through her.

His hand slid up her body toward her breast, cupping it gently, then kneading it, the action unfamiliar and surprisingly arousing, and oh, so different from those other fumbling hands that once or twice had tried to touch her there.

Her need increased yet more when he began to untie the knot of the lacing of her gown and, succeeding, slipped his hand into her bodice. The pads of his fingertips brushed across her taut nipple and a sudden flood of heated longing ran through her, and down, to where the blood began to throb.

She must do something, too. Breaking the kiss, she lifted his hand away and his expression turned to wonder as she kissed his fingertips one by one. Then she reached for the knot at the neck of his dark tunic, untying it swiftly so she could pull the tunic and the shirt beneath over his head to reveal his naked torso.

She ran her fingers over the raised ridges of several scars. "You've had so many wounds," she murmured with awe, and pity, too. "Have you been in many battles?"

"Most were not the sort you mean," he answered, his voice husky.

She bent to press her lips upon the scar nearest his shoulder. "Tournaments and training, too, I suppose."

"Some," he gasped, pushing her gown and the shift beneath lower, exposing her bare shoulders.

There were a hundred other things she wanted to ask, to learn about this man she'd married, but as his lips grazed the bare and rounded curve of her shoulder, she forgot them. All she wanted now was more of his lips and touch. With bold encouragement, she shoved her gown and shift lower, stepping out of them to stand before him as naked as Eve in the garden. She tugged the ribbons from her hair, letting it fall down around her.

She had never seen such a look in any man's eyes as the one in Roland's as he stared at her. It was more than admiration or lustful anticipation. Again she saw the expression that set him apart from every other man she had ever met—a yearning wistfulness that tugged at her heart.

Reaching out, she took his hand and led him toward the bed.

She was a virgin, and he was from a family not noted for gentleness, yet she still felt no fear when she climbed into the bed and held out her arms to him.

He swiftly tugged off his boots and now the wistfulness was gone, replaced with an ardent desire that matched her own.

She turned away when he began to take off his breeches. She had seen him half naked. To see him completely naked seemed…unseemly.

He put out the candle and the chamber went dark. Then the bed creaked as Roland got in beside her.

He began to stroke her hair. "I won't hurt you, Mavis," he crooned in the same soft, gentle voice he had used the first time she had ever heard him, in the stable when he was talking to his horse. She had been fascinated by it then, and she was fascinated—and soothed—by it now. No man she'd met before had sounded like that, as if his throat was made of honey.

Relaxing, she lay still while his hand moved to her cheek, down her jaw and throat, to her shoulder, her arm, her hip, her thigh and back again, the motion teasing and as seductive as his voice, his fingertips barely grazing her warm skin.

She felt the urge to do the same with him, beginning with his hair that curled over his shoulders, to his strong jaw and throat, his powerful shoulders, muscular arm, slender waist and the length of his thigh.

He shifted ever so slightly closer. His hand brushed over her breast and across her belly. Lower. And lower still.

Biting her lip, she slid her hand across his chest, realizing with some surprise that his nipples, too, were taut. Perhaps her attention there could be just as arousing for him.

She lowered her head to flick her tongue across his chest and he moaned softly, proving that he enjoyed that, too. Eager to learn more, she pressed her whole body against him and kissed him deeply. Yes, he was as aroused as she.

He continued to kiss and caress her until she was so full of need, she was ready to beg him to take her.

She didn't have to, for just when the excited anticipation became almost unbearable, he maneuvered her beneath him and then, with almost agonizing slowness, pushed inside her.

She had known there would be pain, and there was—a twinge, quickly forgotten, as he began to thrust inside her. Every motion increased her longing and excitement. Made her feel as if she was seeking some unknown realm of pleasure and passion…seeking… seeking…

Suddenly, abruptly, as surprising as falling from a cliff she hadn't seen, she was *there*, a place where only sensation existed and all else fell away. She cried out, her body arching with throbbing release, a sensation so powerful that only when the pulsing ebbed and Roland laid his head upon her breasts did she recall that he had groaned at nearly the same moment.

Panting, he moved away from her and lay on his back

while Mavis reached for the coverings that had been kicked or pushed away and drew them over their naked bodies. Amazed, delighted, relieved and happy, she lay still awhile, then wondered what was expected of her now. To speak? To remain silent and wait for him to say something? To roll over and go to sleep, or try to?

"Roland?" she said softly.

His only answer was his slow, even breathing. The groom had fallen asleep.

What was that sound? Roland vaguely wondered as he began to wake.

Opening his eyes, he realized at once that he was not at Dunborough. His chamber there was larger than this, and more barren. At home there were no candles on his bedside table, and no chests of clothing save the one... and no beautiful woman wrapped in a cloak standing at the window looking out at the dawn sky.

Mavis. His wife. The woman who had loved him with such passion, such excitement, although they had barely met. Who gave herself so freely, in spite of how this marriage had come about.

He had not come here expecting to find a bride. He had come here to tell Lord DeLac that any plans for an alliance between their two households had died with his father and brother. He'd been about to refuse DeLac's proposal that he marry the man's daughter instead.

And then Mavis had come into the solar.

The moment he had seen her, he had wanted to have her for his wife more than he'd wanted anything in his life, including his family's estate.

Smiling, he was about to get out of bed when he caught that strange sound again, a sort of gasp. It was Mavis, and now he saw that her shoulders were shaking.

She was weeping.

The sudden sharp shock of realization was worse than a blow from a mace or sword. Worse than anything he had felt before. Worse than the beatings he had endured at his father's and older brother's hands. Worse than the worst of Gerrard's mocking torment.

No woman will ever love you unless she's paid. You have no wit, no charm, nothing to recommend you except our father's wealth and title.

Wealth and title and an alliance that her father so clearly desired, now purchased with his daughter's maidenhead?

He was a fool. A simpleton, like the most green country lad come to an unfamiliar town. Despite her blushes and smiles, she must have been forced to marry him, or why else would she be weeping? Shame and humiliation, hot, strong and agonizing, tore apart his joy and hope.

Long ago he had learned to hide his pain. To mask his shame. To pretend he felt nothing, that nothing could touch and wound him, and he would do so again. But first, he had to get away from her, as a wounded beast goes to ground to nurse its wounds in private.

Rising from the bed, he yanked on his breeches, then sat and tugged on his boots.

"Did you sleep well, Roland?" she asked.

He glanced up to see her watching him, her eyes red rimmed and puffy from crying, but a bright and bogus smile on her lips.

Even now, and despite the tears, he wanted to believe she had chosen him for himself alone.

Fool!

If she had been coerced or threatened, he hadn't been aware of it, and it had been done without his consent.

But the wedding was over and consummated. He and Mavis were bound to each other by the church and the law, and nothing could be done.

Their marriage still meant a valuable alliance and a considerable dowry, although his father-in-law was a drunken oaf who would likely never heed a call for help. And Mavis was also Simon DeLac's only child, so he would gain more when the man died, while DeLac had the powerful ally in the north he wanted.

Roland reached for his shirt and drew it over his head. "I trust you can be ready to travel as soon as you've broken the fast," he said, speaking as he would to any underling.

"Yes, I think so."

"I expect so," he replied. He put on his tunic and belted it around his waist with his sword belt.

She hadn't moved, but when he raised his eyes again, he noticed that her feet were bare. So were her ankles.

Was she naked under that cloak?

Desire, hot and strong and vital, surged through him. Memories of the night they'd shared rose up, vivid and exciting.

He must not betray this weakness, for that would give her a hold over him and the power to shame and humiliate him. He had to ignore the feelings she aroused. He must put a distance between them. She must be ever and only just a woman who ran his household and sometimes shared his bed when the need grew too strong to ignore.

His hand on the latch, he spoke without looking back at her. "Since the necessary consummation has taken place, I shall leave it up to you, my lady, to invite me to your bed in future. Otherwise, I shall leave you in peace."

Chapter Two

After Roland had gone, Mavis went to the bed and sat heavily. A lump formed in her throat and her eyes welled with tears, only this time it wasn't because she was leaving the only home she'd ever known and the cousin she loved like a sister.

What had happened to Roland? Where had the kind, gentle lover gone?

She could think of nothing she'd done to anger or upset him…unless he felt she'd talked too much last night. Or perhaps her father's behavior had disturbed him.

It could be that, despite her belief otherwise, he had seen this marriage only as a bargain with her father. He had done what was necessary to consummate the marriage and cared for her no more than that.

As for the tender, gentle way he'd loved her, perhaps that was only because she'd been a virgin.

Maybe he'd found her lacking in their bed.

She knew nothing of a man's pleasure. While her wedding night had been extraordinary for her, perhaps it hadn't been nearly so wonderful for a man of experience. Given her husband's handsome features and powerful body, she was surely not his first.

Then another, more terrible explanation came to mind. She had heard there were men who, having taken their pleasure of a virgin, lost all interest.

No, that could not be so with Roland. She would have seen some hint that it was only her body he wanted. She had encountered that sort of lust often enough before, including from his older brother, and would certainly have recognized it.

She glanced at the bed and noticed the small spot of blood on the sheet. Yet another explanation leaped into her mind, one much more in keeping with her perception of the man in the solar. If he thought he'd hurt her, he might be angry with himself, not at her, and that would explain his parting words to her, too.

Although she was a little sore, the experience had been no more painful than pulling a hangnail, and she must find a way to tell him, once they were alone.

And she would know, by how he acted then, if he had married her because he wanted *her*, as she fervently hoped, or if he saw the marriage only as a means to make an alliance with her father.

A short time later, Roland stood in the courtyard with his arms crossed and his weight on one leg. The wagons were loaded with Mavis's dower goods, the ox to pull it was in the shafts, his horse and her mare were saddled and ready and the morning meal concluded. The clouds parted to reveal the sun, which began to burn off the remaining frost on the cobblestones. A light breeze blew, enough to ruffle his hair and the pennants on the castle walls, and redden the noses of their escort as they, too, waited to be on their way.

"You're a lucky man."

Roland half turned and found Rheged of Cwm Bron at his elbow. "I agree," he said, meeting the man's gaze steadily, keeping his voice even.

"Mavis is a kind and sweet young woman," Rheged continued. "My wife loves her like a sister and we both want Mavis to be happy."

The man's deep voice was genial, but there was a look in his eyes that told Roland this was something more than placid observation. Nevertheless, he replied in the same manner as before. "As do I."

"I'm glad to hear it. We'd be upset otherwise."

Again there was more to the Welshman's comment than just the words. But wordplay and hints and insinuation were the language of cheats and deceivers, and Roland would have none of that. "If you have something of import to say to me, my lord, speak plainly."

"Very well," Rheged replied. "Tamsin tells me you gave Mavis the choice of accepting the betrothal or not, and she accepted. That's all to the good. But Mavis is young in the ways of the world, and she's had enough trouble already with her father, so I hope you'll treat her with the kindness and respect she deserves."

The Welshman spoke as if he were a brute, no better than his father or older brother. He had hoped for better from Rheged, and he wondered what the Welshman might have said about him. If Mavis had been forced to accept the marriage and her cousin's husband had said derogatory things about him, no wonder she'd been crying.

"Considering that you abducted the woman you have taken to wife," he said with a hint of the ire he felt, "it strikes me that you are hardly in a position to offer any man advice on how to treat a woman."

Rheged's eyes flared with annoyance, but his tone was still genial when he replied. "Then don't consider it advice. Consider it a warning. If you or your brother hurt her in *any* way, you'll have me to answer to."

"I do not take kindly to threats, my lord, even from relatives," Roland returned.

The door to the hall opened and Lord DeLac came reeling out of the hall, barely able to stand. He wore the same clothing he had the day before, but the finely woven tunic was now stained with bits of food and wine and his beard was dotted with crumbs. His hair was unkempt, his full face florid, and he was clearly the worse for wine. Again.

Nevertheless, for the first time in their acquaintance, Roland was glad to see him, for his presence silenced Rheged. He didn't take kindly to being threatened and he didn't want to come to blows, not in his father-in-law's courtyard.

"Ah, Sir Roland!" Lord DeLac cried. "There y'are! Time to go, eh? Now you've got the dowry and my daughter, off you trot!"

As if all he'd wanted to do was conclude a bargain. No doubt that was how Lord DeLac thought of the marriage.

Roland had to suppress the temptation to dunk the greedy, drunken lout in the nearest horse trough.

"Mavis!" DeLac bellowed, turning around in a circle and looking up as if he expected to see her on the wall walk. "Where are you, girl? Your husband is waiting!"

"Here, Father!" Mavis answered, appearing at the kitchen entrance and hurrying toward them with her cousin at her side.

His beautiful young wife wore a simple brown traveling gown and was shrouded in a thick brown cloak with a rabbit fur collar. Her attire was almost nunlike and her demeanor that of a fresh young maiden—quite different from the bold wanton in his bed last night.

He'd never experienced such thrilling excitement, such perfect satisfaction, in any woman's arms. He had been sure she felt the same, until he'd seen those devastating tears.

Surely, he told himself, if she'd been forced to take him for her husband, she wouldn't have been so willing and wanton—but why then had she been crying? He couldn't think of anything he'd said or done to otherwise upset her, except make love to her, his exciting, virginal—

She had been a virgin. No doubt there'd been some pain, something he hadn't yet considered, and perhaps enough to cause her tears.

Mavis came to a breathless halt beside his horse and gave him a bright smile. "I'm ready now."

His gaze searched her face as he tried to discern if she was sincerely happy, or only pretending to be.

If she was pretending, she was very good at it.

"About time, too!" her father exclaimed. "Take her, Roland, and safe journey to you both. God's blood, it's freezing out here!"

With that, Lord DeLac hurried back inside without so much as a backward glance at his only child. Meanwhile, Rheged's wife hurried to embrace Mavis while Rheged continued to regard Roland with a look that might have frozen the very marrow of a man's bones, if it were anyone but Roland. He had been subject to intimidation his entire life, and by men harder and crueler than Rheged of Cwm Bron could ever be.

"Godspeed and may you have a safe journey!" Tamsin said to Mavis fervently. "Never forget you will always be welcome at Cwm Bron."

Mavis hugged her cousin tightly. "I'll remember."

"Come, my lady, let us go," Roland said, moving to help her mount her horse.

"As you wish, my lord," Mavis replied, giving him another brilliant smile.

He doubted anyone could feign such sincere happiness so well. He must be right to think that her pain was merely physical, and if so, that hurt would soon heal.

If only there were some way to find out if that was the sole cause of her tears! He couldn't talk to a woman with ease, as Gerrard did.

Once Mavis was in the saddle, Tamsin ran up to his wife's horse and placed her hand on Mavis's boot. "Remember what I said!" she cried. "Anything you need, you have but to ask! If you require our help, send word at once."

She made it sound as if Mavis was going to her doom, and his hope began to fade that he'd found the cause of her tears. Yet whatever the reason for this marriage, he thought as he raised his hand to signal the cortege to depart, he was still Sir Roland, Lord of Dunborough, and his bride would make him the envy of any man who saw her.

Especially his brother.

The day continued to be fine, if chilly, and Mavis would have enjoyed the ride, save for two things: her husband rode several paces ahead as if he didn't want to talk to her, and the men of their escort riding behind her talked far too much.

"S'truth, I wish I was back at Castle DeLac," Arnhelm muttered. He was a tall, slender soldier, bearded and the leader of the escort. "Look at him, riding like he's got a spear up his arse. What kind of lord comes all the way from godforsaken Yorkshire by himself, anyway?"

"One from Dunborough," his short, stocky brother and second in command, Verdan, answered. "And now, God save us, we got to go back with him!"

"This is a bad time to be heading to Yorkshire, all right. At least we don't have to stay there. Mind you, *she* does, poor thing," Arnhelm said, nodding at Mavis. "It ain't right, this marriage."

"Aye, he don't deserve her. He's a hard man, and her as sweet and gentle as a lamb."

Mavis kept her gaze on her husband and tried not to listen, but it proved impossible. Arnhelm had too loud a voice. For his sake, she was rather glad her husband was so far ahead, so he couldn't hear the men's conversation. And Roland did sit in the saddle as if his back would break rather than bend if he tried to lean forward.

Determined not to listen to Arnhelm and Verdan anymore, she moved her horse forward until she and Roland were side by side. He might not want to talk to her, but she would speak to him.

She also didn't want the soldiers returning to DeLac with tales of a silent bride and a brooding groom. While her father might not care, Tamsin would worry. "How much longer will we be traveling today, my lord?"

For a moment, she thought he wasn't going to answer, but he did.

"A few hours." He gave her a sidelong glance. "Unless the riding is too tiring or uncomfortable for you."

"Oh, no. I have spent many a happy hour in the saddle. I'm not sore at all."

He glanced at her again, then looked away just as

quickly, and she wondered if he understood what else she was saying. She didn't want to come right out and tell him he hadn't hurt her much, not with the escort so close. Instead, she tried a different subject. "If we make good time, how long until we reach Dunborough?"

"Six days."

"As long as that?" She had been anticipating three days, four at the most if the weather turned bad.

"The ox cannot go quickly."

She should, of course, have taken that into consideration. "And your castle? Is it as large as DeLac?"

"Larger. It's one of the strongest in the north," he replied, and although his expression didn't change, she could hear his pride.

"The household must have many servants," she ventured, wishing she'd taken on more of Tamsin's duties in DeLac before her cousin had married.

"Enough."

"Come, my lord," she gently chided. "Can you not be more specific? I am to be chatelaine, after all."

He frowned. "I'm not certain. Eua can tell you. Or Dalfrid."

"And they are?"

"Eua has been serving in the household since before I was born, and Dalfrid is the steward."

While Roland's answers were short and to the point, at least he was talking to her, and she took that as an encouraging sign. "I understand you have a twin brother. Does he live in the castle, too?"

"Gerrard is my garrison commander."

"I look forward to meeting him. How fortunate you are to have someone you can trust in that position."

"I trust him to look after his own interests, and that means protecting Dunborough. And the men like him."

"Then I'm sure I'll like him, too."

"Most women like Gerrard," Roland brusquely replied. "He can be a very charming fellow when it suits him."

Given the slightly hostile tone of his response, Mavis answered cautiously. "I have sometimes wished for a brother."

"You are close to your cousin, are you not?"

"She's like a sister to me."

"You set some store on her opinion, then."

"Of course, as your brother's must influence yours."

"I don't care what my brother thinks."

There could be no denying that Roland was absolutely, grimly sincere. And yet… "Except in matters of defense of the castle, I assume."

"Should Dunborough need to be defended, I will take command."

"What, then, does Gerrard do?"

"He assigns watches and trains the men."

She was about to suggest that wasn't much responsibility for the lord's brother when Roland said, "I should perhaps warn you, my lady, that my brother's favorite pastime has always been to mock me."

She simply couldn't imagine anyone mocking Roland. "No one likes to be teased. Some of the young men who came to DeLac were apparently under the misapprehension that I would enjoy such cruel sport. I quickly let them know that if they mocked anyone, and especially Tamsin, I wouldn't even look at them. I would never make sport of you, my lord, or think kindly of anyone who did."

When Roland didn't answer, she decided it might be best to speak of something other than his brother. "I didn't think my father was going to let me take Sweetling. That's my mare. Don't you think she looks sweet, my lord?"

"She's a fine horse," he allowed, his tone somewhat lighter, although his expression was still grim.

"Yours is beautiful. Hephaestus is his name, is it not?"

"Yes."

"That's unusual. Wasn't Hephaestus a god?"

"The blacksmith of the gods, and lame."

"Oh, yes, I remember now! He's also called Vulcan, isn't he? Did you name him Hephaestus because he's as black as the smoke from a smith's forge, or a blacksmith's anvil?"

"I like the name, and he's a clever beast."

"You sound proud of him."

"He is the first horse I have ever truly owned. The first I chose for myself." He slid her another glance, not so sharp or searching. "Despite my father's wealth, I've had little I could call my own."

"I can say the same," she replied, thinking they had this in common, at least. "That's why I thought he wouldn't let me have Sweetling."

Roland raised his hand to halt the cortege. They had come to a bridge over a swiftly moving, narrow river. Tall beeches and aspens lined the banks, and a part of the edge sloped down to the water. The trees were bare, the ground hard and one bold squirrel chattered at them from above.

"We'll rest and water the horses here," Roland announced, sliding from the saddle.

"I'd like to walk about a bit," Mavis said, looking at him expectantly.

He helped her dismount, then abruptly turned and marched off along the bank of the river, away from where Arnhelm, Verdan and the rest of the men were watering the horses and ox.

It was too cold to simply stand and wait, so Mavis gathered up her skirts and followed her husband. His pace was brisk until he came to a halt some distance from the others in a pretty spot shielded by graceful willows and where the clear water rushed over the rocks beneath.

He appeared startled when he saw her. "You should stay with the wagon," he said. "There is a wineskin and some bread and cheese."

"I'd rather be with you."

To that, he said nothing. But since he didn't appear angry and he didn't send her back, she said, "Isn't it a pity winter has to come? I wish it could always be summer."

"I like the cold."

"Because you're from Yorkshire, I suppose. I've heard the dales are quite windy and barren."

"And cold."

Clearly he didn't care if he was painting an attractive picture of Yorkshire or not. Nevertheless, he was talking.

"If Yorkshire is cold, I hope your castle will be warm." She decided she would have to be bold if she were to learn if he desired her, or had only wed her for the alliance. "Although if it's chilly inside as well as out, we'll simply have to spend more time under the blankets."

She might have been wrong, but she thought his cheeks turned pinker, as if he was blushing. She would never have guessed that a man like Roland would blush, yet apparently he did.

But he was also frowning, his eyes hard as stone, and he very sternly said, "It will be warm enough."

Such an answer and such a look might have dismayed

and silenced her before, but because of that blush, she dared to say, "Nevertheless, we shall have to spend some time beneath the blankets if we're to have a child."

"A child?" he repeated, as if such a thing had never occurred to him.

"You do want children, don't you, my lord?" she asked.

"What nobleman doesn't want an heir?" he replied. He tugged down his tunic. "You took me aback. Having only recently become the lord of Dunborough, I hadn't yet considered an heir of my own."

She took some comfort from the knowledge that he hadn't married her only to produce an heir.

"I'm happy to hear you want a child, my lord," she said softly. There was a chance, of course, that the child could be a girl, but she was not going to suggest that. Once, in a rage, her father had told her that daughters were useless except in trade, and she didn't want to learn that Roland shared the same opinion.

"Can I assume then, my lady, that you also wish to have children?"

"Yes." She took a chance that she might hear something that would upset her and added, "A child will also strengthen the alliance between our families."

"I had not considered that."

Did that mean he hadn't considered that a child would strengthen the alliance, or that he hadn't considered the alliance at all when he asked her to be his bride?

He studied her face with even more intensity. "So you will do your duty?"

"I didn't marry you because of duty," she said firmly. "I wed you because I wished to. As for why you married me—"

She fell silent and waited for him to answer. To hear from his own lips why he had married her.

He didn't answer, not with words. He gathered her into his arms and took her lips with an almost desperate passion, that wistful yearning made manifest with his embrace.

As she eagerly responded, she could believe no alliance or the need for an heir had brought them together and made them man and wife. They were united by another kind of need—for affection, for respect, for security in a world that was too often volatile and uncertain.

She put her hands on his broad chest and slowly slid them to his shoulders, wrapping her arms about his neck and leaning into his body. Her legs turned to water when he pressed her body closer to his and slid his tongue between her open, willing lips.

It didn't matter where they were, or that the air was cool, for she was hot with need. Gasping, anxious, ready and willing, she broke the kiss and hurried to untie the drawstring of his breeches while he moved her so that her back was against the wide tree trunk.

The instant he was free, she grabbed his shoulders and kissed him again. He pulled up her skirts and, with his hands beneath her buttocks, lifted her. She wrapped her legs around him and uttered a soft cry of pleasure as he plunged inside her. There up against the tree they made love like wild, primitive creatures with but one need and that was to mate.

In a few short moments she buried her face in his neck to stifle the exclamation that burst from her throat, while he gripped her tight and made a sound like a cross between a growl and a gasp.

"My lord!" Arnhelm called a short distance away.

They stilled at once.

"My lord, the horses are watered!"

Hot, disheveled, embarrassed but not ashamed, Mavis slowly slid to the ground. Red-faced and silent, Roland turned away to tie his breeches while she adjusted her skirts and tucked a stray lock of hair back into place.

Then he held out his arm to escort her back to the cortege as if they'd done nothing more than admire the view.

"Good God, you don't mean t'say they did it right there?" Verdan demanded in a shocked whisper as the cortege once again began to move toward Yorkshire.

"Aye, they did, or I'm blind and deaf to boot," Arnhelm replied equally quietly.

"Poor thing!" Verdan said, looking at Mavis with pity. "He's no better than an animal."

"Aye, like that father and brother of his. I remember when they came to DeLac before. The old goat was after anything in a dress and his son—well, let's just say the day he died was a good day for the rest of the world." Arnhelm looked around to make sure the other men couldn't hear. "I tell you, Verdan, I don't like this at all. Our sweet lady given to that lout. Neither does Lady Tamsin or Sir Rheged. I'd be willing to wager a month's pay they'll gladly come and fetch her, husband be damned, if they think she's unhappy. Let's keep our eyes open and if we see more amiss, we can tell them when we return, and save Lady Mavis."

"I'm willing," Verdan replied with a nod of his helmeted head.

After making love with Roland by the river, Mavis was certain he would be more congenial when they returned to the cortege and resumed their journey.

Unfortunately, that did not happen. He again rode several lengths out in front of her and the rest of the men.

She told herself not to make too much of that. He might be tired, or anxious to find a night's lodging. As for not conversing, it could merely be that he was a naturally reticent man who wasn't used to having a wife, just as she was no more used to having a husband. And if a tendency to silence was the worst that could be said of him as a husband, that was no great hardship.

As the afternoon wore on, however, she began to wonder if he had another fault—a disinclination to consider that if he was not weary, others might be. She was very tired and her back was starting to ache. The soldiers behind her, even Arnhelm and Verdan, had long since ceased talking, too.

Yet whenever they passed an inn or monastery where they might take shelter for the night, he continued past.

Just when she had decided that something *must* be said lest they be benighted on the road, they arrived at an inn with a large yard surrounded by a willow fence. This time, Roland raised his hand to halt their cortege.

A plump man wearing an apron immediately appeared at the door and bustled toward them, shooing geese and chickens out of the way, flapping his arms as he went.

"Greetings, my lord, my lady!" he cried, gesturing for them to enter. "Welcome! Welcome!"

"We seek shelter for the night," Roland replied without dismounting.

"Of course, sir, of course. My wine and ale and beds are the best for miles, and my wife the best cook for miles, too!"

"How much?"

The innkeeper ran a swift gaze over Mavis, the soldiers and the wagon that came creaking to a stop behind them, then named a price that struck Mavis as extravagant even if Roland was obviously a man of means.

Apparently Roland agreed with her assessment. "That is far too much for one night's lodging."

The innkeeper ran his fingers over his upper lip. He named a somewhat lesser fee.

Roland shook his head.

The man quoted another price, lower still.

Roland raised his hand as if to signal the cortege to move on. Surely he couldn't be in earnest, she thought with desperation. It would be dark soon!

"Wait!" the innkeeper cried with a look of panic. He named another price, lower by several pence. "And that is truly the best I can do, sir!"

"Acceptable," Roland replied, "provided there is a separate chamber for my lady and me."

"Of course!" the innkeeper cried, and finally Roland swung down from his horse.

"We are honored to serve you, my lord!" the innkeeper enthused. He gave Mavis a broad smile. "Anything you need, you have only to ask, my lady! This way if you please, my lady!"

He waited while Roland, his expression unreadable, raised his arms to help her down. Holding on to his broad shoulders, she slid to the ground and, given the company, tried not to be aware of his powerful body. "Thank you, my lord."

He only nodded.

Nevertheless, she tucked her hand under his arm as the innkeeper bustled ahead of them into the largest building made of wattle and daub, with a roof of thatch. She could also see a large barn and stable behind the inn.

Meanwhile Arnhelm, Verdan and the soldiers of their escort dismounted and servants appeared from inside the stables to help them with the horses, the wagon and the ox.

The taproom of the inn was a low-ceilinged chamber, the beams dark with age and smoke from the fire in the central hearth. Tables and benches were arranged about it, and rushlights added a little more illumination to the dim room. Sawdust and rushes were on the floor to soak up any spills of food or drink, and she could smell the fleabane sprinkled on them, too.

"The wife's made a fine beef stew, my lord," the innkeeper said as he pulled out the bench at the table closest to the fire.

The aroma wafting through the door across the room proved that beef was cooking somewhere.

"Bring some for my wife and me, and the men, too," Roland said as they took their seats on the bench.

"Aye, my lord, aye!" the innkeeper exclaimed, and he hurried through the door that must lead to the kitchen.

Despite the man's assurances, however, it seemed his wife was not so willing to guarantee the stew.

"Are you mad?" a woman exclaimed. "Stew for twenty? We've not enough meat, you great lummox!"

"But it's a *lord* and a *lady*," the innkeeper replied just as loudly, either unaware or too upset to realize they could be heard in the taproom as easily as if they were standing beside the hearth.

"So of course you insist they stay and you play the happy host while it's up to me to feed them!" the woman retorted.

"It seems we've caused a spat," Mavis remarked,

untying the drawstring of her cloak. "Obviously he sees some profit flying out the door if he can't provide enough stew and she doesn't think they can. Fortunately, such a meal can be stretched with more vegetables and gravy, as she ought to know. I suspect, then, this is the sort of repeated argument that husbands and wives sometimes have."

When Roland didn't reply, Mavis folded her hands in her lap. "I could be wrong, of course."

"I have little experience of husbands and wives," Roland admitted, albeit with cool dispassion. "My mother died giving me birth, and the women who took her place in my father's bed were not wives."

Although this wasn't pleasant information, Mavis was glad to hear it nonetheless, because Roland chose to share it. "My mother died when I was little, too. I don't remember her at all. And my father, for all his faults, never brought his mistresses into the household."

If Roland was going to reply to that, he never got the chance, for the innkeeper returned with their wine, and he was not nearly so merry. "Forgive me, my lord, but my wife fears that we aren't going to have enough stew for all your men."

Mavis didn't want to be the cause of a quarrel, nor did she wish to travel any more that day, so she rose from the bench. "If you'll excuse me, my lord, and if you don't mind, innkeeper—"

"Elrod's the name," the innkeeper blurted, then flushed even more.

"Elrod, I will have a word with your good wife. Perhaps I can offer some suggestions to help with the meal."

Elrod's eyes grew as round as a wagon wheel. "Thank you, my lady, but I don't think—"

"I'm sure there's something that can be done, and I'll try not to upset her," Mavis assured him as she swept her skirts behind her and headed for the kitchen.

The innkeeper, half aghast, half impressed, looked warily at the tall, grim knight sitting in front of him.

The man might have been made of wood for all the emotion he displayed.

"I'll, um, I'll get more ale. It's in the buttery," Elrod stammered before hurrying away through another door.

Roland would willingly have laid out good coin to see what was happening in the kitchen, although he would never admit it. This had truly been a day of surprises, and finding out his wife was willing to offer her aid in the kitchen of an inn was the least of them.

Far more interesting was her assertion that she hadn't married him out of duty, but because she wished to.

It seemed Gerrard had been wrong, and he had found a woman who wanted him…if her words and her smiles and her passion were to be believed.

Yet how had he responded? Like some lust-addled oaf, taking her with no more gentleness than if she'd been a camp follower on a long campaign.

He had been ashamed ever since—too ashamed to even ride beside her. He should have shown more restraint and dignity. They were nobles, after all, not peasants. Worse, he had behaved as if he were as incapable of self-control as his father or his brothers.

He was not his father. He wasn't Broderick. He could control his base urges. He understood denial, knew how to suffer in silence and betray no hint of what he was actually feeling.

So until he could be sure that she was being honest and sincere, he would keep his distance.

And be safe.

* * *

Meanwhile, Mavis discovered chaos in the kitchen. A pot containing what appeared to be soup or stew was bubbling over into the fire in the hearth. A harried-looking woman likely in her late twenties, her face long and narrow, her hands sinewy and work worn, was desperately chopping leeks. At a small, rickety table near the washing trough was a serving girl kneading a mass of sticky dough. Baskets of peas and beans were on the floor, and there was a stack of wood near the back door.

"Close the door, Elrod, for God's sake!" the woman exclaimed without looking up from her task. "And send that lazy, good-for-nothing stable boy to the village to see if he can get more bread. There's barely a loaf left and what Ylda's making won't have time to rise before—"

She glanced up, saw Mavis in the doorway and nearly took off a finger. "Oh, my…my lady!" she cried, swiftly setting down the knife and wiping her hands on her apron. "What are you…? Can I do…?"

"I came to see if I could be of any assistance, since we're such a large party."

"There's enough for you and his lordship, of course!" the woman replied. "We can make more soup for the men. But we don't have enough bread, I'm sorry to say."

Mavis ventured farther into the room, which was, she noted with relief, clean. "You could make lumplings. That is what we do at DeLac when there isn't enough bread."

The woman regarded her warily. "Lumplings? What are they, my lady?"

"You make them out of flour and water," Mavis said, starting to roll back her cuffs. "Then you put them on top of the stew or soup when it's nearly done cooking and cover it all with the lid for a short time."

"If you'll tell me what to do, I'll be glad to try, my lady, and thank you!" the innkeeper's wife said with genuine gratitude and not a little shock as Mavis took down an apron hanging on a peg beside the door and began to put it on.

"There's no need for you to do anything, my lady," the woman protested. She nodded at the girl who was staring at Mavis as if she'd offered to buy the entire establishment. "Ylda and I can make them, if you'll tell us what to do."

"I don't mind," Mavis replied. "And you are?"

"Polly, my lady. My name's Polly and this is Ylda," she added, gesturing at the girl, who was still staring, eyes wide, mouth agape.

"Polly, Ylda," Mavis acknowledged with a smile. "After a long day in the saddle, I'm happy to stand a bit."

What she did not say, but certainly felt, was that it was a delight to be in the kitchen. At home, Tamsin had managed the household so thoroughly, she had had little to do and plenty of time on her hands. While she could sew and embroider and did so often, she most enjoyed helping in the kitchen. She had a knack for pastries, and the cook had let her create several special dainties for her uncle's feasts when Tamsin was otherwise occupied.

Indeed, being in a kitchen and working with flour, even if it was only for something as simple as lumplings, was like being back home, happy and busy and peaceful, if only for a little while.

Chapter Three

Later that evening, Roland strode across the muddy yard to the stable. His wife had retired after an excellent meal of beef stew with warm, soft rolls of dough floating atop that she called "lumplings." Apparently she had shown Elrod's wife how to make them, and they did indeed help to stretch out the portions of stew.

Not that he had said anything to Mavis about the lumplings, or the meal. He saw at once how tired she was and felt guilty that he hadn't prevented her from wearying herself even more in the kitchen. However, he had not, and there was nothing to be done except eat as swiftly as possible, so she could retire all the sooner, as she had. And that meant without conversing.

He pushed open the door to the stable and went to the stall holding Hephaestus. His horse neighed a greeting, while nearby, Mavis's mare shifted nervously. Sweetling was indeed a pretty creature, a fitting mount for such a beautiful woman.

An exciting, passionate woman who could make him forget everything except desire when he held her in his arms.

"Oh, it's you, my lord!" the leader of the escort cried,

popping up like a hound on the scent from behind the wall of the stall. Roland suspected he'd been sleeping there. "All's well, my lord," he assured Roland, who hadn't asked.

Roland stroked his stallion's soft muzzle. The animal nudged his hand, making him shake his head. "No, I don't have an apple for you now."

"Greedy, is he?" the soldier whose name, Roland thought, was Arnhelm, replied with a broad grin. "My lady's Sweetling is just the same."

The soldier went to the mare's stall and, grinning rather weakly, kicked at something in the straw. Another soldier—shorter and stockier—rose, yawning. He snapped to attention when he saw Roland. "My lord!"

"You are taking care of my lady's horse, I assume," Roland calmly remarked.

"Aye, m'lord."

"And you are?"

"Verdan, my lord."

Roland noted their somewhat similar features, despite the difference in their builds. "Are you two related?"

"Brothers, my lord," Arnhelm answered.

Brothers. That no doubt explained the kick.

He was about to dismiss them when he realized he had an opportunity he might want to take advantage of, and not only to delay going to the chamber he would be sharing with his wife. "Lord DeLac seems to have a good eye for horses."

Verdan and Arnhelm exchanged glances, then Arnhelm answered. "Aye, m'lord. We never thought Lord DeLac would let my lady take her, even though she's been my lady's mare since my lady were fifteen."

"And she is now…?"

"Nearly twenty, my lord, so past time she was mar-

ried, so everybody said," Verdan replied. "Lady Mavis
had the boys buzzing around her from when she was
just a lass, and with good reason. Pretty and pleasing,
that's our lady. A man could go far and not find another
like her, so when we found out she was to be married,
we all—"

Arnhelm shoved his brother with his shoulder, a
censorious motion that Roland was also all too familiar with. Unlike Gerrard, however, Verdan seemed to
appreciate that he should, perhaps, be quiet. "We all
wished her joy," he finished rather feebly.

"No doubt," Roland said. "You two are sleeping here,
I take it?"

"Aye, my lord, to guard the horses and the dowry,"
Arnhelm answered. "I'm on first watch."

"See that you stay awake, then," Roland replied
as he abandoned hopes for some time alone. He gave
Hephaestus another pat on his nose, and left the stable.

As he crossed the yard, he paused a moment to look
up at the window of the chamber where his wife had
gone. The shutter was closed, but the slats allowed a little bit of light to shine through. His wife was still awake.

He was tempted to bed down in the stables with the
soldiers on watch. He'd slept in the stables at home often
enough, trying to avoid his father and brothers.

But then he'd been a lad fearful of his father's fists
and older brother's slaps, strangleholds and punches,
not a lord with men under his command. He knew full
well what gossips soldiers could be. He wasn't about to
let rumors spread that Sir Roland of Dunborough did
not sleep with his lovely young wife. He could imagine the speculation that would follow. At the very least,
they would probably say that she had barred the door.

As he continued across the yard, he wondered about

the other men who'd wanted Mavis. Well, any man who saw her would want her. But had she wanted any of them? She'd said she'd married him because she'd wished to; that didn't mean there hadn't been others before him whom she might have considered, too.

It didn't matter what had happened in the past. She was his wife now. He need not be jealous of those other, unknown men.

He marched through the taproom, acknowledging the soldiers bedding down there with a nod before he mounted the steps and entered the bedchamber.

To find Mavis in the bed, with the covers up to her chin as if to shield herself from attack.

In spite of his determination to keep his distance, his heart sank. Nevertheless, he would maintain his dignity. He went over to the small table in the corner bearing a cup and pitcher. After pouring himself some water, he downed it in a gulp.

When he turned back, his wife was no longer in the bed. She stood beside it, wearing only a shift, her golden hair loose about her shoulders. She had her arms clasped in front of her and looked like an angel, while his thoughts were far from pure.

But he would resist the lust of his body. He would ignore the desire coursing through him like waters at the flood. He would not remember their wedding night or that afternoon beneath the tree, except for the shame he'd felt afterward. He wasn't like his father. Or his brothers.

He must remember, too, that only that morning she had been weeping, so her smiles and her willingness to share his bed might only be for show. "Go back to bed, Mavis."

She nodded and obeyed, but her expression...it was like seeing a flame snuffed out. It took all his resolve to go to the bed, take a pillow and pull off a blanket. "I shall sleep on the floor," he said, regarding her steadily, watching for a flicker of relief.

Instead, she lifted the covers in a gesture of invitation. "You need not, my lord."

Every particle of his being urged him to join her, to share her body and her bed, to believe that this exceptional woman wished to be his wife.

And yet he dare not give in, not if he would prove to himself that he was different from his family. "You are weary, my lady, and should rest."

"So should you, and it need not be on the floor."

He was not going to admit that she tempted him beyond all reason, or that he'd seen her crying. "I will sleep where I choose, my lady," he replied.

Without another word, she turned onto her side and faced the wall.

That was for the best, he thought as he made his simple bed, lest she continue to try to persuade him and he prove too weak to resist.

The next morning, Mavis awoke to the sound of birds singing. The chamber was dim, for the shutters were still closed. It was bright enough to see that she was alone, however, and a pillow and folded blanket were on the end of the bed.

Rising, she sighed with both weariness and dismay. It had been a long, anxious night, half of it spent waiting to see if Roland would join her in the bed.

He did not.

She tried not to feel hurt or disappointed, although he had to realize now that making love wasn't painful for her. And even if he didn't want to make love with her, there was no need for him to sleep on the floor.

A soft knock sounded on the door and, after her response, Polly entered with a ewer of steaming water in one hand and linens in the other. "Beg pardon, my lady, but Sir Roland asked me to bring you water and linen to wash. He wants to leave as soon as you've dressed and had a bite to eat."

That was more than he'd said to her. "Thank you."

Polly set the ewer on the washstand. "Elrod's still talking about them lumplings, my lady."

"I'm glad he liked them."

Polly grinned. "He likes that they're cheap. I like that they're easy. Your husband must be some proud of you, my lady."

"I hope so," she replied. "I can wash and dress without assistance, Polly. I'm sure you're needed in the kitchen."

"As a matter of fact, my lady, I am. Ylda could burn boiling water," she said with a grateful grin before she bobbed a curtsy and hurried from the room.

Mavis watched her go with a sigh, then washed, combed her hair and put on her traveling gown. She picked up her cloak and made her way to the taproom.

Roland wasn't there, either. Nor were any of the men. Elrod was, though, beaming at her as if she were the light of his life. "Ah, my lady! Here you are and looking lovelier than ever!"

The man would have done very well at court. "Thank you. Where is my husband?"

"In the yard overseeing your men saddling the horses and getting the ox into the yoke."

Polly came into the room carrying a tray bearing a bowl, slices of thick bread, a smaller vessel covered with waxed cloth and two mugs. "Don't stand there boring the poor woman, Elrod! Go out and see if you can help."

As he started to obey, she set the tray down before Mavis. "Here's porridge and bread and honey, and mead or ale if you like, my lady. Eat hearty now. It's warm and the day's cold, and I hear you've got a long journey ahead of you."

A long, lonely journey, Mavis thought, unless Roland—

"It's time to leave, my lady," Roland declared from the door leading to the yard before Elrod reached it.

She rose immediately, as an obedient wife should. "As you wish, my lord."

"She has to have something to eat, my lord," Polly protested.

Although Roland nodded his agreement, he didn't sit down. He stayed standing, his gaze upon her. Mavis quickly ate a slice of bread, sipped some mead, then got to her feet. "I'm ready, my lord."

He nodded once again before reaching into his belt and pulling out a small leather purse. "For you, innkeeper," he said, tossing it to Elrod, who deftly caught it. "With our thanks," he added before he took Mavis's arm to lead her into the chilly yard where the escort and horses waited.

Walking beside him, Mavis glanced at the sky. She was glad that there were no dark clouds today. She was also aware that the men were watching, and so were Elrod and Polly at the door, so she made sure that she smiled.

"Godspeed, my lord!" Elrod called out.

"God bless you, my lady!" his wife added.

After Roland helped Mavis onto her horse, she waved a farewell, wondering how soon she might travel back this way to visit DeLac or Cwm Bron. Roland, meanwhile, mounted Hephaestus, raised his hand, and once again the cortege started on the journey to Yorkshire.

* * *

This time, when they stopped to water the horses, Roland stayed with the soldiers, although keeping a little apart from them.

Nor was her husband any more inclined to speak to her as they traveled along the road. He was again riding several paces ahead, making it clear he had no wish for conversation.

What was she to make of this, and him? That he did indeed crave only her body? That she had been wrong to think there was more to his longing than lust? That she had only imagined that wistful look in his dark eyes? That she had been completely wrong about him?

Yet if he only lusted after her, surely she would have known it from the first, and especially on their wedding night. And he would be forcing his way into their bed, not sleeping on the floor.

He was a mystery, an enigma she was beginning to fear she might never understand.

One thing was different today, though. He sent Arnhelm and Verdan on ahead. She could think of a few reasons why: that he feared danger (which she truly hoped was not the reason) or to send word to Dunborough that he was on the way home, or to seek a place to stop for the night. She hoped it was the latter, but nevertheless prepared herself for another long day in the saddle. Fortunately, the right answer was indeed the last. They stopped much earlier at an inn, and it appeared the host was waiting for them.

Unfortunately, this inn was not quite so prosperous looking as Elrod's. The main building was rather small, the yard untidy, the wall missing several stones. The host was a thin, sallow fellow, and none of the servants who came to help with the horses and the wagon seemed any healthier or more robust.

The taproom was dim, for the shutters were open only a little. Nevertheless, she could see that it wasn't as clean as Elrod's establishment. At least there was a good fire blazing in the hearth.

She joined Roland there, removing her gloves and tucking them into her belt, then holding out her hands to warm them.

She hadn't intended to speak to Roland, but silence was not her natural state. "It seems we were expected, my lord. Was that why you sent Arnhelm and Verdan on ahead?"

"Yes," he replied, looking around. "Elrod suggested we stop here. I begin to doubt his recommendation."

"We can ride on and seek another," she offered, and despite her fatigue.

He slid her a sidelong glance. "No. You are too tired."

Mavis didn't disagree nor did she say anything else. She sat quietly by the fire, waiting for wine and refreshment, while Roland sat just as silently beside her, staring grimly at the fire.

"He don't look pleased," Verdan said to Arnhelm as they entered the taproom along with the rest of the men after seeing to the horses.

They took their places on benches some distance from the hearth. It was colder there, but they didn't want to get too close to Sir Roland.

Looking around, Arnhelm spoke quietly, so that only his brother could hear. "I've stayed in worse, and we could have found worse."

Verdan nodded his agreement as the innkeeper—a reed of a fellow who'd been only too happy to have such a large company and for even less than the last innkeeper—hurried toward the keg that had caught Arnhelm's eye the moment he'd walked in.

"Here, Halldie!" the innkeeper called out to a not-so-young serving wench who scurried into the room like a squirrel on the hunt for nuts for the winter. She had a pitcher in her hand and two goblets that she set in front of Lady Mavis and Sir Roland before she faced the innkeeper.

"Bring mugs for these men," he ordered.

As she hurried to fetch them, the innkeeper addressed Verdan and Arnhelm. "So, where are you from?"

"Castle DeLac," Arnhelm replied.

"That's his lordship's daughter, newly wed," Verdan added.

"DeLac? You're a ways from home," the innkeeper replied as the serving wench returned with a tray full of clay mugs.

"We're her escort to Dunborough."

The tray of mugs crashed to the floor. The serving woman's face flushed and her whole body began to shake, while the innkeeper regarded Roland with a glare of hate. "And who might he be, then?" he demanded.

Before Arnhelm or Verdan could answer, Sir Roland slowly got to his feet. "I am Sir Roland, Lord of Dunborough."

The innkeeper straightened his slender shoulders. "Your men should have said who you were. You aren't welcome here, neither you nor your wife nor your men!"

Lady Mavis turned as pale as snow while the stony visage of Sir Roland didn't alter by so much as a wrinkle.

"Aye! Go! Get out!" the serving wench cried, pointing at the door.

Arnhelm rose and motioned for the other men to

join him as he sidled toward the door, his gaze darting from Lady Mavis to Sir Roland, who did not move, to the innkeeper and the serving woman. "I am willing to pay—" Sir Roland began.

"I don't give a tinker's damn how much you'll pay," the innkeeper exclaimed. "We know the kind of man you are."

"Aye!" the woman cried again. "Your father and your brother showed us! They stayed here, and played their disgusting games with my sister, a poor simple creature who'd never harm a fly. She's with the holy sisters now, and likely to stay there for the rest of her life, thanks to them! So get out, all of you! I'd rather starve than take your money! Get out, get out, *get out!*"

Arnhelm quickly led the men outside. "Get the horses and the wagon," he ordered, but he held his brother back. "There's goin' to be hell to pay now. We should have—"

"Sssh!" Verdan hissed as Sir Roland, grim as death, and Lady Mavis, white to the lips, came out into the yard.

"Let's go see to the ox," Arnhelm muttered, but before he could, Sir Roland called out his name.

"Heaven preserve me," he murmured under his breath. There was no help for it, though. He had to face the wrath of the lord of Dunborough.

"Aye," Verdan whispered as he followed his brother, ready to share the blame and take the punishment with him, too, whatever it might be, as they faced the irate nobleman.

"You didn't tell the fellow who I was?"

Arnhelm kept his gaze focused somewhere over Sir Roland's left shoulder as he answered. "I said I was looking for lodgings for a lord and his lady and their escort, my lord. He didn't ask me your name or where you was from."

Arnhelm waited, trembling, for he knew not what— but he didn't expect Sir Roland to simply say, "Ride on to the next inn and see if there's room for us. And this time, Arnhelm, make sure you tell them it is Sir Roland of Dunborough who seeks lodging there."

Nearly fainting with relief, Arnhelm glanced at his brother before replying. "Yes, my lord. And Verdan?"

The nobleman regarded his brother coldly. "What of him?"

"Well, my lord, there might be thieves and outlaws on the road, and a man alone—"

"Take him, then. Just be quick about it."

"Aye, my lord!" Arnhelm replied, turning smartly and hurrying to the stable with Verdan at his heels.

"That was a close one," Verdan said after they entered the stable.

"Aye, and we'd best make sure we find a better place," Arnhelm replied. "If there's one who'll take him."

When the cortege left the inn yard, it was Mavis who didn't want to talk. She'd been aware that Roland's family was not held in high esteem and with good reason, yet the vehemence of the innkeeper and that serving woman's reaction disturbed her greatly. Now she was glad that Roland rode ahead as she tried to decide what she would do if such a thing happened again.

But before they had gone very far, Roland came back to ride beside her.

Even more unexpectedly, he spoke. "Given my family's reputation, I should have considered such a thing might happen. I would have spared you that humiliation."

The admission was more than she'd expected from him. "Elrod was glad to have our custom."

"We were closer to DeLac."

That was true, and yet… "It wasn't your fault, my lord, any more than your father's reputation is your fault. In time, reputations can be changed, if good deeds replace the bad."

"Do you truly believe that, my lady?"

"Indeed I do, my lord."

He said no more, and neither did she as they continued for some distance, until Mavis wasn't sure how much longer she could sit in the saddle. She was about to propose they stop, even if it meant making camp at the side of the road—not something to be wished at this time of year, even if it didn't rain—when Arnhelm and Verdan appeared in the distance, riding back toward them.

"At last," Roland muttered.

Unfortunately, as the two soldiers got closer, it was apparent from their expressions that they didn't have good news.

"I'm sorry, my lord," Arnhelm said as he reined in, his expression as mournful as his brother's, "but there's no inn for the next ten miles willing to have you…us, for any amount of money."

It seemed word had already spread about the cortege and who led it. Given their slower pace because of the wagon and the ox, a swift rider or even a fast lad on foot could have taken the news from that other tavern ahead of them.

Another glance at the sky confirmed that if they didn't find a place to sleep soon, they would be benighted on the road.

Nor were the rest of the men pleased, judging by

the few muttered remarks that reached her ears until a sharp look from Arnhelm silenced them.

If Roland heard, he gave no sign, although he was sitting even more stiff and upright in the saddle. "Join the rest of the men," he said to Arnhelm and Verdan, then he motioned the cortege to begin moving forward again.

"What are we to do, my lord? Make camp at the side of the road?" Mavis asked, trying not to sound dismayed. "We can't go much farther before nightfall."

"No wife of mine will sleep out like a gypsy," he grimly replied. "There is a manor nearby. I passed it on my way to DeLac. We shall seek shelter there."

Mavis was too tired and too worried to voice any doubts or protest, but what if the lord of the manor didn't want them, either?

They rounded a corner of the road and there before them lay what had to be the manor of a well-to-do farmer or minor nobleman. The low walls surrounding the manor house were made of stone, as was the house, and it had a slate roof. Several chickens clucked in the cobbled yard, and there was a stable and a good-sized barn, as well. A sprawling kitchen garden was at one side, and on the other, a pen holding six cows. In another meadow farther away, a herd of sheep grazed and bleated.

A young woman carrying buckets on a yoke from what might be the dairy toward a back door of the house paused and stared when Roland rode into the yard and dismounted. "Whose holding is this?" he asked.

"S-sir Melvin de Courcellet," the girl stammered, the buckets swinging beside her.

"Tell him he has guests."

"Y-yes, my lord," she replied, setting down the yoke and running into the house.

"We will spend the night here," Roland announced just before a plump man dressed in a long robe, his round face slightly greasy and with a chicken leg in his hand, came barreling out of the main door. "Who is this who dares to—"

He skittered to a halt and fell silent as his gaze took in Roland, the soldiers and Mavis. He tossed the chicken leg away and wiped his hands on his tunic. "Greetings, my lord. Who might you be?"

"I am Sir Roland of Dunborough," her husband replied, "and we seek shelter for the night."

"Roland of..." Sir Melvin cleared his throat and looked a little sick. "Dunborough, you said?"

"Yes. And this is my wife, Lady Mavis, the daughter of Lord Simon DeLac."

Roland had never mentioned her father anywhere else, so this had to be an attempt to make the man more amenable. He might have done better to speak with less force and authority. From his tone, it sounded as if he was ordering Sir Melvin to take them in.

"DeLac, eh? His daughter, is it?" Sir Melvin said, running a nervous hand around the neck of his tunic. "Of course you're welcome to stay, my lord. And your lady, too, and your escort. Just, ahem, allow me a moment to tell my wife how fortunate we are. If you'll excuse me..." He hurried back inside.

"Perhaps, my lord, you should have asked, not demanded," Mavis said.

"My wife will not sleep rough on the road."

Behind them, Arnhelm and Verdan gave each other a wary look.

Roland went to help her down, but Mavis shook her head. "I'll wait until I'm sure we're welcome."

"As you wish," he replied, turning to look at the manor.

She noticed that the back of his neck and tips of his ears were red. Was he ashamed of what he'd done? Or as anxious as she after all?

When Sir Melvin came out of his house, he was followed by a slender, rather homely woman. "This is my wife, Viola. Please, come in and be welcome."

"Thank you. We are most grateful for your hospitality," Mavis said, getting down from her horse without waiting for her husband's aid.

"Come along with me, my dear, and rest awhile," Lady Viola said to Mavis. "You look done in."

Mavis smiled, grateful as much for the heartfelt kindness in the woman's voice as for the offer itself. "I *am* tired," she agreed.

"We'll join you in the hall for the evening meal," Lady Viola said to her husband as they passed. "I leave it to you, Melvin, to see that Sir Roland's men are taken care of."

"Right you are, my dear! Now come along with me, Sir Roland, and we'll get your horses settled and then your men. There should be room enough in the stable for your horses, and we've a building behind it for the ox and your wagon. Your men can all sleep in the hall.

"That's a fine beast you're riding, I must say! Speaking of fine, your wife is quite a beauty. Mavis, you said her name was? Lovely name, lovely girl. We've heard nothing of Lord DeLac's daughter getting married, though…"

Lady Viola led Mavis to a small, comfortable chamber on the second floor of the manor house. Tapestries covered the walls and a large bronze brazier of glow-

ing coals provided warmth. There were cloth shutters
as well as wooden ones to keep out the cold and drafts.
The furniture was simple, but well made, consisting of
a bed, two low chairs near the brazier, a chest for clothing, a washing stand and a stool, where a maidservant
sat rocking a cradle.

The servant, a rosy-faced, neatly dressed lass, rose
when they entered.

"How is my lambkin, Annisa? Still asleep?" Lady
Viola asked.

"Aye, but making little noises like he'll be waking
soon."

"You go and eat, and I'll tend to Martin until you return." As the maid nodded and left the chamber, Lady
Viola said, "Then it should be time for the evening
meal."

"I must thank you for your generous hospitality, my
lady," Mavis said at once. "I'm sorry you were forced
to take us in, but we could find no other accommoda-
tion. Unfortunately, it seems that the reputation of my
husband's relatives has preceded us, and innkeepers are
reluctant to give us shelter."

"It's indeed unfortunate that you've had such a recep-
tion so near our home," Lady Viola replied, "but we're
happy to be of service."

She spoke with such sincerity, Mavis believed her,
and was even more grateful.

"I'm surprised your husband didn't realize that might
be the case."

Mavis remembered what the groom had told her the
first night Roland had arrived at Castle DeLac. "He only
stopped once on the journey to DeLac, so he might not
have encountered anyone who had any dealings with
his family, or knew their reputation."

"And you did not suspect there might be any such trouble?"

Mavis shook her head. "No," she replied, suddenly feeling foolish. Sir Blane and Broderick had journeyed to DeLac. She should have expected that they'd behaved just as loutishly along the way as they had when they reached DeLac.

The babe began to fuss. Lady Viola picked up the squirming, swaddled baby with a tuft of light brown hair and, holding him to her shoulder, sat in the chair near the brazier. "Please, lie down, my dear, and rest. You look worn out."

Although Mavis was tired, she sat in the other chair. "I assure you, Lady Viola, that Roland is not like his father and older brother. I've met them, and I can vouch for the difference."

That was certainly true, especially when it came to their treatment of women.

When the baby continued to fuss, Lady Viola opened her gown and put the wee lad to nurse. "And the other brother, Gerrard? Have you ever met him?"

"No. Have you, my lady?"

"Only by reputation," she replied. She studied Mavis a moment. "I would rather not be the bearer of bad tidings, but ignorance is no protection for a woman, so I will tell you what I've heard about Gerrard of Dunborough—that he's devilishly handsome and devilishly clever, too, and without an honest bone in his body. He cheats at games of chance and refuses to pay merchants, or the tavern keepers whose wine he drinks, or the women he…" She delicately cleared her throat. "To put it in the simplest way, I am afraid, my dear, that he is a thorough reprobate."

Although Mavis was dismayed to hear her husband's

twin painted in such a terrible light, she tried not to betray it. "Then he, too, is nothing like Roland. But since Roland is the lord, and Gerrard the younger, I should have little enough to do with Gerrard in Dunborough."

"I hope so, my lady, yet that might make him all the more dangerous."

"Surely there is little he can do to hurt me, and even if he tries, my husband will protect me."

"For your sake, I would that it were so, but Gerrard's a sly fox, my lady. He could try to make your husband hate you."

"Why? What could he possibly gain?"

"From what I know of the men of Dunborough, his brother's unhappiness may be enough."

Mavis had no answer to that, nor did she wish to hear any more. "You've been blessed with a fine, healthy child," she observed.

Lady Viola kissed the top of her nursing baby's head. "Children are indeed a blessing and a joy, my dear."

Mavis instinctively rested her clasped hands on her belly. "I would do anything to have children. They are our comfort and support."

"Beg pardon, my lady," Annisa said as she reentered the chamber. "The evening meal is ready."

Lady Viola handed her sleepy child to the maid-servant, who laid the baby on her shoulder to burp him.

"I'm sorry. You didn't get a chance to rest after all," she said to Mavis as she closed her gown.

"It's quite all right," Mavis replied, even though she wished she'd taken a nap so she wouldn't have heard so much about her husband's brother before they rejoined the men in the hall below.

Chapter Four

"I suppose the women must have their time to gossip, eh, my lord, and we men must wait for them to finish, even if we're starving," Sir Melvin said to Roland as they sat together in the main room of his manor house.

Roland did not reply, in part because he didn't know if Mavis indulged in gossip, but also because it didn't matter if he answered. He had already learned that Sir Melvin would keep talking regardless. Since returning to the house he had talked about the state of the roads, last year's harvest, the king and the latest news of the church in Rome.

Roland could believe the man would keep talking even if he were knocked unconscious.

"Mind you, it's easy for a man to wait for a woman as beautiful as your wife," Sir Melvin continued. "Such eyes! Such skin! Not that I envy you, my lord, for Viola won my heart when I was just a lad, and she says the same of me, hard as that may be to believe."

Roland did find that rather difficult to comprehend. He supposed it was possible that Sir Melvin had been thinner, and quieter, in his youth.

Roland's gaze wandered to the soldiers of his escort,

who were likewise awaiting the evening meal. They were clustered around a trestle table at the far end of the room, chatting quietly among themselves and only occasionally glancing their way. No doubt they were discussing what had happened that day, and he was sure nothing good was being said of the men of Dunborough.

He noted the two brothers sitting close together, head to head, one speaking, the other listening, paying attention and nodding agreement as if they were friends, not mortal enemies locked in battle for a father's notice.

"You've made a most promising alliance, too," Sir Melvin went on, snaring his attention again. "Lord DeLac is a wealthy and powerful man."

"Who will probably soon be dead of drink," Roland replied, trying to silence the fellow, at least for a moment.

Unfortunately, his plan did not succeed.

"Yes, well, ahem, we have heard he imbibes overmuch at times. The better for you, though, perhaps, eh, my lord?" Sir Melvin said. "You and your charming wife will inherit since he has no son. You'll have an estate in the north and one in the south."

"Unlike my father or my elder brother, I take no pleasure in any man's demise, and I doubt my wife will feel any delight in her father's death, however the man's behaved."

"N-no, of course not. I didn't mean to imply… Forgive me," Sir Melvin stammered.

"I have taken no offense," Roland answered as his wife and Lady Viola finally appeared.

He saw at once that Mavis didn't appear any more rested. She was still too pale, with dark circles under her eyes.

Perhaps Lady Viola was as talkative as her husband

and he would have done better to continue on until they found an inn or abbey willing to take them, no matter how desperate he'd been to find a night's lodging.

Unfortunately, it was too late now.

The men rose as the ladies joined them on the dais at the high table, Mavis to Sir Melvin's right, Lady Viola on his left. Lady Viola was plain, but far from ugly, and when she smiled indulgently at her husband, Roland could believe theirs was indeed a love match, as surprising as he would have found it when he first arrived.

"Your son is a lovely child," Mavis said as the servants began to serve a thick ham pottage in trenchers, with fresh-made bread and unexpectedly good wine. "You are very blessed."

"Yes, very blessed and fortunate," Sir Melvin agreed with proud complacency. "I'm after a dozen children at least. The more, the better, I always say. I suppose you'll be wanting sons soon, my lord. Nothing against daughters, for where would we be without them, but a son first, eh?"

Roland didn't risk even a glance at Mavis before he replied. "I hope to have many children."

"Then you're in agreement with your wife," Lady Viola noted, and he felt a surge of pleasure and relief. "As she says, children are our comfort and security."

Comfort—as if he'd been harsh and cruel.

Security—as if he couldn't keep her safe.

Did Mavis think him incapable of the most basic duties belonging to a husband and a father? Did she believe that he would be as negligent as his own, or hers?

To be sure, his father had been cruel, capricious, selfish and demanding, always pitting one son against the other in a never-ending competition, but that only made Roland more determined to be a better father, if God blessed him with children.

"I look forward to fatherhood," he said firmly, and then he added, because he was certain it would be true, "I'm sure my lady will be an excellent mother."

Sir Melvin smiled and began to talk about the weather.

Later that night, Mavis sighed and rotated her head as she ran her comb through her long, blond hair. Her back and shoulders ached from many hours in the saddle, and although the food had been good, it had been a most awkward and uncomfortable meal. Roland had said very little, especially after Sir Melvin mentioned children. She supposed she should take comfort in Roland's faith in her ability as a mother, yet after that he had barely said another word and never smiled, no matter how entertaining Sir Melvin's stories were, and the nobleman could be quite entertaining. She had tried to make up for her husband's silence, but between the long day and the good food, and her lack of sleep from the night before, she had retired as soon as etiquette would permit. Now she could scarcely finish undressing and getting ready for bed because of the yawns that would not stop.

Until she heard the scrape of a heel on the stone floor and turned to see Roland standing on the threshold, silhouetted by the light of the torch in the corridor behind him, his angular face in shadow.

Her heartbeat quickened and her body warmed with a blush as she thought of how she must look, clad only in her shift. She went to cover herself, then stopped. He had every right to look at her, as well as share this chamber and the bed. She was, after all, his wife.

He came into the room, his tread as quiet and smooth as a cat's.

"I thought perhaps you would stay longer in the hall," she said, trying to speak calmly and not betray any sign of her tumultuous emotions.

He crossed his arms and leaned against the wall near the door, as if he didn't want to get any closer. "Sir Melvin pleaded weariness and went to join his wife, who retired shortly after you did. It was either drink with the men or come here, so I came here."

It was hardly a flattering response, but she had already discovered that her husband would never be a diplomat. "Do you intend to sleep on the floor again, my lord?"

"Yes."

A single word, with no explanation offered. Very well, she would ask for none.

She went back to combing her hair, although it was a struggle to keep her hand steady. "Lady Viola is a very kind, thoughtful woman."

"And quieter than her husband, thank God."

"I think he's very kind, generous and amusing, too."

"You didn't spend the afternoon with the man." He pushed off from the wall and came closer. "I don't think you rested, either."

She put down her comb and turned to face him. "I was being a good guest, as you should have been, considering you all but forced Sir Melvin to take us in."

He regarded her steadily, his gaze inscrutable. "I am a plainspoken man, Mavis. It would be a mistake to expect flattery and flowery words from me. You were exhausted, and so were the men. I couldn't take the chance we'd be benighted on the road."

"I, too, care little for insincere flattery or empty

praise, my lord," she honestly replied. "I have heard
enough of that in my lifetime and know how false it is.
But not all praise is false, or spoken for a selfish purpose." She rose and faced him squarely. "For instance,
I would simply be stating a fact if I said you are a handsome man."

His frown deepened.

"Surely you know that, my lord. Women must have
told you that before."

He slowly shook his head.

"What, no one has ever said you're a fine-looking,
well-made man?" she asked incredulously.

"Not in my hearing. I suppose you're used to compliments."

"That were often not sincere." She approached him
cautiously, both determined and yet afraid to say too
much, lest he spurn her again. "It would also be true
if I said I am happy to be married to the lord of Dunborough."

His eyes narrowed as if he couldn't believe that,
either. "Are you?"

"Yes, and hope to be happier still."

"How?" he asked, and she saw again that wistful,
yearning look come to his eyes, the same look she had
seen in her father's solar. That Roland *did* exist, and she
had brought him back again.

"By getting to know you better," she replied. "By
becoming a part of your household and helping you as
a wife and chatelaine should. By having children. By
sharing your bed."

She went closer still.

"I want to have your children, Roland. I want to share
your bed," she whispered before she took his face be-

tween her palms and raised herself on her toes to kiss him gently.

As always when she touched him, she was aware of the passionate desire lurking, ready to come forth—but not until she had shown him tenderness, something she now doubted he had ever known.

She moved her lips across his, as light as the brush of a feather. He stood still a moment, then his arms went around her and she heard his quick, sharp breaths as he pulled her close. Excitement raced through her, and she pressed more featherlight kisses along his jaw and neck. She wrapped her arms about him and slid her hands slowly up his back. Then she stepped back and took his hand to lead him to the bed. She drew him down to sit beside her and as he looked at her, she ran her fingers through his dark hair. "Husband," she murmured before she leaned close to kiss him again.

At the same instant, a loud crack of thunder rent the air and rain began to pound against the wooden shutters of the chamber. Just as suddenly they heard shouts and voices raised in alarm from the yard.

Roland strode to the window, and she hurried to join him. Regardless of the rain, he opened the shutters and they both gasped.

A huge oak beside the stable had been split down the middle by lightning, sending a massive limb crashing onto the stable roof and setting the trunk ablaze. Despite the rain, the stable was on fire. Whipped by the wind, the flames danced and moved across the thatched roof like a starving creature seeking food.

"Stay here," Roland ordered as he ran from the room.

Mavis couldn't stay in the chamber. She grabbed her cloak and threw it over her shift, shoved her feet into her

boots and hurried to the empty hall below. She opened
the outer door and stopped, stunned by what she saw.

Arnhelm, Verdan, the rest of their soldiers and Sir
Melvin's servants ran back and forth from the well with
buckets, pots or anything that would hold water, spilling half the contents in their haste to throw water at
the stable. Geese and chickens squawked and flapped
and got underfoot. Two huge workhorses stood quiv-
ering and neighing with fear near the gate. The ox bellowed not far away. Sir Melvin dashed from one side
of the yard to the other shouting, "Oh, sweet Jesus! Oh,
Mother Mary!"

Where was Roland? And Sweetling? And Hephaestus?

Before she could ask one of the servants running
past, the stable door opened and Roland himself appeared leading Sweetling and Hephaestus. As soon as
they were outside, he handed them off to one of the
younger servants who might be a stable boy, with an
order to take them to the far side of the yard. Then he
called out to Arnhelm and Verdan, ordering them to
make certain all their horses were accounted for.

He pointed to some other men. "You four, round up
all the livestock and keep it out of the way. The rest of
you, form a line from the well to the stable and pass
the buckets! Now!"

Mavis rushed to the well. "I'll turn the handle," she
said to the servant standing there, determined to do
something to help as the men formed a line. "You fill
the buckets."

Roland, meanwhile, stayed close to the stable and
threw the buckets of water on the burning building over
and over and over again. Out of the corner of her eye,

she saw Sir Melvin, although still agitated, leading their ox to join the horses near the gate.

Then the rain stopped. There was a hush, a pause, as everyone looked up, but only for a moment, because the wind continued to blow. The fire blazed into new life, heavy smoke from the damp thatch filling the air. Although no one abandoned their post, they all began to cough and choke.

Nevertheless, thanks to their efforts, the flames finally lessened, and then the rain began again, putting out the last of the fire as it dwindled and ceased and turning the courtyard into a sodden morass of straw and mud and ash.

Exhausted, Mavis slumped against the side of the well. The men in the line likewise put down their buckets, pails and pans. Some collapsed on the ground, regardless of the mud.

"S'truth, I'm done in," Arnhelm groaned. Verdan simply sat with his head in his hands, until Lady Viola appeared in the doorway of the kitchen.

"There's ale and wine and bread ready," she called out. "Come in, come in, all of you!"

Arnhelm, Verdan and the rest of the men obeyed at once. Mavis started to go with them, until she saw Roland, his wet tunic and breeches clinging to his powerful body, his boots caked with mud, his hair plastered to his forehead and his face black with soot. He was heading toward the far end of the stable, where the charred limb of the tree lay among the smoldering ruin of the building.

Although she was exhausted, wet and hungry, her curiosity was stronger. She followed him, stepping carefully around the growing puddles, skirting the downed limb from the tree that was probably centuries

old. When she rounded the corner of the ruined building, she saw Roland standing motionless, his hands on
his hips, looking at what was left of another, smaller
building that had been close by the stables. Cinders and
sparks from the stable had set it alight, too, and burned
it to the ground.

She sighed to see such destruction.

Roland started and turned toward her. Frowning,
he ran a swift gaze over her. "You should go inside at
once."

"As should you," she replied.

With a nod, he took her arm to lead her around the
stable and through the puddled yard.

"You should have stayed inside with Lady Viola,"
he said as they skirted one particularly large puddle.

"I wanted to help."

"Not at risk to your health."

"You are just as wet," she noted. "Were all the animals saved?"

"Yes, but not the wagon."

The wagon? *Their* wagon? The one with—

"My dowry!" she cried, turning back.

"The coin is safe," he said, blocking her way. "I kept
it with me. As for the rest..." He shrugged. "There's
nothing to be done about it."

She stared at him, aghast at his dismissal of this
tragedy. "But I have nothing left to call my own except
the clothes on my back and the few extra things in my
little traveling chest. When we arrive in Dunborough,
I'll have no other clothes, no table or bed linens, not
even extra undergarments."

"You can get new clothes in Dunborough."

"What will your household, your tenants, your
brother, think if I arrive with next to nothing?" she cried

with frustration and dismay as she started to shiver. "That my father didn't value me enough to provide a dowry?"

Cupping her shoulders, his hands warm, he said, "If anyone wonders why I wed you apparently without a dowry, I will say…" He paused and let go of her and stepped back. "Enough of this. You're cold and wet and you'll get sick if we stay outside much longer."

He took hold of her arm again and started toward the kitchen. She slipped in the mud and he immediately bent down and scooped her up in his arms.

She wanted to protest, but she was freezing and he could walk faster, so she didn't object until they entered the kitchen.

"You can put me down now," she whispered as Sir Melvin, Lady Viola and everyone else gathered in the large, warm room turned to look at them.

Either Roland didn't hear her, or he chose to ignore her request as he continued through the kitchen. "I want a hot brick for our bed, more blankets and hot water to wash," he ordered. He spoke as if this was his castle, and she blushed with embarrassment.

She was even more embarrassed when they left the kitchen and entered the main room of the house lit only by a few spluttering torches that threw grotesque shadows on the walls. Two maidservants rushed past them. One carried what looked like a brick wrapped in linen, the other a ewer of steaming water and she had clean linen over her arm.

"Put me down," she said more sternly.

Still he ignored her.

"I said, put me down!" she commanded, pushing at his chest.

"No. You're wet, you're tired, and the sooner you

get in a warm bed, the better. I am quite willing to be pushed or pummeled or whatever you choose to do, but I will not put you down. And you should cease your efforts to prevent me. I've been beaten too many times, my lady, by my father and older brother to be affected by any efforts of yours."

He had been beaten by his own family? Her father struck her rarely, but she vividly recalled the pain beyond the physical, the heartbreak and humiliation, and she said no more.

When they reached the corridor leading to the family apartments, the two maidservants who'd hurried ahead of them from the kitchen came out of their chamber. Seeing Roland and Mavis, they dipped a curtsy, then scurried in the opposite direction, taking another set of stairs.

Roland carried her over the threshold, then finally set her down.

The room was much as they'd left it, except for the extra blankets on the bed, a pile of fresh linen on a stool nearby and two more rushlights kindled. The shutters were closed, and the rain had started again.

Very aware of her husband's presence, Mavis took off her wet cloak, laying it over the one chest of clothing she now possessed. When she straightened, she found Roland staring at her as if he'd never seen a woman before.

Her soaking shift was nearly transparent.

Mavis grabbed the top square of linen and wrapped it around herself. Holding her breath, her heart racing, she stood trembling as he came farther into the room.

He halted near the pile of linen. He pulled off his wet tunic and shirt, tossing them to the floor before he, too, reached for a square of linen. He began to rub his chest vigorously. "You should get out of that shift before you catch cold."

He was right, so she did. Keeping the linen wrapped around her, she wiggled out of the shift until it puddled around her feet. He, meanwhile, stripped off his breeches and stockings and wrapped a square of linen around his narrow waist, then began to dry his long hair with another piece of linen.

As he moved it back and forth over his head, his eyes closed, she couldn't help noticing his nearly naked body and the scars on his back and chest. He'd said he'd been in different sorts of battles, and she'd assumed some sort of armed skirmish with outlaws or practice battles. Now she suspected they were mostly from one-sided encounters, beatings administered by his terrible father or equally monstrous older brother when he was too young to fight back.

He suddenly opened his eyes and caught her looking at him.

No doubt blushing like an innocent maid, she went to get another square of linen to dry her own hair. She draped it over her head and began to rub, until she felt his strong hands cover hers and he said, his voice low and husky, "Let me."

She swallowed hard and said nothing as he began to dry her hair, although she was well aware that save for two pieces of linen, they were both naked. And standing very close together.

The linen around her began to slip and she instinctively clutched it and pulled it back into place. At the same time, he stopped and stepped away without a word, going to the leather pouch in the corner and taking out some breeches.

She would not be sorry he was getting dressed.

Trying to ignore him, she sat on the bed and started to comb her hair, working through the damp, tangled mass of knots with her fingers.

As she struggled with one particularly troublesome tangle, the linen slipped below her breasts. She quickly reached for it, tucking it more tightly about her, and looked up to find Roland once again regarding her like a hungry man at a feast, his clean, dry shirt clutched in his hands.

His obvious desire enflamed her own. His need caught hers and held it. "I should see that the horses have been stabled somewhere. And the ox," he said huskily.

Mavis went back to working on her hair, despite her trembling fingers. "If you think that's best, my lord."

"Best?" he repeated in a murmur.

It was the closest she had ever heard him come to doubtful hesitation. Did that mean he wanted to stay?

Despite her dread that she might be mistaken, encouraged by his kisses before the lightning struck, she rose and faced him. "I'm sure Arnhelm and the others will take good care of our animals. Do you not agree, my lord?"

He nodded his head.

"Then perhaps you ought to stay."

Her husband neither moved nor spoke until she let the linen fall to the floor. Then he dropped his shirt and crossed the space between them in an instant. In the next moment she was in his arms, her naked breasts against his bare chest, their arms wrapped about each other, lips and tongues and torsos touching.

Her weariness dissolved. Her yearning blossomed. His throbbing heartbeat matched her own. As if they had one mind, they broke the kiss. She hurried to the bed while he tossed aside the linen that had been wrapped around his waist.

He joined her in the bed, and once again his caresses excited her beyond measure, although this time was like the first, tender and gentle. His tongue and hands teased and coaxed until she whimpered with unmet need.

Just before she was about to tell him she was ready, he pushed inside her. She arched toward him, seeking even more union, while his thrusts grew stronger and quicker, and their soft cries filled the chamber. A last, final, feral growl signaled the completion.

As her body slowly stilled, a great weariness overcame her, and after he withdrew, she fell asleep beside him.

Roland looked down at his slumbering wife in wonder. *No woman of any worth will ever want a cold stick like you.*

Again Gerrard's mocking words ran through his mind, but this time, he knew that Gerrard was wrong. Mavis wanted him, at least in her bed. That was not all that *he* wanted, but it would be a start.

And did her willingness to make love not prove that it had more likely been the physical pain of losing her virginity that had made her cry? And if so, why then *should* he resist the powerful urges of his body, and the desire of his heart?

He lay awake for a long time trying to think of a way to tell her how she made him feel. As no woman had ever made him feel. But the task seemed hopeless. He was not like Gerrard, who had an easy way with words and women both. Perhaps, in time, Mavis would come to understand that she was growing more precious to him every day, and every day he was thankful she'd agreed to be his wife. Or so he could hope.

Yet when he eventually fell asleep, he dreamed he was trapped in a burning building while his father, his brothers and Mavis stood outside and laughed.

Roland awoke with a start to find Mavis still nestled beside him. He had only been dreaming that harsh, mocking laughter. His father and older brother were dead. Mavis had never laughed at him. Neither would Gerrard when he returned with such a wife.

Who had lost much of her dowry to the flames.

Thankfully he still had the bag of silver coins that had been part of her dowry.

He gently moved away from her and got out of the bed.

He washed and dressed quickly and quietly, and hurried to the hall below where the men were stirring. Sir Melvin was there and already eating, much to his surprise.

"I barely slept a wink," Sir Melvin confided as Roland joined him at the table. "How much do you suppose your wife's dowry was worth? Of course, I'll repay it all as soon as—"

"That will not be necessary," Roland interrupted. "The loss was not your fault, so you owe us nothing."

His host regarded him with genuine dismay. "But it was my shed and—"

"You gave us shelter when we were in need and you may have the ox, with my thanks."

Sir Melvin's brows furrowed. "Your wife's dower goods and a wagon are destroyed while you're my guest, and you'll give me an ox?"

"My wife's dower goods were destroyed in a fire that

was not your fault, so I expect no recompense, nor will I accept it. And we can make better time without the ox."

"But Sir Roland!"

"But Sir Melvin, I will not hear another word on the matter," Roland firmly replied.

For once, Sir Melvin had nothing at all to say—for a moment, at least. "By God, you are a generous man, my lord!"

Roland smiled, just a little. "I am not my father, Sir Melvin."

"From what I've heard of the man, no, I should say you're not!" his host heartily agreed.

Chapter Five

Once again Mavis awoke to find herself alone, but this time, she smiled. Roland was proving to be an amazing husband and not only in their bed. He'd been so impressive taking command last night. How well he'd directed the men's effort and, silhouetted by the fire, he'd looked like a well-formed Hephaestus.

Then she remembered that all her dower goods that had been in the wagon had been lost, and her joy lessened. What would the people of Dunborough say about her when she arrived with no fine clothes or other dower goods at all?

She rose and studied her traveling gown and cloak. She'd look little better than a beggar!

Unfortunately, as Roland had said, there was nothing to be done. She could at least take some comfort from Roland's acceptance of the loss. If he'd married her for her dowry, he would surely have been more upset. Of course, he did still have the silver...

Putting such mercenary thoughts from her mind, telling herself he wouldn't make love to her as he did if he had married her only for gain, she dressed and hurried to the large chamber below. The men of their escort were already gathered there, eating bread and porridge and drinking ale, while Roland and Sir Melvin sat at another table.

She couldn't help blushing when her husband looked at her and she remembered what they'd done last night—and rather loudly, too. Roland, however, betrayed no such recollection, which was just as well. Otherwise, she would have blushed even more and probably had to stifle an embarrassed giggle.

"My wife makes her apologies, my dear," Sir Melvin began as she joined them and a servant brought her some porridge, bread and honey. "The babe's a bit fractious—I don't think any of us slept well last night— and my wife prefers to look after the child herself."

"A good rest will make us all feel better," Mavis replied, not daring to look at her husband.

Roland rose from the bench and straightened his tunic. "I shall see that the horses are ready for our departure. Again I give you my thanks, my lord, for your generous hospitality and a most memorable night," he said, glancing at Mavis in a way that made her face grow hot again.

"And I thank you for all your help," Sir Melvin replied, blissfully unaware of the undercurrent between Mavis and Roland that was making it difficult for her to listen. "And of course, your gift of the ox. Are you sure you won't reconsider? It's a fine beast."

Mavis regarded her husband with surprise. "You're giving the ox to Sir Melvin?"

"So he says, but really, my dear, it's too much!" Sir Melvin quickly replied. "You lost all your things and—"

"It was not your fault," Roland said. He regarded Mavis steadily, stoically. "And as I have explained, we'll make better time without it. Now if you'll excuse me."

As Roland strode from the chamber, Arnhelm, Verdan and the men of the escort jumped to their feet and hurried after him, some cramming the remains of their bread into their mouths.

While Mavis watched them go and contemplated her husband's unexpected generosity, Sir Melvin leaned toward her and said, "He didn't tell you?"

"No," she had to admit, "although I'm glad he gave you the ox."

"Not only has he given it to me as thanks for our hospitality, he won't accept anything in compensation for your dower goods."

Again she was pleased, and she agreed. "The fire was not your fault."

"I confess I've heard nothing good of the lords of Dunborough, but I must say that while Sir Roland is a stern fellow, he's not at all what I expected."

Arnhelm came to the outer door. "My lady, we're ready to leave."

Mavis got to her feet. "Thank you, my lord, for everything," she said, lightly kissing Sir Melvin on both cheeks. "I shall always remember your kindness."

"And I shall always remember how you both helped us fight the fire, and your kind generosity afterward," he said as he escorted her to the yard and their waiting horses.

Verdan helped her into the saddle while her husband swung onto his black horse. He nodded to their host and raised his hand to signal their departure.

Mavis waved her farewells, then moved her horse so that she was riding beside her husband. "I'm so pleased you gave Sir Melvin the ox to thank him for his hospitality. It was generous of you, my lord."

"We had no more need of the beast," Roland replied, "and we'll reach Dunborough all the sooner without it."

She wasn't going to be dissuaded from giving praise where it was due. "Nevertheless, it was good of you, and I *will* say so."

The tips of his ears turned red, and she thought she saw the ghost of a smile at the corners of his lips. Delighted, she forged ahead. "I'm glad to discover my husband is such a generous man. My father, alas, has grown miserly in later years, except when it comes to feasting."

Roland made no comment.

Still not dissuaded, she continued. "Do you have many feasts at Dunborough, I mean besides the harvest, and Christmas, Easter, of course, and May Day and Saint—"

"We don't have feasts at Dunborough," he interrupted. "The servants, tenants and villagers have their celebrations, but my family is not welcome to join them. My father wasn't sorry it was so."

"And you?" she prompted, hearing an undercurrent of sadness in his deep voice. "Were you sorry?"

He looked at her quickly, then just as swiftly away. "Sometimes."

That glance gave her a vision of a dark-haired lad standing alone, uninvited and unwanted, at the edge of a village green while other boys and girls danced around a Maypole.

"Perhaps we can have a feast for All Saints' Day," she suggested. That was still some ways off and would give her time to learn about the household and servants of Dunborough.

To her dismay, he didn't look pleased by her suggestion. "I may be a lord, but I'm not a wealthy man, Mavis, and that fire did cost us something. A feast will strain the coffers even more."

She tried not to be, or to sound, disappointed. If he hadn't been to many feasts, or thought of them only with pain, she shouldn't be surprised he wasn't anxious to host one. "Very well, my lord. But Christmas—"

"Will be celebrated with little fuss and feasting. I don't believe in spending lavishly on frivolities." He slid her another glance, this one expressionless, before he announced in a louder voice, "I'm going to ride ahead to seek a place to water the horses."

Arnhelm and Verdan spurred their horses to move forward, but Roland shook his head. "Alone," he declared, leaving the soldiers no choice but to drop back before he kicked his heels into Hephaestus's sides and rode off at a canter.

Roland drew Hephaestus to a halt and glanced back over his shoulder to make sure he was well ahead of the cortege, then nudged his horse into a walk. He'd wanted—needed—time alone to collect his thoughts and, most of all, decide what to say to his wife.

"I fear it's hopeless, Heffy," he said aloud. He often talked to animals because they didn't mock or criticize him. "I want to talk to her, but I don't know how to speak, how to act, how to *be* with her, except when we're in bed."

When they were, it was wonderful. Beyond anything he'd dreamed or hoped for. "Perhaps that's a start, eh, Heffy?" he said, with more cheerfulness. "And maybe one day, if I'm patient, and even if I can't tell her how I feel, she'll come to care for me."

And then he might finally know what it was like to have somebody love him.

As Roland disappeared around a bend in the road, Arnhelm shook his head. "I ain't never going to understand the nobility," he said to Verdan, keeping his voice low so Lady Mavis wouldn't hear. "What's he doin' ridin' off like that and by himself? S'truth, if I had a wife like that, I'd never leave her side."

Verdan guffawed. "If you had a wife like that, I'd never leave her side neither."

"Be serious, you nit. I tell ya, it ain't natural."

"Oh, they're 'natural,' all right," Verdan replied. He dropped his voice even lower. "One of Sir Melvin's maidservants—that pretty one with the fair hair—told me she heard 'em goin' at it like rabbits last night."

That baffled Arnhelm even more. "Then why's he ridin' off like that?"

"How do I know?" Verdan answered with a shrug. "He's a lord, she's a lady, who knows what goes on in their heads—or beds," he added, laughing at his own joke. "Look, you, she's happy enough, ain't she? You ain't seen her weepin', have ya? And didn't he do a fine job fightin' the fire last night? That blonde girl thought he was like some hero out of a song."

"In other words, she didn't give you the time o' day," Arnhelm replied with a smirk.

"I was too tired," Verdan said virtuously. "And I don't think he's so bad as you think. You're seein' trouble where there ain't none. Don't you want her to be happy? Ain't you the one always sayin' she deserved better?"

"Aye, but I ain't so sure Sir Roland's goin' to make her happy."

"And *I* say he is," Verdan declared, his voice louder. "What more d'ya—"

"Enough, you big lummox!" Arnhelm warned. "She's gonna hear you!"

Mavis didn't hear them. Not that day, or the days that followed, as they continued north. Nor did Roland ever speak much to her. She found it difficult to find a subject that interested him beyond a few words.

That would have been more disturbing had they not shared their nights, their bed and their bodies. Roland continued to be an exciting, tender lover and she took comfort from the way he loved, telling herself that was more important than being a witty companion on the road.

Despite the pleasure of the nights, however, she was getting weary of traveling and longed to reach their destination, especially once they got to Yorkshire. It was truly wild, and rough and cold, with the wind whipping across the dales as if it had a mind to strip the clothes from your back.

Mavis wrapped her cloak more tightly about her. At least she could comfort herself with the realization that they were indeed making much better time without the wagon and ox.

Nevertheless, she had stopped asking Roland when they would reach his home, for he only ever replied, "Soon."

Today, however, while he was some distance ahead, he was still in sight, and it was already past the noon, so perhaps they were close to Dunborough at last.

Reaching the top of a ridge, Roland pulled his horse to a halt. He sat motionless a brief moment, then turned Hephaestus and returned at a gallop.

Mavis tugged Sweetling to a standstill.

"What the...?" Arnhelm muttered, drawing his sword.

Verdan and the other men did the same, while Mavis tried not to panic.

"What is it, my lord?" she called out.

"Mounted and armed men coming this way on the

road," he said not to her, but to Arnhelm and the escort. "Arnhelm, you and Verdan ride ahead with me. The rest of you, stay here and guard my lady."

"Aye, my lord," Arnhelm answered, but before any of them could move, four riders appeared at the top of the ridge and galloped down the slope toward them. They wore no mail or armor or helmets, although they all had broadswords at their sides.

Sweetling whinnied and refooted, as nervous as her mistress. Some of the other horses shifted anxiously, too.

The riders were still some distance away when Roland swore under his breath. "Sheathe your swords," he ordered.

"Are they friends?" Mavis asked, still wary in spite of Roland's command.

"No," he replied as the four riders drew their horses to a halt a short distance away, blocking the road. All were young, wearing clothes that bespoke wealth. The tallest wore a bright blue tunic, the shortest forest green and the cloak of the middle one was dark red. Their spirited horses nodded their heads and stamped as if chafing at having to stop.

Yet it was the man who rode ahead of them on a snow-white horse that held her attention. He was dressed in black with a thick belt embossed with brass and as he got closer, she could see that although his boots were mud spattered, the leather was of a high shining gloss.

He was also the spitting image of her husband.

They shared the same high cheekbones, the same broad shoulders and lean, muscular legs, even the same long, dark hair. But there was one difference. This man smiled broadly as he brought his horse to a halt in front of them, something her husband never did.

Nor was she the only one who noted the uncanny resemblance, for she heard Arnhelm's gasp "S'truth!" and the equally astonished mutters of the other soldiers of the escort.

"Greetings, brother!" the stranger exclaimed.

Roland's twin sounded like Roland, too, although Gerrard's voice was slightly higher pitched. Up close, she could also see that Gerrard's face was slightly rounder and less angular, as if someone had rubbed off all the sharp edges of her husband's features.

Gerrard looked the lesser for it.

"And who is this charming young woman who is no doubt responsible for the delay in your return?" Gerrard asked, regarding Mavis with the leering sort of speculation she was unfortunately familiar with, and detested.

"My *lady*, this is my brother Gerrard," Roland replied. "Gerrard, this is *Lady* Mavis. My wife."

Gerrard's grin died on his lips. "Your...? Is this a jest?"

"It is the truth," Mavis said as she nudged Sweetling closer. Now more than ever she wished her pretty gowns hadn't been destroyed in the fire. Nevertheless, she held her head high. She was, after all, the daughter of a lord and wife to another. "I'm pleased to meet my brother-in-law."

Gerrard gripped his reins tighter and spoke not to her, but to his brother. "Lady Mavis—Simon DeLac's daughter?"

"The same."

"So you've made an alliance with DeLac?" he asked his brother.

"Yes."

"I thought you were going to tell him any hope of that died with our father and Broderick."

Mavis tried not to reveal her surprise, but this was the first time she'd heard that Roland had not come to Dunborough with an allegiance in mind. Hard on the heels of surprise came a vast and joyous relief. If he didn't want the alliance and he cared little about her dowry, he must have wed her for herself alone.

"I can see why you reconsidered. You are truly the most fortunate of men, brother," Gerrard continued. His lips curved up again, but this time, it was more of a sneer than a smile. "A wife beautiful enough to sate any man's desire, a most excellent political alliance and no doubt a fine dowry to boot. You should have sent word home of this wondrous event."

"There was no time."

Gerrard's brows rose. "Time to wed and bed, but not to send word?"

Roland's frown deepened. "We shall discuss what happened at Castle DeLac when we are at home and in private. What are you doing so far from Dunborough?"

"Why, I came seeking you, brother," Gerrard replied. "You left in such haste and without an escort, and then were so long delayed, I feared you'd fallen prey to outlaws on the road, or perhaps had hurt yourself."

He made Roland sound like a child who needed tending.

"As garrison commander, it was your duty to remain in the castle."

"So much for brotherly gratitude for my concern," Gerrard said lightly, but there was anger in his eyes. "However, you must allow me and my friends to escort you the rest of the way, and you can send these soldiers back from whence they came."

Arnhelm and Verdan exchanged wary looks.

Gerrard rose in his stirrups and looked down the road. "Where is the dowry, or was it all in coin?"

"Enough questions, and we have no need of your company. I will say when the escort is dismissed." Roland raised his hand and signaled their party to start moving again.

Mavis maneuvered her horse beside her husband's while Gerrard turned his onto the verge to let them pass and gestured for his friends to do the same. She could hear Gerrard and his friends whispering and laughing as they rode by.

"Gerrard needs better manners," Roland growled.

Mavis didn't disagree, yet because she was so happy, she didn't want to add to the enmity between them. "It was good of him to be worried about you since you hadn't sent word you would be returning later than he expected. He was right to think you might have been attacked or hurt, even if his way of expressing that concern was less than respectful."

Roland's only answer to that was a sniff.

"He looks very like you. I should have realized that he would, and yet I never really thought about it. Is he like you in other ways?"

"No."

Clearly Roland did not wish to discuss his brother, so she said no more as they rounded a curve in the road.

The massive earthworks and walls of a sizable castle rose in the distance. "Is that Dunborough?" she asked with awe, amazed at the sheer size of the fortress.

"Yes," Roland replied with pride in his voice.

"I had no idea it was so impressive."

"It's the largest castle for miles around. My father spent thousands of marks on its construction."

Despite his pride, she also caught an undercurrent of

displeasure in his words. "It will surely make any man think twice about trying to attack it," she said.

"That was his explanation for the cost."

"The people must feel safe knowing they have such a sanctuary in times of war."

"I hope so, for it was their tithes and taxes that paid for it."

As they neared the first houses at the edge of the village clustered at the foot of the protective walls of the fortress, Roland rode ahead several paces again. This time, though, she was not distressed. That must simply be his way.

The village seemed a prosperous place, with more than a few buildings of two stories. Most were wattle-and-daub, and those around the village green had shops on the lower level. A stone church stood on a rise a short distance away. There was also a smithy, judging by the smoke rising from one of the buildings near an oak tree, and there were signs for a chandler, a baker and a tavern, too.

Gerrard, who must have followed after all, rode up beside her as they headed toward the castle gatehouse. "So, my lady, has my brother been bragging about his castle?"

Roland might be several feet away, but given that Gerrard made no effort to speak softly, Mavis was sure Roland—and every soldier behind them—had heard his mocking, sarcastic words.

Whatever was between these two men, Roland was a nobleman, the lord of an estate and her husband. She wasn't about to let him be treated in such an insolent way, even by a brother. She couldn't challenge Gerrard with sword or mace, but she had other weapons, and she would use them to put this fellow in his place.

"No, he hasn't really spoken of Dunborough," she replied with a little smile that hinted at pleasant reminiscences. "We spoke of other things when we were alone...or didn't speak at all."

Her reward was the brief flicker of surprise that crossed Gerrard's features before he replied. "I'm shocked he managed to speak to you at all. He's usually tongue-tied around women."

She wished she had known that before. It would have saved her much dismay.

"Even ones he's known for years," Gerrard added.

"It's true that he doesn't chatter on as so many shallow young men do," she replied with cool politeness while trying not to wonder who those "other women" might be, and if any of them were pretty. "But then, he has no need to talk to be impressive. He has a certain... how shall I put it? Commanding presence? Aura of invincibility? Strength? A woman has only to look at him to know that she would always be safe and protected by such a man and then there's..." She delicately cleared her throat. "Well, there are some attractions that are perhaps best kept to oneself."

She had hoped her implications would silence Gerrard. Unfortunately, she was wrong.

"No doubt she'll have something in common with Audrey, then, eh, brother?" he called out. He looked back at Mavis and smiled with triumphant glee to see her surprise—and something else that she couldn't quite hide. "He hasn't told you about the lovely Audrey D'Orleau? Why haven't you told her about Audrey, brother?" he shouted. "Why haven't you mentioned the woman everyone in Dunborough assumed you'd marry?"

This was more than a vague mention of other nameless, faceless women. This was a specific woman, a lovely woman, and one expected to marry Roland.

Then she remembered who was speaking and what Lady Viola had said about him. She wouldn't take Gerrard's words and implications seriously. "We had more interesting things to do than discuss old friends of the family."

"I can think of a few interesting things I'd like to do with you, too," Gerrard said, his very voice a leer.

Roland reined in abruptly and jumped down from his horse. As Mavis and the others halted their mounts and watched in stunned surprise, he marched up to the grinning Gerrard, grabbed him by the leg and dragged him from his horse.

"S'truth!" Arnhelm gasped again.

"Aye!" Verdan replied with equal shock, while Mavis could only stare.

"Have you gone mad?" Gerrard demanded as he scrambled to his feet.

His friends trotted up from the back of the cortege, clearly angry.

"What the devil are you doing?" the one in red demanded, while the other two looked on with eyes as wide as children's.

The man in red also seemed about to dismount until Roland's brother held up his hand to stop him. "There's no need for you to interfere, Walter," Gerrard said. "This is between my brother and me."

Roland paid not an ounce of attention to his brother's friends. "How dare you speak to my wife in that insolent manner?" he demanded. "And why should I tell my wife about the daughter of a wool merchant?"

"Why not, unless you wanted to keep your past liaison from her?"

A knot formed in Mavis's stomach.

Roland strode closer to Gerrard, until they were nose to nose, mirror images glaring at each other. "I had no *past liaison* with Audrey, as you well know," he said sternly, and with such fierce conviction, the seed of jealousy that had been planted in Mavis's heart withered. "And in future you will treat my wife with the respect that is her due."

His hands on his hips, Gerrard barked a laugh. "You're the lord of Dunborough only because you were born minutes before me. As for Audrey, everyone in Dunborough's seen you go to her house. What for? A friendly chat? With the richest and most beautiful young woman for fifty miles?"

"To offer her advice, because she sought it."

"Advice? Is that what it's called these days? Perhaps it is, by callous, arrogant men like you. As for respect, I will grant it when it's earned and not before."

Turning to Mavis, Gerrard made a sweeping bow. "Nevertheless, my lady, I do beg *your* forgiveness for my impertinence. My mind was boggled by such loveliness and I forgot my manners."

He once more addressed his scowling brother. "If you want to impress your wife, Roland, I can think of better ways to do it than by attacking me—although such other means might well be beyond your powers."

"Shut your mouth and get back on your horse," Roland ordered as he stalked back to Hephaestus and put his foot in the stirrup.

"Mustn't make a spectacle of ourselves, is that it?" Gerrard replied, slapping the dust from his breeches. "It's too late for that."

While Roland mounted with stern dignity, Gerrard

threw himself onto his horse with reckless abandon, to the obvious entertainment of his friends.

"A fine fellow you've married, eh, my lady?" he said to Mavis, his horse prancing. "A proud prude of a man who stole his brother's birthright and uses women only for gain."

"That's a lie, as well you know, while you spread rumors that are based upon the gossip of idle tongues," Roland retorted.

Laughing scornfully, Gerrard punched his horse's sides with his heels and rode through the looming gatehouse at a gallop. His friends likewise put their spurs to their horses and followed, the one in red named Walter smirking and the other two young men grinning like jesters.

"God save us," Arnhelm whispered to Verdan. "What a—"

"Aye," Verdan interrupted. "Ain't he just?"

Mavis silently agreed with their sentiments and unspoken epithet. She'd been warned that Roland and Gerrard hated each other, but even so, she hadn't expected their animosity to be so blatant and so fierce. As for this woman Audrey... Thanks to Lady Viola and the knowledge that Roland hadn't married her for financial or political gain, it was far easier to believe Roland's stern refutation than Gerrard's mocking accusation.

Without a word, without any readable expression at all, not even anger, Roland led the cortege through the gatehouse, under the portcullis and across the outer ward. They went through another gate in another wall to enter the inner ward, and through the final gate into the cobblestoned courtyard. Rows of soldiers stood on the wall walks, watching as they passed, and in the yard, more soldiers waited stiffly at attention, clearly

mustered there for Roland's return. Several servants
likewise waited near what had to be the hall. Only one
man stood at his ease, leaning against a wall, his ankles
and his arms crossed and an insolent grin on his face.

Gerrard.

Ignoring his brother, Roland dismounted and helped
Mavis from her horse. He moved with even greater dignity here, as if he was a king and this was his country,
while Mavis was all too aware of the shabbiness of her
attire, and that her arrival was unexpected.

"This is Lady Mavis, my wife," Roland announced
in a loud, clear voice.

The soldiers didn't move. The servants only glanced
at one another. No one said a word, not even in a whisper or muttered aside, including Arnhelm and Verdan.

Mavis suspected news had already reached Dunborough that Roland had a wife, no doubt thanks to the man
leaning against the wall.

"Where is Eua?" Roland called out.

A serving woman, narrow hipped and middle-
aged, pushed her way through the knot of servants.
Her clothes were clean, her dun-colored hair mostly
covered by a wimple, and there were lines around her
mouth as if a frown was her usual expression.

She was certainly frowning now.

"Show my wife to my chamber," Roland said. "It's
been a long journey and she should rest before the evening meal." His gaze scanned the yard. "Where's Dalfrid?"

"At the mill. We've sent someone to fetch him," the
serving woman replied. She spoke without deference
or even respect, although Roland was the lord.

But then he had only recently come into the title. At

least Mavis hoped that was the explanation for her insolence. Otherwise, this did not bode well.

"When Dalfrid returns," Roland continued, "tell him I wish to speak with him in the solar." He wheeled around and fixed Gerrard with a glare. "After I've talked to my brother."

Gerrard's only answer was a shrug of his broad shoulders before Roland started toward the hall.

God save her, surely they all wouldn't be so insolent to Roland!

She was so taken aback, it took her a moment to realize Roland had left the courtyard without speaking to her.

"I look forward to seeing you later, my lady," Gerrard said as he passed her, his tone amused, and he impertinently winked.

Eua grinned at that, while Arnhelm and Verdan frowned.

Mavis drew herself up and regarded Eua with all the dignity she possessed. She must make it clear at once that she was to be treated with respect. She was as certain of that as if Tamsin was there to tell her so. "I am your lord's wife, Eua, and the chatelaine of Dunborough. You had best remember that, or you will be shown the gate. Now please take me to my chamber."

The woman flushed, but gave no other sign that she felt chastised before she led Mavis toward the hall and what must be the family chambers beside it.

Chapter Six

Gerrard sauntered into the solar that had been their father's and slid down into one of the ornately carved chairs. Crossing his arms, he put his boots on the massive table in the center of the chamber and raised a brow as he regarded his brother. "Well, Roland, here I am," he said, his tone as much of an insult as his smirk.

Roland wanted to wipe that mocking grin off his brother's face. It wasn't just the disrespect he'd shown to him. He was used to Gerrard's impudent mockery. It was the way Gerrard had addressed Mavis and looked at her, too, and while she'd acquitted herself admirably...

Yes, she had—and come to his defense, as well. Indeed, she'd succeeded in a way he never had in a battle of words with his brother.

That was cause for some satisfaction and pride, so it was with considerably less force than he might have used that he struck Gerrard's feet from the table.

He also should have known better than to believe Gerrard would show any sign of envy, even though it had to be there. He had seen the way Gerrard had looked at Mavis and then his awestruck expression when he'd found out she was his brother's wife. He didn't doubt that explained a good portion of Gerrard's anger, too. For once, Gerrard would know how he had felt when his brother did something unexpected that affected them both.

"Are you drunk?" he asked as his brother's boots hit the flagstones. "That would be the only excuse you could have for speaking to my wife as you did."

"Ah, yes, your wife," Gerrard replied, putting his feet back up on the table. "Your very unexpected wife. How did that happen, I wonder? It couldn't be because you were stirred by her beauty. Not you. And it couldn't be because you wanted an alliance with DeLac. You were against that even before our father announced his betrothal to the man's niece. DeLac wasn't to be trusted, you said. He would play us false. He'd find a way to deceive us or refuse to come to our aid, should we have to ask him. Yet here you are with Simon DeLac's daughter for a bride. I'm sure the dowry was substantial, but she's still Simon DeLac's daughter, and unless he's undergone some kind of miraculous change, he's still the same deceitful rogue."

"I don't have to explain myself to you," Roland replied, once again striking his brother's boots from the table.

Gerrard jumped to his feet. "No, you don't, *my lord*. I'm only the garrison commander you left in charge with barely a word of warning. Yet lo!" He made a sweeping gesture. "The castle is still here. Nothing has crumbled. There's been no riot or insurrection. So you see, dear brother, I am not completely incompetent. But what of *your* heedless actions? You ride off like a madman after hearing of our father's and brother's deaths and that you're now the lord, then don't come back for days. And what do I discover when I go to look for you? That you've married the daughter of Simon DeLac!"

Marching closer, he jabbed his finger into Roland's chest. "Were *you* drunk when you took that woman for your bride?"

Roland swatted his brother's finger away. "Don't touch me!"

"Is that what she said on your wedding night?"

Roland's hands balled into fists as he fought the urge to strike his brother. "I should know better than to expect you to speak with any respect, but you will not mock my wife."

"I wasn't mocking her. I was mocking *you*."

"Get out!"

"Not until you tell me why you married her," Gerrard returned as he planted his feet and crossed his arms. "Let me hear your sound and logical reasons, for there's no way under heaven love or desire had anything to do with it, in spite of how she looks."

Roland straightened his shoulders and lied. "For the same reason our father and then Broderick agreed to wed her cousin. We need allies in the south and DeLac is a powerful man. I will never trust him, but he's still our ally for all that."

"And the dowry? Considerable, no doubt."

"Enough."

Gerrard's eyes narrowed. "How much?"

"As lord of Dunborough, I need not—"

"God's blood, did that old buzzard manage to give away his daughter without a dowry—and to you?"

"There was a dowry, and I need not say more to you."

"He got you to take her for nearly nothing, didn't he?" Gerrard crowed. "I never thought I'd see the day that any man ever got the better of you in a bargain, not even when it's for a woman who looks like that."

Roland took out the purse of silver that had been part of Mavis's dowry and tossed it on the table.

Gerrard picked it up and weighed it in his hand. "Is this all? Audrey will be outraged."

"Audrey's feelings are her own affair. I made her no promises." Indeed, she'd barely paid attention to him while his older brother was alive, and he had *never*, for one moment, considered marrying her, no matter what Gerrard said. Hopefully, he'd made that clear to Mavis, too. "The wagon carrying the rest of my wife's dower goods was destroyed in a fire when we stopped for the night."

The moment Roland saw the skeptical look that came to his brother's face, he was sorry he'd bothered to tell him. "Whether or not you care to believe me, that's the truth."

Gerrard's expression changed to one of bogus, wide-eyed innocence. "Why, of course I believe you, brother. That would explain the lack of baggage in your cortege. How unfortunate for your bride, among so many other misfortunes. Tell me, Roland, when you and DeLac were making your bargain, did you ever spare a moment's thought for her?"

Roland had barely thought of anything *but* Mavis since the first time he'd seen her, but that was a weakness he would certainly never divulge to Gerrard, or anyone else. "She chose to be my wife."

"Chose? Probably as much as we *chose* to be our father's sons."

"She did choose, and that is all I'm going to say on the matter."

"No doubt that's all the gentle love talk you've shared

with her, too. 'Marry me or not—what is your choice?' God's blood, to think of a beauty like her married to a cold fish like you!"

"No doubt *you'd* rather see her married to a wastrel who drinks and wenches away his nights."

"At least I know what to do with a woman in my bed."

"Or so the whores let you believe."

The mocking grin that Roland despised came back to Gerrard's face. "Perhaps I should offer her some brotherly comfort."

Roland took a step closer. "Stay away from her, Gerrard, or by God, I'll—"

A low cough came from the direction of the door. Both men turned to see the steward standing on the threshold.

"Come in, Dalfrid, and tell my brother all my latest transgressions," Gerrard said to the slender, gray-haired man holding several scrolls. "He can tell you all about his wife, too. Oh, don't try to look surprised, Dalfrid! I'm sure Eua told you he has come home with a wife. But you can also lose that gleam in your eyes. She doesn't have a dowry—or at least not much. He says there was a fire and her dower goods lost. If that's so, though, I wonder why my coldhearted, ambitious brother didn't send her back to her father."

"Leave us, Gerrard!" Roland ordered.

"Gladly," his brother said with an airy wave of his hand as he continued toward the door. "I have no wish to listen to the both of you discuss accounts and other mundane matters."

Clearing his throat again, Dalfrid sidled into the room, bowing humbly and glancing at the purse of coins as he put the scrolls of account on the table. "Naturally

I was told of your marriage, my lord," he said in that smooth-as-curds voice of his. "And that your bride is quite beautiful. I wish you joy, my lord."

Roland threw himself into the chair behind the table, then rose again when he realized he'd just sat where his father used to preside like a king upon his throne. Issuing orders. Making threats. Meting out what passed for justice in his twisted mind. "Thank you, Dalfrid," he said, coming around the table, then leaning back against it and crossing his arms. "Now, what has been happening here while I was gone?"

Dalfrid glanced again at the purse of coins, then gave Roland one of his meaningless smiles. "Cuthbert has paid what he owes, my lord. He understands you're not the sort of man who would allow his father's and brother's deaths to disrupt the business of the estate."

"No, I am not."

Dalfrid put on an expression of sorrow nearly as false as his smiles. "Alas, my lord, I have some news that you will not be happy to hear. Gerrard and his friends have caused some, um, trouble in the village. They got into a brawl in the Cock's Crow and there was considerable damage done. Tables and benches broken, as well as a shutter. There was also the loss of a large keg of ale. It was shattered and the contents spilled."

Roland suppressed an annoyed sigh. "How much does the tavern keeper want?"

"Ten marks, my lord. Naturally I went to the tavern myself to survey the damage."

"Naturally."

"It was as Matheus said. There was something else, my lord." Dalfrid delicately cleared his throat. "One of the serving wenches claims she was attacked."

Roland fixed his gaze on Dalfrid's fawning visage

and waited to hear the news he'd been dreading ever since Gerrard had discovered girls.

"Not Gerrard, my lord, and not raped," Dalfrid quickly explained. "She claims one of your brother's cronies blackened her eye, as well as inflicting some other bruises. I paid her for her, uh, difficulties."

"Where was my brother during this brawl and the beating of the maidservant?"

"Out cold, my lord, in the stable."

That he should be relieved to hear that his brother had passed out from drink! "Is there more?"

"No, my lord."

"Thank God for that," he muttered, finally picking up the purse of coins. "My wife needs new clothes. Her own were destroyed in a fire on our way here, along with most of her dower goods save for the coin."

"At least something was saved, my lord, and you also have the alliance with her father. Lord DeLac is not without influence at court. A most valuable connection, my lord."

Given his expression and enthusiasm, one would think the marriage had been Dalfrid's idea.

"And of course there is the lady herself," the steward continued. "She alone is surely worth—"

"Yes, she is," Roland interrupted. He didn't want to hear Mavis's "worth" discussed by Dalfrid, or any other man. He put out his hand holding the coins. "I also want you to help her with the wedding feast."

Even as he reached for the purse, Dalfrid's already beady eyes narrowed even more. "Wedding feast, my lord?"

"Yes, and there is the money for it," Roland replied. "Since I am lord of Dunborough and Lady Mavis is new to Yorkshire, there should be a proper celebration so she can meet the other nobles."

It would also make her happy, but he would not say that to Dalfrid.

"As you say, my lord," Dalfrid replied as he tucked the purse into his wide belt, "a wedding feast is indeed called for. When should this take place?"

"Soon."

"Say, a fortnight?"

"If Mavis agrees that is enough time."

Dalfrid nodded.

"I shall expect you to come to me for approval of any costly items, especially if you've already spent what's in the purse."

"Of course, my lord."

"I will see that she keeps the expenses reasonable."

"I'm sure you will, my lord," Dalfrid said with another smooth smile. "I'm sure you will."

Arnhelm threw his leather pouch onto a cot in the barracks of Dunborough. "Well, men, we're here," he said to the rest of the escort from DeLac as he looked around the long, narrow room lined with cots. Two pegs had been hammered into the stone wall beside each one, and a long wash table ran along the far wall. "Could be worse."

"Could be better," Verdan said as he tossed his pouch onto another cot and lay down, pillowing his head in his hands and crossing his legs at the ankles.

The other men likewise disposed of their baggage and milled about.

"When do we eat?" Teddy asked, scratching his beard.

"When we're told," Arnhelm replied, sitting on his cot.

"When do we go home?" Rob asked more urgently.

"When we're told."

"I hope tomorrow!" Teddy muttered. "Yorkshire's too bloody cold!"

"Game of draughts?" Rob suggested, and the men moved off to play in the corner where the lone brazier stood, to watch or make wagers on the outcome.

Verdan sat up and regarded his brother with a frown. "Don't you really know when we're leaving?"

"No, and I ain't goin' to ask," Arnhelm replied. "It's our duty to see our lady's safe and by God, I want to be sure she is. And you know as well as I do that Lady Tamsin's going to come and ask us how she was when we left here, sure as we breathe."

"Aye."

"So we stay as long as we can."

Verdan nodded at the rest of the men now engaged in a lively and loud game. "They aren't goin' to like it."

"Good thing they aren't in charge, then, eh? Besides, it ain't them Lady Tamsin and Sir Rheged'll talk to."

Eua led Mavis through the yard toward the hall of Dunborough Castle, the largest building within the inner curtain wall. There was a squat, square tower close behind it, likely the original keep and perhaps attached by some kind of walkway. Another half-timbered, two-storied building with shuttered windows on the upper level, none on the lower, spread out to the left of the hall.

The massive hall itself was chilly and drafty and rather bare, the walls supported by thick stone pillars, with huge oaken beams on plain corbels spanning the roof. There were few windows, and those were at the top intended to allow smoke from torches and the central hearth to escape. A wooden dais was at the far end.

They continued through another, smaller door at the

far end of the hall and to the right of the dais. Opposite that was a wider opening to the left. Judging from the sounds that came from the corridor beyond, that led to the kitchen.

Opening the smaller door revealed a corridor that went along the outside of the long, two-storied timber building attached to the hall.

"His lordship's solar's in the tower," the dour maidservant explained as they entered the corridor, "but you can't get to it from here. Only from outside." She paused at the first door. "This was Sir Blane's chamber. Broderick's was this one," she noted in that same flat, emotionless tone as they passed a second door.

They came to a third door. "That's Gerrard's, not that he uses it much," the maidservant said, her tone vastly different. She spoke as if she expected Mavis to be impressed that Gerrard apparently slept elsewhere, no doubt with a variety of women.

Mavis found that anything *but* impressive.

Eua pushed open the door to the fourth bedchamber. "This is Roland's. And yours now, I suppose."

Mavis tried not to show her dismay as she surveyed the barren chamber, but even the servants at DeLac had better quarters. The only furnishings were a narrow bed more like a soldier's cot covered by a thick woolen blanket, a washing stand, a stool, a wooden chest that no doubt held Roland's clothes and a small table with an unlit oil lamp upon it. When she looked at the bed again, she regretted the loss of her dower goods, especially the linens, even more.

But that was not all that was wrong. "My husband and I require a larger bed. That is barely big enough for one."

"There's his late lordship's, I suppose," Eua replied with a shrug of her shoulders.

"No, not that one." Mavis could all too well imagine the sort of things that had happened in that bed, whether the women were willing or not. "A new one."

"Anything costs money, you have to talk to Dalfrid, my lady," Eua replied. "You know who that is?"

Mavis was not pleased with the woman's question, or the manner of asking it. "Of course. He's the steward."

"Then you ought to know anything requires money, you go to him. Where should I tell the men to put your things?"

"I have only a small chest of clothes and toilet articles." She tried to sound unconcerned, but a blush stole up her face nonetheless. "There was a fire on the journey here and all my other clothes and dower goods were destroyed."

"A fire, eh? Too bad," Eua replied with another shrug of her shoulders and a skeptical expression.

Who did this woman think she was, to speak to her lord's wife in such a manner? One thing was certain, it could not continue. If Mavis had learned anything from Tamsin, it was that respect was essential when dealing with servants.

Mavis drew herself up and spoke in her best imitation of her cousin. "It *was* too bad. Now fetch me some hot water and a brazier to warm the chamber. At once!"

Finally Eua made a show of deference, bobbing a curtsy before she left the chamber.

Hopefully, all the servants wouldn't be like Eua, Mavis thought as she watched her go. Then there was Gerrard, but at least she had some experience dealing with vain and arrogant young men.

Mavis again surveyed the spartan chamber and

sighed. This was not what she'd been expecting. Not at all.

"By God, you are a beauty."

Forewarned by the slight difference in pitch, Mavis turned to find Gerrard standing in the door.

"All alone, eh?" Gerrard noted with a smile as he strolled, uninvited, into the chamber.

Yes, he was like her husband, but vastly different, too, and not just because he smiled so broadly, so easily and so often. Roland was a strong, silent warrior who would surely fight with grim determination. Gerrard was undoubtedly bold and probably did well in tournaments, but she wouldn't be surprised to learn he lacked the stomach for a real battle.

"If I were your husband, I would never leave you waiting, especially in such a godforsaken excuse for a bedchamber. But then, Roland never concerns himself with anyone's comfort."

"Including his own," she replied. "I'm sure he has many things to attend to since he's returned."

"If I had a wife as beautiful as you," Gerrard said, sauntering closer, "the business of the estate could wait."

She backed away. "Perhaps, then, it's better you don't yet have either a wife or an estate of your own."

That wiped the insolent grin off his face. "My brother has robbed me of my inheritance."

"If he was the eldest, the estate was his by right of primogeniture."

"Only if he *is* the eldest. No one can prove that."

"Wasn't it also a provision of your father's will that Roland inherit?" she asked, even though she wasn't sure that was the case.

Fortunately, judging by Gerrard's sullen scowl, she'd

guessed aright. "I don't doubt my late father was influenced by the greedy, ambitious son who slavishly followed his every command."

Instead of the insolent one? she silently asked. Aloud, she said, "As a son, it was his duty to obey."

"As you obeyed your father when you married Roland?"

"I would have fled my father's household and sought sanctuary in the church rather than marry against my will," she answered honestly and although her marriage was none of his concern.

Gerrard laughed and came closer still. "I'd sooner believe my horse can talk than a woman like you would marry Roland willingly."

A shadow fell across the floor. "What are you doing here, Gerrard?" Roland asked from the doorway.

Mavis smiled with relief. Meanwhile, Gerrard crossed his arms, leaned his weight on one leg and regarded Roland with another mocking grin. "Well, brother, it seems you've finally remembered you have a wife."

"And you've apparently forgotten this is my chamber, not yours."

"You didn't tell me your brother was so amusing," Mavis said, walking past Gerrard to take her husband's arm. "He was just telling me he believes his horse can talk."

"I said I can sooner believe my horse can talk than that she wed you willingly."

Mavis smiled up at Roland's stoic face. "And since I did marry you willingly, he must either believe his horse can talk, or admit that he was mistaken to make such an assumption. But perhaps we should excuse him. I've only just arrived and he does not yet know me."

"I look forward to getting to know you better, my lady."

She gave Gerrard another smile, albeit a more brittle one, and her eyes were not amused. "I look forward to learning more about my husband's brother, too."

Especially why Roland had made Gerrard his garrison commander. Having seen them together, that was a mystery. "Is the evening meal ready, my lord?" she asked.

Roland's hand covered hers as he nodded, the action not without a hint of possessiveness. "Yes. Come, my lady," he replied, turning to escort her from the chamber and leaving Gerrard to follow.

Mavis didn't have to look back to see if he did. She could hear him following behind them like a smirking, impudent shadow. Nevertheless, she tried to enter the hall with confidence and poise—but what she would have given then to have her green gown and silken veil!

Regardless of her attire, Arnhelm and Verdan and the men of DeLac greeted her with smiles and nods. The soldiers of Dunborough watched her more warily, and others who looked to be men of some responsibility such as the huntsman, the fletcher and smith, did likewise. The three young men who'd been with Gerrard on the road were also there, unsteady on their feet in a way she was unfortunately familiar with, while a tall, slender man, well dressed in a long woolen tunic of dark blue, waited close to the trestle table on the dais. She spotted Eua at the farthest corner of the hall.

The hall was still rather barren. There were no linen coverings, and the only chairs were at the high table, with benches at the others. Torches now burned in the sconces.

Gerrard sauntered past them to join his friends, while

the man in the blue tunic hurried toward them, pausing a moment to give Gerrard a bow that was not acknowledged.

"My lady, this is Dalfrid, steward of Dunborough," Roland said. "Dalfrid, this is my wife, Lady Mavis, the daughter of Lord Simon DeLac."

"It's an honor, my lady!" Dalfrid cried, bowing deeply. "I must confess my breath is quite taken away by your beauty."

In spite of his effusive welcome, there was something about the man Mavis immediately didn't like. She wasn't sure if it was his long, narrow face or his wheedling way of speaking or the way he rubbed his hands together, but something seemed amiss.

"Dalfrid will show you the stores tomorrow," Roland said, "and give you any assistance you require to prepare for a wedding feast."

"Wedding feast? I thought you didn't have feasts at Dunborough," she said, too surprised to hide it.

"I decided our wedding was a worthy occasion to celebrate, and a feast will give you the opportunity to meet our neighbors and tenants and the more important villagers."

As pleased as she was that he considered their marriage important enough for a feast, a thousand thoughts, questions and worries burst into Mavis's mind—first and foremost that although she'd asked Roland about feasts, she had never planned one. Tamsin had been in charge of such events in recent years. Yet now she was to not just take control of this unfamiliar household, but plan her own wedding feast, too?

"We should have more than enough stores," Roland continued, "and there is no great hurry. Let us say in a fortnight's time." He fixed his penetrating gaze on her. "That will be sufficient, will it not, my lady?"

Whatever her concerns and doubts, she didn't want to imply she wasn't up to the task. "Certainly, my lord."

"Good. I've also told Dalfrid to see that you have whatever new garments you require."

That was much more welcome news. "Thank you, my lord."

"Any request you have that requires purchase or payment, you should make to Dalfrid. If there are concerns, he will bring them to me."

"Then, Dalfrid, we require a new bed," she said to the steward. "The one in Sir Roland's chamber is much too small."

In the silence that followed, Mavis could have heard a raindrop fall. Roland's head slowly swiveled toward her. Dalfrid's eyes widened and his jaw hung slack, while everyone else in the hall was apparently equally stunned, except for Eua. She let out a snort of laughter that was more embarrassing than the silence.

Blushing, Mavis desperately tried to mend her mistake. "I thought the sooner... That is, it's small for two."

Dalfrid recovered. "I'll see to it at once, my lady."

"Tomorrow will do," Roland said evenly.

"Tomorrow, then, my lord," Dalfrid replied.

By now several servants had appeared at the entrance to the kitchen bearing trays and trenchers. The steward made another bow and went to a table on the opposite side of the hall where Arnhelm, Verdan and the escort from DeLac were sitting. Gerrard and his friends were still smiling with amusement and exchanging whispers.

Mavis looked around again. "Where is the priest to bless the meal, my lord?"

"We have no priest in the castle. Father Denzail serves in the church in the village."

The manner in which Roland replied told her that was another of his father's edicts he had yet to change, should he wish to do so.

They took their seats and the maidservants started toward the high table. Eua, she noted, stayed where she was, although she gestured and pointed to direct the servants like a general leading a battle from afar.

"I didn't mean to embarrass you about the bed, my lord," Mavis said before the servants got to the high table. "I didn't think—"

"No, you did not," he said, his voice low. "You shouldn't have made your request in the hall."

Gerrard rose with a goblet in his hands and another disrespectful, mocking grin on his face.

"I don't think we need wait for a wedding feast to drink a toast to the bride and groom!" he called out, his eyes gleaming in the torchlight. "To my brother Roland and his beautiful bride! May she give him many children—but never twins!"

Another silence descended on the hall as Gerrard downed his wine in a gulp and wiped his mouth with the back of his hand.

Roland got to his feet. "Let us also drink to my brother. May he one day find a wife willing to overlook his many shortcomings."

"As you have?" Gerrard retorted. Then, scowling, he threw his goblet at the high table, right at Roland's head.

With a cry, Mavis moved to avoid it, while Roland lunged in front of her and caught it. He angrily threw it back, narrowly missing his brother. The metal goblet hit the wall with a metallic clang, then fell, dented, to the floor.

"Leave the hall!" Roland commanded.

For a moment, it looked as if Gerrard wasn't going to obey. Fortunately, he did, gesturing for his friends to follow him from the hall. They did, and not with very steady steps.

After they were gone, there was another moment of silence before the rest of those in the hall began talking among themselves, casting occasional wary glances at the high table and its occupants.

"I would ask you to excuse my brother, but there is no excuse for him," Roland said to Mavis as he sat down again.

"He's had too much to drink, like my father in recent days," she replied. "I'm sadly familiar with how that can affect a man."

"That's no excuse, either. He's always been insolent and now he believes he has more cause to be."

"Perhaps, in time, he will come to accept that the estate is rightfully yours."

"I doubt it."

"Then it might be better if he were not your garrison commander," she suggested.

"I am the master of Dunborough, my lady, and I decide such things."

"Of course, my lord," she replied, trying not to feel rebuffed and to remember that he hadn't married her for gain.

Chapter Seven

After Gerrard and his friends had staggered from the hall, Arnhelm and Verdan looked at one another, then rose in unison from their places at the table where they sat with the rest of the escort.

"We'll be back later," Arnhelm said to Teddy. "There's a tavern in the town and we've a powerful thirst."

Teddy laughed. "And no serving wench worth looking at here, eh?" he teased.

Verdan frowned. "It ain't—"

Arnhelm nudged his brother in the ribs. "Aye, just so," he said, grabbing Verdan's arm. "We'll be back before the cock crows."

"Sooner than that, I'll wager," Rob said with a wide grin as the two men hurried from the hall. Once in the yard, they made their way swiftly to the gate and through the wards until they caught sight of the four young men strolling, more or less, toward the village.

Gerrard and his friends didn't go to the large tavern off the green with a rooster on the sign. Instead, they turned into a narrow alley and knocked at a narrow door. It opened a crack, then wider, and the four men were ushered inside.

"Worth a try," Arnhelm whispered and he and his brother stepped up to the door and knocked.

The door opened enough to reveal half a man's bearded face and one wary eye.

"We're two thirsty fellows come from DeLac who don't much want to drink in the hall with that grim bastard of a Sir Roland looking on." Arnhelm heard his brother's sharp intake of breath and willed him to keep quiet. "We've got money," he added, pulling out the purse that contained all the money they had in the world.

The door opened wider and Arnhelm and Verdan found themselves in an unexpectedly large room, with heavy beams above and lit by several lamps. Three braziers made it warm, and so did the presence of several young women in various states of undress.

As Verdan stared, openmouthed, Arnhelm spotted Gerrard and his friends seated at a table across the chamber. All of them had wenches on their laps. One of the men—not Gerrard—also had his hand on a naked breast.

Other men, villagers by the looks of them, filled the room and engaged in talking, arguing or games of chance, making the room buzz with noise.

Arnhelm led Verdan across the room to an empty table that was dark in shadow close to Gerrard and his friends.

"What kind o' place is this?" Verdan whispered to his brother in a tone between horror and wonder.

"It's a brothel, nit."

"S'truth!"

Arnhelm angled his stool closer to Gerrard and his friends. "Sit quiet and don't call for ale—or nothin' else, or what would Ma think? We're just here to listen."

Verdan nodded and leaned back against the wall.

Meanwhile, Gerrard had pushed the young woman off his lap. "Enough ale, Bella!" he cried, slapping a fat purse of coins on the table in front of him. "Bring us wine—the best you've got. After all, we're celebrating my brother's marriage—lout that he is!"

Bella pulled her somewhat disheveled bodice back into place, grabbed the purse and hurried to obey.

"I tell you, boys," Gerrard began with a deep frown, his elbow on the table as he pointed at them, "something is wrong with the world when *Roland* gets both an estate *and* a beautiful wife."

"You're right!" James, dressed in blue, cried.

"Eggsactly!" added Frederick, wearing green.

"Absolutely," Walter agreed, proving he was by far the most sober of the bunch.

"What if I went to the king?" Gerrard proposed. "Don't you think John will give me the estate?"

This time, his friends were not so quick to agree, until Walter nodded his head. "I'm sure he will." He dropped his voice so that Arnhelm had to strain to hear. "If you pay him enough."

"What need I to pay?" Gerrard demanded loudly. "It's mine by right! Roland tricked our father. He stole the estate!"

Walter hissed at him and urged him to be quiet. "It's not enough to suspect, even for John. You've got to have some evidence."

"Eua'll swear I'm the oldest. Eua'll do anything I say and she was in the household then."

"She's only a servant," Walter reminded him, and the other two nodded their heads.

Bella returned with a wineskin and a saucy smile.

"You think I should be lord of Dunborough, don't you?" Gerrard asked her.

"Aye, m'lord," she agreed, once again sliding onto his lap. Laughing, she put the wineskin to his lips and poured.

He drank until he began to splutter. He pushed the wineskin away, then kissed her, his hand roving over her bodice and up her leg.

James grabbed the wineskin and likewise took a swig while also fondling the slattern on his lap.

Arnhelm turned to his brother, gave him a look and together they got up and left the young men to their sport. They managed to slip out unnoticed when the man at the door had his back turned.

"Do you think he'll really go to the king?" Verdan said as they walked back to the castle.

"Might, or might be just a lot of talk. He seems the kind more interested in drinking and whoring and complaining than doing anything else. Still, we ought to say a word o' warning to our lady before we go."

Verdan nodded. "Aye."

"And I'm thinkin' we ought to tell Lady Tamsin and Sir Rheged about him, too, just in case he does make trouble."

"Aye," his brother agreed.

After Mavis had retired and the people in the hall began to disperse or bed down close to the long central hearth, Roland sat in his chair with a goblet in his hand and cursed himself for a fool. He shouldn't let Gerrard goad him and he shouldn't have lost his temper, even if Gerrard wasn't the least bit grateful he was the garrison commander.

Gerrard condemned him for being hard-hearted, yet

he'd never once tried to interfere when his father acted with cruelty. Nor had Gerrard ever lifted a hand to help the townspeople or tenants. Gerrard begrudged him this estate, but he'd done nothing to earn even a portion of it. He had left it to Roland to do what he could while he drank and wenched and gambled, and then he'd mocked his brother, calling him a stiff, coldhearted fellow who would never find a wife.

Gerrard had never known the bitterness of standing in the shadows watching his more popular brother joke and laugh with his friends, even if the friends were blackguards and toadies. He had never had to envy a brother's easy way with women who vied for his favor even when they knew where he came from and who his father was.

Nevertheless, by some miracle, he had found a wife who seemed to like him and who welcomed him into their bed, who made love with passionate abandon. Yet how had he behaved tonight? Like a petulant child, and he was sorry for it.

Determined to make things right with Mavis, Roland rose from his place, tugged down his tunic and left the hall, heading for his bedchamber.

Yet when he reached the door to his chamber, doubts began to assail him. He had never apologized to anyone, for anything, in his life. Was that not a sign of weakness? If he was to rule Dunborough, if he was to be master of his estate, he must appear to be powerful and invincible.

Even to his wife.

Even if he wanted her so much, his longing seemed to have a strength that no rational thought could overcome.

He sighed and laid his hand flat on the door, silently bidding Mavis good-night.

The door abruptly opened to reveal Mavis standing in the chamber illuminated by a single rushlight.

Clad only in that shift.

"Do you require something, my lord?" she asked, her brow furrowed.

Require? "No."

The wrinkle in her forehead disappeared and she tilted her head as she studied him, while he felt rooted to the floor as if he'd been nailed there.

Then she stood aside to let him enter.

Mavis had heard Roland's footfalls and recognized his bold tread. She'd realized that his steps had slowed and halted beyond the door. She'd wondered what he would do. He had been so angry, so brusque in the hall.

Yet when she heard his deep, heartfelt sigh, she hadn't been able to ignore it.

Now she watched him as he came into the chamber. His back was as stiff and straight as it had been in her father's solar, and for a moment, she wished she hadn't opened the door, until he turned to face her. Then, in those dark, often forbidding eyes, she saw again that look of wistful yearning.

But even then, he didn't apologize for his rough manner. He said, "As long as I am the lord, Gerrard will have a place in Dunborough."

"As you will, my lord," she replied, hiding her disappointment.

"I will not have people say I cast my brother out."

What could she say to that? She half expected him to leave then, but he didn't. He seemed to be struggling with something inside himself, engaged in an inner battle that silenced him, except for the desperate determination in his eyes.

"My lord?" she said softly, wondering if there was some way she could help him.

"Roland! My name is Roland, and I'm not like my father or my brothers."

"Of course not," she returned, taken aback by the intensity of his declaration. "You are by far a better man, or you wouldn't have asked me for my hand. You would have demanded it, if you acknowledged me at all."

His eyes widened and his whole posture changed, like a man whose fetters had been stricken from him.

She walked slowly toward him, as she might approach a wounded animal. "I heard you in the stable the day you arrived, when you were talking to your horse. I knew the kind of man you are even before I saw your face."

"You were there?" he asked in a rough whisper.

"I was planning to run away, until I heard your voice." She smiled then, a little smile of wary sincerity. "And then the groom saw me." She took hold of his strong hands. "When I saw you in my father's solar, I was glad I'd failed."

The look in his eyes changed again, to one that made her heart race and her blood warm, before he pulled her into his arms and kissed her with a tenderness that was different from his other embraces. She felt different, too, even as that fervent longing blossomed.

Here, in what had been his home, she had seen something of the trials he had endured. She better understood him now and cherished him all the more.

Once again passion and need arose. Their kisses deepened and their caresses fired their desire. They soon discovered that although the bed was small, it was large enough for two when they were making love.

* * *

Early the next morning, Mavis nestled against her naked husband and sighed with satisfaction. "Perhaps we should tell Dalfrid we don't need a larger bed after all.

"And have to explain why you changed your mind?" Roland said with a wry little smile she found completely delightful.

"No, you're right. I've already embarrassed myself—and you—enough."

"Your request was rather unexpected," he admitted, toying with a lock of her hair. "On the other hand, the look on Dalfrid's face was…"

And then she heard him laugh, a low rumble of a sound, deep and rich and full of joy. "I've never seen him look like that. Still, I think we must tell Dalfrid to buy us a bigger bed, or one of us is going to end up on the floor."

Although she didn't wish to spoil the lightness of his mood, there was something she had to say, and no doubt the sooner, the better. She raised herself on her elbow and regarded her husband gravely. "I have a confession to make, Roland. I've never planned a feast before."

His surprise, for once, was obvious. "Did your father not have feasts? Indeed, they are renowned."

"They are, and justly so, but that's been my cousin's doing. Tamsin always planned the feasts. She ran the household, too. She was good at it, you see, and the servants were swift to obey her. I did try to learn as much as she could teach me before she left DeLac, but there was little time."

Roland's smile was as welcome as his kisses. "Set your mind at ease, Mavis. It need only be a small feast.

And you'll have Dalfrid to help you with the merchants, and Eua with the servants."

Although the thought of dealing with those two people didn't please her, with Tamsin for an example, surely she could manage, or have as little to do with them as possible. "May we invite Sir Melvin and Lady Viola? And Tamsin and Rheged?"

"You may invite whomever you wish. I'll give a list of the Yorkshiremen and their wives who are likely to attend. As I said, it need only be a small feast, and that will be a very short list."

Mavis lay back down beside him. "I hope the new bed fits in this chamber. Is there none larger?"

"Only my father's and that is one I shall never use," Roland replied, stroking her hair, feeling her warm soft body against his, the stirrings of desire momentarily quelled by the thought of his father and his father's chamber and the sordid things he did there.

No, he would never use that room. It was far too tainted, and he would not bring that shadow upon their marriage.

"Then I shall make this one as comfortable as possible," Mavis said, and his heart grew lighter.

"Now you, my lord Roland, may be able to lie abed all day," she said as she got out of bed, "but I had best meet the household of Dunborough and be about my duties."

With a sigh of reluctance, he sat up. "I had best be about my duties, too, but first kiss me, wife, lest I come seek you out later when both of us should be doing other things."

Mavis gave him a hearty kiss. And then another. And it was some time yet before they broke the fast.

* * *

Moaning, for his head felt as if little demons were at play inside it, Gerrard stumbled into the barracks and threw himself down on the first cot he encountered. He put his arm over his eyes to block out the light.

He'd left his friends in the brothel to finish their sport. He had come back because while he indulged in drinking, gambling and kissing and a little more, he never slept with whores, despite what Roland and most of Dunborough thought. Not that he was a monk, not by any means. But if you had to pay, it was simply a transaction. There were always serving maids or lasses from the village who were glad to share their favors with the younger son of a lord, even a lord of Dunborough.

Gerrard became dimly aware that he wasn't alone. "Who's there?" he muttered, moving his arm and cracking open his eyelids. He didn't recognize either of the two men looking down at him. "Who the hell are you?"

"Men of DeLac, my lord," the taller one responded, while the other one's mouth hung open like a landed fish.

"What do you want?" He sat up. "Where are my men?"

"The ones not on watch are out in the field with Teddy and the rest of the escort. Sword drill and such," the tall one answered.

"Oh." Gerrard lay back down. "Why aren't you with them?"

"We was just goin'. Anything we can do for you?"

More awake now, Gerrard sat up again. "You can tell me about Lord DeLac. I've heard the man's a sot."

The two soldiers exchanged glances.

"Go on, you can tell me. I should know if my brother's father-in-law is a trustworthy fellow."

"He may be, or he may not," the tall soldier replied. "Still, I'd be careful about upsetting our lady. Her father might be past his prime, but her cousin's husband isn't."

"Oh, and who's that?" Gerrard replied as if he didn't give a damn.

"Sir Rheged of Cwm Bron."

Good God. Gerrard certainly remembered that Welshman. He'd been the only man to ever defeat Broderick, even though his older brother cheated. Broderick always dosed his opponent's wine with a poison before a tournament. It wasn't enough to kill, but it was enough to render the man weak. He'd been sure Rheged had had the wine, but he'd beaten Broderick nonetheless. He'd never seen any man fight with such skill and determination, not even Roland.

Both he and Roland had stayed far from the castle for a few days after that, in case Broderick attacked them in his rage. As it was, more than one servant sported bruises and cuts and gashes for weeks afterward because they fell under Broderick's angry gaze.

Now Roland's marriage made a lot more sense. DeLac might not be a worthy ally, but Rheged would be.

Once again his brother had managed to beat him.

"Leave me," Gerrard muttered, and the soldiers obediently departed.

He wanted to be alone, to think and nurse his aching—

"Here's my lamb!" Eua cried. "Out carousing again, and why not?"

"I need to sleep, Eua," he said with more than a hint of impatience as the woman appeared beside the cot and regarded him with a sympathy he did not need. All his life she'd mothered him, in no small part because she liked to be noticed and flattered and given little presents of money, something Roland never seemed to understand. It was easy to get on Eua's good side, if you were willing to make the effort, lie a little and pay.

Now that he was older, though, he more often found her attention annoying, and this morning was no exception. "Maybe you could find me something to eat," he suggested.

"At once! You look so pale and worn out. You ought to tell your brother you want your father's chamber if he doesn't."

Gerrard would rather sleep in a cave full of bats. "Just bring me some bread and ale, if you will. And maybe some cheese." He reached into his belt, but didn't find a single coin. No matter. He'd get more from Dalfrid later. "That merchant from Lincolnshire should be by soon. Perhaps you'd like a new bracelet."

The woman's homely face lit up as if he'd offered her a chest of gold instead of a cheap trinket. "Lord bless you, Gerrard, and make you lord of Dunborough, as you ought to be!" she cried before she hurried away.

"From your lips to His ears," Gerrard said before he sighed and lay back down, and thought of all the things he'd do when he was rightfully named lord of Dunborough by King John.

First, though, he'd have to make his case before the king—whatever that entailed.

After she had broken the fast, Mavis sought out the steward and found him in the solar, a large, comfortable chamber with a wide table, carved chairs and a painted wooden chest in the corner. Tapestries depicting hunts covered the walls, and two braziers of glowing coals warmed it.

Wearing a robe of very fine black wool, Dalfrid was at the open chest when she entered. He quickly closed the lid and turned to face her. "Oh, my lady! May I help you?"

"Yes," she replied, her unease about the man increasing, although she couldn't put her finger on a reason. "I'd like to meet the cook and the other servants."

Dalfrid gave Mavis the sort of patronizing smile she had seen on men's faces all too often. She half expected him to pat her on the head and call her a good girl before he replied. "It will be my pleasure to make the introductions, my lady."

Mavis wasn't at all sure about that. It was much more likely that Dalfrid saw her as a costly addition to the household, and one whose value had yet to be proven. Well, prove it she would, to him and to anyone else who doubted her abilities. Including herself, she inwardly added.

Dalfrid locked the chest, tucked the key into his belt, then led the way from the solar to a kitchen that was as immense as the rest of the fortress. A fire burned in the hearth wide and tall enough to fit three women upright, and a pot of bubbling stew dangled from a hook. The rich smells of beef cooking and chickens roasting filled the air, joining the aroma of fresh-baked bread. Smoked hams hung down from the rafters above, along with strings of onions. Baskets of beans, peas and neeps were under the long, scarred wooden table in the center of the room. Two doors were opposite the one they'd just entered. One likely led into the yard or kitchen garden, and the other was probably a storeroom.

A man of indiscriminate age in a long white apron kneading dough at the long, flour-covered trestle table stopped and stared, as did a slender girl about eighteen with chestnut-brown hair who'd been chopping leeks. Another young woman pouring peas into a cauldron froze, although the peas continued to rattle into the iron pot. She was more plump and a bit older than the other girl, although with a prettier face. A spit boy, thin as a twig and freckled, had been crouched on the floor as he kept three chickens turning. Brushing soot from his breeches, he scrambled to his feet.

Eua was there, too, putting a loaf of bread, something wrapped in a cloth and a mug on a tray.

"My lady," Dalfrid began, "I believe you already know Eua." He gestured at the man in the apron. "Florian." He nodded at the girl chopping leeks. "Lizabet." The one pouring peas abruptly straightened, sending a few peas spilling onto the floor. "Peg." He frowned at the spit boy. "Tom."

Mavis acknowledged each in turn, including the grim Eua, with a nod and a smile.

"Lady Mavis wishes to speak to you," Dalfrid announced, then moved behind her.

Before Mavis could say a word, Eua came to stand directly in front of her, as if daring Mavis to cross an imaginary line in the floor.

Mavis silently vowed she would not let the woman upset her. She would act calm and confident, like Tamsin, even if she felt otherwise.

Looking past Eua to the other servants, she said, "As you may already know, my husband has decided that there's to be a wedding feast in a fortnight. It is my hope and expectation that it will be a fine feast, of the sort my father is known for."

"He's known for being a miser and a sot," Eua declared with breathtaking insolence.

Mavis regarded the woman coldly, as Roland might. "Do you not remember that I am your lord's wife and the chatelaine of Dunborough?"

The smirk disappeared from Eua's face, replaced by a scowl as Mavis addressed Florian. "You are the cook?"

"I...I am, my lady," he stammered, red-faced. "I've been cook here for th-three years. We never had a feast in all that time, my lady, so I don't know... That is, I never..." He fell silent and stared at the floor as if she'd threatened to have him whipped.

This was a setback she hadn't foreseen and not just that he'd never prepared a feast before. She wanted respect, but she didn't want the servants to be afraid of her, either.

So she spread her hands, not in surrender, but to suggest that she was fallible and willing to let them know it. "I am new here, and new to the duties of a wife and chatelaine. Nevertheless, I plan to do my utmost to assure the good reputation of my husband and my household. I trust you all are willing to do the same."

She spoke directly to Florian. "Good plain food, well cooked and seasoned, is often better and more welcome than elaborate dishes with unfamiliar ingredients." As the man relaxed, she gave him a warm smile. "We shall have to learn together, Florian."

Relief spread over Florian's features, followed by smiles of equal relief from the other servants, except Eua, who sniffed scornfully.

"And if we fail?" she demanded, her arms crossed, her expression openly hostile.

Out of the corner of her eye, Mavis saw the steward shifting nervously from one foot to the other. "You all had best see that we don't," he said, moving forward. "My lady, let us go and—"

Mavis waved him away and stood her ground. Eua wanted a battle and she would have it here and now.

"If honest mistakes are made, there will be no punishment, but if there is neglect or laziness, there will be consequences. I wouldn't want it said that the people of the household of Dunborough are lax or lacking, would you, Eua? Wouldn't you rather help me show everyone that Sir Roland's household is one he can be proud of?"

Eua continued to scowl. "Sir Roland's household, you say? Gerrard should be the lord here, not that cheat of a brother who took his birthright, so I don't give a tinker's damn what some high-and-mighty nobleman—or you—has to say about this household until Gerrard's in his rightful place."

This was impudence and disrespect that could not be overlooked or excused and, Mavis was sure, unlikely to change, so she pointed to the door leading outside. "Go, Eua, from the kitchen and from this household. There is no place for you here anymore."

The servants exchanged wide-eyed glances, while Eua glared.

"You...you can't do that! You can't make me!" she spluttered, her face flushing and flecks of spittle forming at the corners of her mouth. "Gerrard won't let you do that!"

"Gerrard is not the lord of Dunborough, nor am I his wife."

"But...but you can't!" Eua's eyes narrowed and her body began to tremble. "You don't dare! I know things—about this household, about your husband. Aye, and his father, too, that stinking old bastard!"

If not for the gleam of hysteria in Eua's eyes, Mavis might have been worried about her threats. But she had seen that look of panic before, in the eyes of a servant Tamsin had caught stealing red-handed. That man, too, had claimed to know secrets and made threats. But he'd known nothing, or he would have used that knowledge to save himself when he was brought before the court. "Tell me, then," she said evenly. "Tell us all what you know so that I don't dare send you away."

Eua's frantic gaze darted from one to the other before coming back to Mavis. "I...I..."

"Well? I am waiting."

"Your husband isn't the firstborn twin!"

"How do you know? I understand his father never said, his mother died and so did the midwife."

"Because...because I know, that's how." She drew herself up. "The old lord himself told me!"

Mavis crossed her arms. "Sir Blane told you, a serving woman, something that he kept from everyone else?"

"Aye! When we was in bed!"

"Since you were never his wife, I must assume you were nothing more than a temporary bedmate. I find it very difficult to believe that the Sir Blane I met—and believe me, Eua, he was a man one doesn't forget even on short acquaintance—confided such a thing to you."

"He *did* tell me!" she cried.

"And since you've told me, and everyone in this room, you may go."

Eua stared at her in stunned disbelief, then raised her hand as if she meant to strike her. At the same time, both Florian and Dalfrid moved to stand in front of Mavis.

Eua shook her fist instead. "Aye, I'll go, and happily so—and you can go to the devil! You and Roland, too!" she cried. She ran to the door leading to the yard, knocking over the tray as she did, sending the loaf and wrapped parcel flying and spilling the mug of ale.

The wrappings unraveled to reveal a round of cheese,

which the spit boy hurried to put back on the table, along with the bread and empty mug.

Dalfrid turned to Mavis with a stricken expression. "I fear, my lady, you're going to have cause to regret that rash decision. Even if Eua's claims are groundless, she's been here a long time. I doubt Sir Roland will be pleased, and I know Gerrard won't be."

In spite of Dalfrid's remarks, Mavis wasn't frightened. She felt...triumphant. She was certain Eua's threats were harmless, and she didn't care what Gerrard thought. The only opinion that mattered to her was Roland's and after last night, she was confident he would listen to her and accept what she'd done. "As chatelaine, it was my decision to make."

Dalfrid gave her a somewhat sickly version of his usual obsequious smile. "As you say, my lady, it was your decision—and you must abide by the consequences."

If she wasn't going to be intimidated by Eua, she certainly wasn't going to let Dalfrid intimidate or frighten her, either. He was a servant, too, after all, and she was Roland's wife. "You may go, Dalfrid."

His eyes flared with surprise before he nodded and bowed and glided noiselessly out of the room.

"I'd wager good money he's going straight to Sir Roland," Lizabet said warily.

"Doesn't matter if he does," the cook boldly declared. "As you said, my lady, you're the chatelaine, and I, for one, am glad we've seen the last of Eua. She's a bad 'un and always has been."

"Aye," Peg began, "and she ruled this household like a...like a..."

"Dragon!" the little spit boy supplied.

"Aye, like a dragon," Peg confirmed. "Had the breath of one, too."

"She made a pet of Gerrard," Florian explained. "He was the only one ever pretended to like her, so she was furious when she found out Sir Roland was the oldest. Wouldn't believe it. Said it had to be a lie. Sir Roland had either forged the will or lied to his father or brought it about some other way. And then when she heard he'd brought home a wife!"

The other servants all shook their heads.

"Hellfire," Peg said. "Knew her days here were numbered."

"Should have gone then," Lizabet remarked.

"Thought she could rule you, too, no doubt," Florian said to Mavis with a shrug of his shoulders. Then he grinned. "More fool her."

"Still, there'll be hell to pay when Gerrard finds out," Lizabet warned.

"As long as he blames me, and not his brother," Mavis said. "I'll go to Sir Roland now and explain, and afterward I'll go through the food stores with you, Florian."

"Anything you want, my lady," he said. "I heard one of the men saying Sir Roland'd be in the stable."

"Then that's where I shall go," she replied.

Chapter Eight

Mavis opened the door to the stable, then hesitated. It wasn't that it was dim, or that she was disturbed by the scent of leather, manure and hay. Those smells were as familiar to her as wool or apples. It was the sound of Roland's low voice crooning comforting words to his horse, sounding just as he had the first time she'd heard him.

"It's only a stone in the shoe, Heffy," he murmured. "You'll be right as rain soon."

She walked toward the stall where the tall, dark horse stood and saw Roland bending over, holding his horse's right back hoof in his hands as he examined it.

He caught sight of her and let go of Hephaestus's foot. The animal limped a bit as it moved back, and Roland came forward with that rare little smile playing about his lips. "I didn't think to see you here. Not that I'm sorry."

Perhaps Dalfrid had not, after all, rushed to tell her husband what she'd done. It was very tempting to forget why she had come to the stable, but that would only be delaying the inevitable. Still, a little delay wouldn't hurt anything. "Your horse is lame?" she asked, her hands behind her back as she leaned against the nearest post.

"Not badly," he replied, putting one hand above her on the post and bending closer, "but I won't be riding him for a few days. I might have to think of something else to do."

Again she was tempted to forget why she'd come there. Again she knew that he was going to learn what she'd done eventually. It would be better if he heard it from her.

She took a deep, steadying breath before she spoke, and her smile was tremulous at best. "I have dismissed Eua from the household."

Roland's brows lowered as he straightened.

"I've sent her away," she continued. "She's too insolent, too disruptive. Such a disrespectful servant is like a poison in the household. I know you're the master of Dunborough, but I am chatelaine, and I must do what I see fit when it comes to the servants, and despite the threats she made."

Roland's frown deepened. "Threats? What sort of threats?"

"She claims that your father told her Gerrard was born before you."

Roland's skeptical grin was a relief and a confirmation of her own estimation of the truth of Eua's words. "If that were so, she would have been saying so from our childhood. She never did, not until my father's will revealed that I was the eldest. She's always favored Gerrard, so no one will believe her on that score, and especially now."

"I was sure she was lying, too," Mavis said. "There was too much desperation in her eyes for me to believe otherwise, and the other servants told me how she preferred your brother."

Roland cupped her shoulders and drew her into his

strong embrace. "I should have sent Eua away before I left for DeLac, but I was in too much of a hurry. That was even before I knew of the bride that awaited me there."

The door burst open as if blasted by a winter's gale and Gerrard, his face red with rage, marched into the stable. Roland and Mavis parted, although Roland kept a warm, firm hold of her hand.

Gerrard ran a disdainful gaze over Mavis before he addressed Roland. "Do you know what this woman has done?"

"Are you referring to my wife?"

"Do you see anybody else here?" Gerrard retorted, his hands on his hips, looking more like a petulant boy than an enraged man. "Who does she think she is, to send Eua away? Or was that your order and she merely the instrument to carry it out? I can well believe you'd use—"

"He had nothing to do with Eua's dismissal," Mavis interrupted. "Since I am chatelaine of Dunborough, it's my right to dismiss servants as I see fit, and I saw fit to send Eua from the household."

"Because she wouldn't bow and scrape? Because she knows that I should be the lord and not your husband?"

"Because she was insolent and disrespectful, and likely to stay that way. I cannot and will not have such a servant in my household. As for her claims of superior knowledge, even you must wonder why your father would tell a servant what he'd tell no one else except the attorney who made his will—not even you."

"He kept everything to himself, all the time. Ask Roland."

"Eua tells you what you want to hear, Gerrard," Roland replied, "and she's still no more than a servant.

Why should the law believe her and not my father's own will?"

His face even more red, his gaze more hostile, Gerrard glared at Mavis once again. "Whatever the law says, what of me, your insolent and disrespectful brother-in-law who will never bow down before your husband? Will you make Roland send me away? For I assure you, my *lady*, he'll never get respect and deference from me until he deserves it and that will *never* be!"

"You would treat him thus even though it undermines his position as lord of Dunborough and therefore yours, as well?" Mavis countered. "What must the tenants think if their lord's brother behaves like a spoiled child? And the merchants with whom he trades? What must they think of *you*? Or are you truly so selfish, so blind, so shortsighted, that you don't see what harm it does to both of you?"

Gerrard took hold of her arm. "Beware how you speak to me, my lady, lest you—"

Roland grabbed his shoulder and yanked him away. "Take your hands off my wife," he growled as the two men faced each other like enraged lions, ready to pounce.

"Oh, dear me, am I interrupting something?"

Mavis started and turned to see a woman in the doorway. She wore a very fine cloak of light brown wool trimmed with fox fur. The hem of a brilliant scarlet gown was visible at the bottom, and her hands were encased in pale kidskin gloves. She pushed back the hood to reveal dark hair, delicately arched black brows, red lips and a pale and beautiful face.

Whoever she was, this was no time to have visitors,

not when she feared Roland and Gerrard were about to come to blows.

"Audrey!" Gerrard cried, his anger apparently gone in an instant as he smiled at her.

So this was Audrey D'Orleau, the woman gossip said Roland would marry. She was indeed beautiful and certainly smiled at him as if she would gladly have accepted, although she smiled at Gerrard, too.

Again Mavis felt the small sting of jealousy, and tried to ignore it.

As for Audrey, she didn't seem to notice Mavis, although Mavis had caught the swift perusal, the quick assessment. But she was used to that, from women who were trying to determine who was the prettiest. Nevertheless, she had to subdue the urge to smooth down her hair and gown, and to pinch her cheeks to ensure they were lightly, becomingly pink.

"The guards said you were both here, but I never... I didn't..." Audrey covered her rosy lips with her gloved fingertips. "Perhaps it would be best if I returned tomorrow."

Mavis could tell when a woman was acting flustered, as opposed to being so, and this woman was merely acting.

Gerrard spoke first. "My brother and I were having a discussion."

Roland took Mavis's hand to lead her forward as if they were in the king's hall, and her confidence returned. "My lady, may I present Audrey D'Orleau."

"Audrey's a very good friend," Gerrard slyly noted.

Roland ignored him. "Audrey, this is my wife, Mavis."

The woman's smile was lovely and she had perfect teeth, too. "I am delighted to meet Roland's wife. Welcome to Dunborough, my lady." She looked at them all with every appearance of concerned confusion. "Now perhaps I had best be on my way."

"Please, you must have some refreshments," Mavis said. She may not be attired as befit the wife of a lord, but she could still behave like one.

Audrey looked from her to Roland, then Gerrard. "No, I think not. I wouldn't want to disrupt your... discussion."

"The discussion is over," Roland replied.

"So of course you must stay," Gerrard added.

"Well, then, I shall," Audrey said with a pleased smile.

Mavis wasn't overjoyed by the invitation, but it was her duty to be courteous and welcoming.

"If you will excuse me, my lord," she said, smiling at Roland, "I should go ahead to tell the servants to bring wine and ensure that the fires are kindled."

Then she raised herself up on her toes and kissed her husband. Whether she intended to show Audrey that she was Roland's choice and both were glad of it, or to prove to Gerrard that he couldn't upset her, or both, she couldn't have said, but the kiss was no peck on the lips.

Regardless of the audience, Roland responded as if they were alone, too, holding her close and moving his lips over hers with slow and sinuous purpose.

Unfortunately, they were not alone, so she reluctantly broke the kiss and gathered up her skirts. "I shall await you in the hall, my lord," she said, more than a little breathless as she hurried past Gerrard and the red-faced Audrey.

"Forgive me, Audrey, but I've just remembered I've promised to meet my friends in the village," Gerrard said, his expression full of disdain as he addressed Audrey and his brother. "Enjoy your afternoon with Roland and his bride," he added as he strode from the stable, leaving Audrey and Roland alone.

Before he had married Mavis, this was a situation Roland would have gone miles to avoid. Now, however, and especially after that kiss, Audrey had to be aware that any hopes she might have harbored—and without any encouragement from him—were completely dashed. He could simply treat her as he would any other guest.

He held out his arm. "Shall we?"

She took his arm and as they left the stable and started across the yard toward the hall, moved a bit too close. "I see Gerrard doesn't approve of your marriage."

"It is not his place to approve or not."

"No, of course not, and now that I've seen your bride, I understand why you married her. Such a pretty little thing!"

Roland was not pleased with Audrey's implication that he had taken a mere girl for a bride. "She is far from a child."

If Audrey realized he was displeased, she gave no sign, but continued to smile. "What does she think of Dunborough? Is she not impressed?"

"I believe so, yes."

"I do hope Gerrard hasn't been too rude to her. The poor boy was surely upset when he heard about the marriage, and with no warning, too. One day you are here, the next you're gone, and then you return with a bride even though you sent no word to say that you'd been wed. Or if you did, the messenger did not arrive."

Roland's jaw tightened and he refrained from pointing out that Gerrard was no boy. "I sent no message because none was necessary. Marrying Mavis was my decision to make, and Gerrard will come to accept what must be."

"I trust you're right. It will be so difficult for you and your sweet bride if he doesn't," Audrey replied with a sigh that implied otherwise, reminding him of another reason he would never have married her. She was subtler than his family, but no less demoralizing. Without openly criticizing him, she always made him feel that anything he said or did was not quite right.

When they reached the hall, Roland opened the door and stood aside to let her enter.

A roaring fire blazed in the hearth, the table was spread with linen he recognized from a feast held long ago and Mavis was standing by the chairs on the dais, waiting.

Pride and happiness soared through him. To think he had such a wife—beautiful and poised, clever and kind, passionate and loving. He, who had been told all his life that he was too serious, too cold, too hard-hearted, to have a woman love him. Who had given up hope that any woman of merit would ever want him.

"I had heard there was a most unfortunate accident on your journey here, my lady," Audrey said as she took the offered chair on the dais, "and all your dower goods were destroyed. I had hoped that was just a rumor, but..." She ran another swiftly measuring gaze over Mavis. "I see it must be true. How terrible!"

Roland was suddenly sorry that Audrey was still there.

However, he never should have doubted that Mavis could hold her own, whether with Gerrard or anyone else. She gave Audrey the most blatantly bogus smile he'd ever seen and her eyes said she was quite aware that she'd been insulted. "It was unfortunate and of course I regret the loss of my clothes and linens. Still, it could have been much worse, if my lord and his men hadn't helped to put out the fire. You should have seen him! He took command like a general and looked like a god."

Roland had never understood the notion of a man's chest swelling with pride, until now. "And Mavis will have new clothes as soon as possible," he said, smiling at his wife.

Audrey shifted in her chair. "I'm sure it was all very exciting." She gave Mavis another false smile. "I shall have to send you my dressmaker. She is a marvel, from France, and most reasonable."

"I'll look forward to it. I shall need some shifts, too, although Roland prefers me without them."

Roland choked back a burst of laughter. He could hardly believe his wife had said something so outrageously wanton—even if it was true—while Audrey blushed as red as her gown.

He had never, in all the years he'd known her, seen Audrey blush.

However, she recovered quickly and cleared her throat. "Yes, well, I believe Dominique will be happy to oblige. Anything I can do to help." She gave Mavis the most insincerely sympathetic look he had ever seen. "I understand your poor father isn't well. I do hope he'll recover."

"I hope so, too," Mavis calmly replied as she smoothed her skirt over her knees. "I'm sure you've heard other things about my family, too. Perhaps you'd like to ask me about them, so I can dispel whatever false stories are going about."

"I did hear that he gave a prize that proved to be made not of true gold, but only painted metal."

"Yes, that is so, and I am not proud to admit it," Mavis replied without a hint of shame. "He has grown somewhat miserly over the years."

"Except for his daughter's dowry," Roland interjected. "He was most generous there."

Audrey didn't seem to take any notice. "I heard something even more shocking about your cousin, so shocking I'm sure it can't possibly be true."

"I suppose you mean that she was abducted and married the man who took her. It's quite true and she's quite happy, as am I, for her sake. They were already in love before he rescued her."

"Rescued?"

"Rescued," Mavis said firmly, "from a marriage she did not want."

Audrey slid Roland a questioning glance, but he wasn't about to suggest Tamsin was wrong to flee a marriage to his father.

Instead, she asked, in the same way she might have asked if Rheged was poxed, "Is it true her husband's also a Welshman?"

"Yes, and proudly so."

"Well! I shall be surprised by nothing I hear in the village after this—nothing!"

Lizabet appeared at the entrance to the kitchen carrying a tray bearing wine and hurried over to them. "I'm sorry, my lady," she said to Mavis, "but the cook has a question about the evening meal. And Peg wants to know about the linen, and there's a fishmonger at the gate asking if you want eels."

Mavis gracefully got to her feet and bestowed a smile on her husband and Audrey. "If you will excuse me, I had best attend to these household matters."

"Of course," Audrey said, likewise giving Mavis another blatantly false smile. "And I suppose I should be on my way."

She waited as if expecting someone to invite her to

stay. Roland certainly wasn't going to, and he wasn't surprised by Mavis's silence. She had offered Audrey food and drink. More was not required.

As Mavis nodded her goodbye and started toward the kitchen with a graceful gait and swaying hips, Audrey rose abruptly. "Farewell, Roland," she snapped before she walked briskly out of the hall without waiting for his response.

Roland sat back in his chair and sighed. He had never liked Audrey, but now he could only feel pity for her.

As for Mavis—he wanted to go to her at once and tell her how proud he was to be her husband.

But that could wait until they were alone.

Walter, James and Frederick said nothing as they sat in the brothel and watched Gerrard. They had seen him in a black mood before and knew it was better to keep silent and let him talk.

At this time of day, the only other customers were two soldiers seated across the room, their heads together, drinking ale and sizing up the women who were likewise warily steering clear of Gerrard.

"How dare she?" Gerrard muttered into the goblet of wine that was not his first. "Who does she think she is? She's just some sot's daughter. She's no right to give orders. Or to criticize me. God's blood! She calls *me* insolent, then all but insults Audrey to her face! I should have guessed there was something wrong with her, or why else would she have married Roland?"

He took another drink before glaring at his silent friends. "And yet Audrey wanted to marry him!"

"She said so?" James asked.

Walter shot him a look as Gerrard answered. "No, but I could tell."

"She never let Gerrard touch her," Frederick whispered to James as, after another look from Walter, they took their drinks and moved away.

Meanwhile, Walter shifted closer to Gerrard. "Audrey can't marry Roland now," he said quietly. "And she's still rich as Croesus."

Gerrard looked at him over the rim of his goblet. "She is, isn't she?"

"A man could do a lot of things with her wealth," Walter noted. He lowered his voice still more. "Even to bribing a king."

"What's that?"

Walter leaned closer and spoke in Gerrard's ear. "You would have enough to bribe the king. Then you could be sure the king will rule in your favor. Everyone knows John can be bought, if a man can pay the price, and nobody disputes that you and Roland were born the same day and the same hour. If your father had said which of you was the eldest from the first, it would be different, but since he didn't, it shouldn't be too difficult for John to name you heir instead. All these wars in France cost money, after all. Of course, you'd have to marry Audrey first to get enough to make it worth John's while to go against your brother."

Gerrard grinned. "As if that would be a hardship for any man. You've seen her, haven't you? And she likes me."

While both men shared a companionable chuckle, neither they, nor James or Frederick, saw the two soldiers get up and leave.

"That's it, then," Arnhelm said with determination as he and Verdan marched back to Dunborough. "They're planning something and we've got to tell our lady."

"What?" Verdan asked. "They was just talking."

"I tell you, he's up to something, whispering like that."

"Other than getting drunk and bedding whores, we ain't seen nor heard—"

"Aye, we have," Arnhelm declared. "We seen him sneakin' about with those others."

"That ain't enough and what if we're wrong?"

"It's enough to warn our lady to be on her guard, and that's what I mean to do before we go back to DeLac."

"What are ya going to say? Beg pardon, m'lady, but we don't trust your brother-in-law and we don't trust your husband to keep you safe neither?"

That silenced Arnhelm for a moment. Then he said, "I'll just tell her she oughta watch out for that Gerrard because he might be up to no good. And when we get home, I'll go to Lady Tamsin and her husband and tell them the same thing."

"What good'll that do?"

"To let them know she might need their help. Now come on, it's gettin' dark and I want to wash. That brothel's probably got fleas."

Mavis enjoyed the evening meal that night. Gerrard wasn't in the hall, nor was Eua or Dalfrid, who had gone to tend to some business in York. More important, Roland seemed lighthearted, at least for him. They talked about the wedding feast, and who Roland planned to invite. There were three knights and ladies with small estates nearby, several tenants who were doing well with their crops, the chandler, the butcher, the fletcher, who made all the arrows for the garrison, and two cloth merchants from the village.

"Bartholomew and Marmaduke," Roland said, naming the merchants and giving her a little smile as he did so. "They are very successful and very persuasive. Their goods are not cheap, though, because they're the best to be had outside of York."

"I'll try to restrain myself," she said with every appearance of solemnity, "although it may be very difficult. I feel like I've been wearing this gown for years."

Roland raised her hand to his lips and kissed it. "You're lovely in whatever you wear."

"My father didn't think so," she remarked. "Even when he was most miserly, he would spend a great deal on my gowns. A proper setting, he would say, as if I were a jewel."

"You *are* a jewel."

"I'll accept such a compliment from you, but I should warn you, my lord, that I am not a woman who wants to sit and be admired."

His eyes sparkled when he replied, and it wasn't just the torchlight. "So I've already discovered."

Mavis flicked back a lock of hair from her shoulder and regarded him with a pert expression. "I like adventure, too. I used to climb trees when I was a girl, to see how far I could get, until I gave it up."

"I thank God you didn't fall. I suppose you grew too old for such larks."

She shook her head. "It wasn't that. Tamsin has a fear of being up high and she would get too upset."

"Tamsin…that's an odd name."

"It's short for Thomasina."

"You miss her, I suppose."

"Not as much as I thought I would," she honestly replied. "That reminds me, Roland. Arnhelm and the others are going back tomorrow. I want them to take the invitation for our wedding feast to Tamsin and Rheged.

I'll tell Arnhelm and Verdan now, and then I believe I shall retire."

Roland nodded, regarding her with a seductive little smile that made her blood rush. "I'll join you shortly, after I give the watch the password for the night. It seems Gerrard has not deigned to come back to the castle."

Although she longed to say something about this lapse and Gerrard's lax manner in general, Mavis only nodded and left the table to join Arnhelm, his brother and the soldiers of DeLac. They rose at once when they realized she was coming to speak to them until she motioned for them to remain seated.

"I wanted to make sure you won't leave without seeing me in the morning," she said, addressing them all. "I want to thank you for coming with me, and for helping to fight the fire at Sir Melvin's. I was proud of all of you."

The men grinned and smiled.

"I also have a commission for you, Arnhelm, and your brother, too. I'd like you to take the invitation to my wedding feast to Lady Tamsin and her husband."

"And your father, too," Verdan added, clearly thinking she'd forgotten to mention him.

In truth, however, Mavis hadn't yet decided to ask her father to make the journey. Given his propensity to be drunk before the noon meal, that might not be wise. Nor had he seemed particularly sad to see her go. "I shall see you in the morning," she said instead of answering directly.

"Aye, my lady," Arnhelm replied, and she was somewhat surprised to see that he looked almost…relieved. Because she was going to say goodbye?

He could simply be glad to be returning, she thought

as she left the hall and went to the chamber she shared with Roland, now a much cozier room. The servants had found some old tapestries in a chest in a storeroom, beaten the dust from them and hung them on the walls. They were so old, the pictures were hard to see, but they appeared to depict some kind of garden. Whatever they showed, they helped keep the room warmer, along with two bronze braziers that had been cleaned and polished.

Lizabet had also found some candles and rush mats. Peg had discovered another table somewhere, and a stool, so she had a dressing table.

Best of all, though, was the bigger bed that had arrived that afternoon. It stood large and solid against the wall opposite the window, with curtains around it to keep them safe from drafts.

All in all, it was a pleasant chamber, and with the bigger bed, she was sure it would be even more comfortable.

She removed the gown she was growing to hate and, clad in her shift, drew one of the blankets from the bed around her shoulders, then went to the window and opened the shutters to look out at the moon. She and Tamsin had often defied her nurse's admonition to avoid the night air, lest they fall ill, to gaze at the moon and the stars. The heavenly bodies seemed so miraculous, hanging in the sky and twinkling.

She wondered if Tamsin was looking at the moon from her bedchamber window. Maybe Rheged was with her, holding her in his arms and whispering gentle words of love in her ear. Roland never whispered sweet nonsense in her ears, but if the way he made love to her were any indication, she should be just as content.

If only they didn't have to deal with Gerrard. If only Roland would send him away as she had dismissed Eua.

A noise behind her made her turn, to see her husband closing the door to their chamber. "You'll catch a chill if you stay there," he said, his deep voice low and soft.

She closed the shutter.

"I don't want you to fall ill," he said, wrapping his arms loosely around her waist. He looked around the room, then nodded at the new piece of furniture. "I see the servants have been busy and Dalfrid has found a bigger bed."

"Yes," she whispered as she slid her arms around his waist.

"I was proud of you today. I've never seen any woman hold her own so well with Audrey."

"She's a very beautiful woman. I'm not surprised people thought you'd want to marry her."

"*I* never did, so you can put that thought out of your head."

He spoke firmly, and as if she were being completely ridiculous. Yet surely it was only natural to wonder if there had been anything serious between them when he was so handsome and commanding, and she was so lovely and nearby. "Did you never once—"

"No, as I have already said."

"But you have been with other women," she persisted. Even though she feared it was a mistake, she simply had to know.

"Of course. I'm a man, with a man's needs, but there was never any affection. It was a business transaction and no more. Whatever I shared with those others, it was nothing to what I feel when I'm with you."

She wanted to believe him. She needed to believe that she alone could give him the love he sought, and that he would love her—and her alone—in return. She searched his dark, seeking eyes, and once more saw the need that was not only physical. That spoke not of lust, but heartache and loneliness, of a longing for love that had so long been denied.

The blanket slipped from her shoulders and fell unheeded to the ground as her lips captured his.

"Shall we see how soft the bed is?" she whispered.

Stepping away, she untied the drawstring at the neck of her shift and, turning her back to him, pulled it down. When it was low on her hips, he put his hand between her shoulder blades, warm and strong, moving close enough that she could feel the heat of his body as he slid his hand lower, followed by his mouth, the sensation making her shiver.

"Are you cold?" he whispered as his arms went around her, one hand rising to her breast, the other moving lower, then in small, slow circles in a way that made her legs weak.

"No," she gasped as her shift puddled at her feet. He pressed her back against him, so that she could feel that he was as aroused as she.

Although he was still dressed.

Turning, she worked to undo the knots at the neck of his tunic and shirt while he cupped her face and pressed light kisses on her forehead and cheeks. She lifted off both his tunic and shirt, then laid her hands on his bare chest, feeling for a moment the heartbeat of the powerful man she'd married before she bent down to pull off his boots. He lifted her hand away to remove them himself, and when he straightened, he tugged at the drawstring of his breeches, trying to undo the knot, until she lifted his hand away and did it herself. That done, she insinuated her hand inside to grasp the evidence of his need. He grabbed her shoulders while she stroked, his head thrown back as a groan issued from deep in his throat before he pulled her close for another long, deep kiss.

Surely, oh surely, those other women didn't matter now, she thought as, still kissing her, he kicked off his breeches and maneuvered her toward the bed while she continued to caress him. Her legs met the bed and she broke the kiss to get beneath the covers.

"It is a very soft bed," Mavis noted as he joined her.

"A bed of rock would be comfortable if you're beside me," he replied with a seductive look in his brown eyes.

He slid backward, brushing his hands down her thighs as he moved.

"What are you—"

She gasped as he pressed his lips where she had never thought a man's lips would go, and his tongue began to tease a part of her she didn't know existed until that moment. That incredible, unforeseen moment. "Oh, Roland!"

She could say no more. All she could do was grasp his long, dark hair and pant as the excitement built.

Just when she could stand the growing tension no longer, he moved forward and slid inside her.

Moaning, she arched and wrapped her legs around him while he, with a low, rough groan, began to thrust. She lost all awareness of anything except their bodies and their need, as if they were the only people in the castle. In Dunborough. In England.

Until all too soon—or so it seemed to her—the delicious tension snapped. She cried out as her body throbbed and gripped his shoulders so hard she left marks, while he growled like a wild creature. Then, panting, he laid his head upon her breasts.

She stroked his back until he rolled away and looked

up at the canopy of the bed. "I must thank Dalfrid in the morning," he murmured. "This is a wonderful bed."

"A very wonderful bed," she agreed. "I'm happy to be your wife, Roland. I believe we can have a happy life if…"

She fell silent. Perhaps it would be best to say no more tonight.

But it seemed she'd already said too much, for Roland raised himself on his elbow and regarded her gravely. "If?"

She felt she had to answer. "I fear that as long as Gerrard is…as he is…and you allow him to stay your garrison commander, we'll never have peace in the household."

"Ah," he breathed. He sat up and regarded her intently. "You wish me to send him away?"

She was sorry she had started this, but answered truthfully. "I want a peaceful household, Roland, where you're honored and respected as you deserve."

"It's Gerrard's household, as well," he replied. "He, too, is my father's son and his childhood was as full of suffering as mine. For that, and because he is my brother, I will never cast him out. Indeed, it has been my plan that should Gerrard prove, in time, to be worthy of his own estate, I will give him a portion of this one."

"You would give away your inheritance?"

"A part of it, as he should have had from my father. There is enough for us both."

He spoke as if he expected her to disagree, but his inheritance was his alone. "Your estate is yours to do with as you will."

"I would rather have your approval as well as your acceptance, Mavis."

Again she saw that need, that yearning, and realized

that he truly did want her to agree that it was the right thing to do. And so it was, if it would help keep the peace. "I do agree, Roland, and I have never heard of anything so generous. I wish everyone who thinks badly of you could know you as I do. But if you've made that offer to Gerrard, why does he still treat you so badly?"

"Because I haven't made it yet, nor have I told him, or anyone else, what I plan to do, until now. I must be certain he's worthy without knowing a reward awaits. In that way I can be sure he truly is deserving."

She was glad that he was confiding in her about such an important matter. That had to mean he trusted her, and cared about her opinions, too. "How long before you decide if you'll make the offer?"

"A year."

That seemed a long time, but he was wise to take his time, and at least she could foresee a day when Gerrard would have less cause to complain. However, there was another problem to consider. "What about those friends of his? I suspect they encourage the worst of his behavior. Can you not make them leave Dunborough?"

Roland drew her down beside him. "That I can, and I will," he said as he stroked her cheek and pressed another kiss upon her brow. "I already know exactly how."

Nestling against her husband, Mavis told herself she'd been worried about Gerrard and jealous of Audrey for nothing. She was indeed a most fortunately married woman, with a kind, generous and passionate husband.

Whose hand began another exploration.

She responded eagerly, and it was some time yet before they were asleep.

Chapter Nine

Roland watched Gerrard's supposed friends stumble into the solar the next morning, all obviously the worse for a night's carousing.

"Here y'are, m'lord," the fair-haired young soldier who'd been sent to find them said. "They were just where you'd thought."

"And my brother?"

"Not there, m'lord," Hedley replied, his voice betraying nothing. The man was young, but could keep his own counsel, which was why Roland had chosen him for that task.

"Thank you. You can go."

Hedley nodded and marched away, leaving Roland alone with Gerrard's supposed friends.

"Sit down," Roland said to the bleary-eyed Walter, the son of a well-to-do merchant from York. The other two, James and Frederick, had poorer beginnings, but might have made something of themselves had they not run afoul of Walter and, yes, Gerrard, too—rich young men with too much time on their hands and chips on their shoulders.

James and Frederick slumped into two of the chairs.

Walter stayed on his feet, although he swayed slightly and squinted in the early morning sunlight.

"Do you know where Gerrard is, Walter?" Roland asked.

"I'm not his keeper," the young man muttered, tugging his disheveled tunic into place and running a hand through his greasy, light brown hair. "If you want *him*, what are we doing here?"

Roland lowered himself into his father's chair. It had taken him some time to use it, even if the chair itself didn't have anything to do with his father's behavior. Three bags of silver coins were before him on the table. "I want to make you an offer."

He shoved one of the bags of coins toward Walter. "There are twenty marks of silver in each purse, one for each of you. You are welcome to them, on one condition—that you leave Dunborough at once and never return."

James and Frederick sat up a little straighter and eyed the purses, then one another, while Walter's lips twisted with a skeptical scowl. "Twenty marks—just like that?"

"Just like that," Roland confirmed, "provided you leave Dunborough and don't come back."

"There has to be more to it than that," Walter muttered even as James and Frederick were reaching for the purses.

"No, there isn't. I want you gone from here, and I'm willing to pay."

"And Gerrard? Are you paying him to leave, too?"

"No. Gerrard can stay."

By now, James and Frederick had their coins in their hands. Apparently the weight of silver in their palms was enough to awaken them, in more ways than one. "Come on," James said, rising with an alacrity he had not displayed even before today. "Let's take it and go before he changes his mind."

"Come, Walter," Frederick said, likewise getting to his feet. "Gerrard can find us after, if he's a mind to."

Roland realized Frederick was, unfortunately, right, but it was more likely Gerrard would stay as long as he still believed Dunborough should be his.

Roland started to reach for Walter's purse. "If you don't want it, then—"

Walter snatched it up. "Yes, I do—and it's less than I deserve for acting as nursemaid to your brother."

"If you were truly acting in that capacity," Roland grimly replied, "you would know where he is."

"The stable," Walter retorted. "You'll probably find him in the stable."

The same place they'd both sought refuge as children.

"Now good riddance to you and this godforsaken place!" Walter snapped as he started for the door, his two comrades following like dogs after their master.

When they were gone, Roland went to the window that overlooked the courtyard.

He kept watching and after a moment, he saw the three young men walking swiftly toward the gate, past the escort from DeLac that had already assembled in preparation for departing.

"Good riddance to you, too," he said softly before his gaze went to the stable.

As he closed the shutter, he decided he would let Gerrard sleep.

As Mavis crossed the yard toward the soldiers from DeLac, she saw Gerrard's three friends hurrying out the gate as if they were being chased by hornets.

Roland had said he had a way to make them go and obviously he'd been successful.

"My lady," Arnhelm said, bowing his head in greeting when she reached him.

"Good morning, Arnhelm." She nodded at the rest of the men, then held out three letters written on parchment and sealed with wax. "This is for Sir Melvin and his lady," she said, handing him the first message. She pointed to the little drawing of a pine tree that she had made in the corner since she was sure Arnhelm couldn't read. She gave him the second letter that had a little rendering of Castle DeLac on it. "This one is for my father. And this is for Lady Tamsin and Sir Rheged," she finished, showing him the picture of the sword and shield on the third.

"Right you are, my lady," Arnhelm replied. "We'll deliver 'em safe and sound."

"I'm sure you will." She looked up at the clear sky. "It appears to be a fine day for traveling. I hope they all are."

"As do we, my lady," Arnhelm said before he frowned. "But there's other sorts of clouds and bad weather to watch out for."

Mavis had no idea what he was talking about, and her confusion must have shown, for he handed the letters to his brother and came closer. "A word o' warnin', my lady, that I hope you won't take amiss," he whispered. "That brother-in-law o' yours bears watchin' and I wouldn't trust him far as the next tavern. We been keepin' an eye on him while we was here, and he's a bad 'un. Bitter and angry and he drinks too much. Dangerous, that sort."

"I...I see," she stammered, not sure what to say. Then she thought of Roland. "I thank you for your concern,

Arnhelm," she said, meaning it with all her heart, "and I do appreciate your warning, but I'm sure my husband will protect me from anything his brother might do."

Arnhelm nodded and she could see he was trying to look as if he shared her confidence. "Aye, my lady. But a word o' warnin' nonetheless."

He said no more, for Roland appeared at the door to the hall and came to join them. After bidding them farewell, Roland took Mavis's hand and she held it tight. Whatever Arnhelm had seen or heard while he was at Dunborough, she truly believed Roland would keep her safe from any foe.

Including his bitter, angry brother.

A short time later, an irate Gerrard lurched into the solar, where Roland was again trying to make sense of the accounts. Gerrard's face was pale, there were heavy bags beneath his bloodshot eyes and he had bits of straw in his hair.

"What have you done with my friends?" he demanded as he put a hand on the back of a chair to steady himself. "I heard you had them brought to you this morning even though they could barely walk."

"If they could barely walk," Roland replied from where he sat on the other side of the table covered with scrolls and lists and worn-down quills, "it was because they'd gotten drunk the night before with you."

Gerrard straightened his disheveled tunic, ran a hand through his messy hair and licked his obviously dry lips. "Where are they? The dungeon? What for? Being my friends?"

Roland leaned back in his chair and regarded his brother with the inscrutable expression that drove Gerrard nearly mad. And ever since Roland had returned, there'd been something else about it—a sort of proud satisfaction that grated even more.

"Your so-called friends are gone, never to return."

Gerrard gasped. Roland was a coldhearted fellow, but even so— "You killed them?"

"Of course not," Roland replied with disgust, and as if Gerrard was a dolt.

"I offered them twenty marks in silver if they left Dunborough and didn't come back. James and Frederick grabbed the coins without a moment's hesitation. Walter took a little more convincing, but not much. They're probably halfway to York by now."

Gerrard splayed his hands on the table and leaned toward his brother. "Are you telling me you paid my friends to go?"

"Yes, and they went," Roland freely admitted. "What kind of friends were they, after all, if they could be so cheaply purchased? At least it was your own brother who bought them, not an enemy. If you truly considered them your friends, you should be ashamed you chose so unwisely."

Gerrard regarded his brother with scorn. Once again the clever, sly Roland had outmaneuvered him and he could guess what his plan was. "This is another part of your scheme to get me to leave without my due, isn't it, so you can claim I forfeited any rights to either the title or the estate."

"I have no such plan," Roland replied with infuriating calm.

"What about your wife? I'm sure she wants me gone."

"Mavis understands that is my decision to make, or yours, if you so choose."

Gerrard drew himself up. "If I stay, am I still the garrison commander, or will you take that from me, too?"

"You are still garrison commander until I say otherwise." Finally an expression came to Roland's stony visage, and as always, it was critical. "Getting drunk is not likely to enable you to remain in that position."

"Getting drunk is the only comfort I have!" Gerrard retorted, hating his brother's haughty manner. "You've taken everything else—money, title and now even my friends!"

Roland rose. "I've *taken* nothing from you, and I've earned what I have."

"So you say!"

"So I have!" Roland returned. "While I did my duty and tried to protect the people, you were off drinking and wenching and gambling. When Father and Broderick were at their worst, you disappeared and left me to bear the brunt of their displeasure. So, yes, I've earned what I have, and if you lose your position, it will be because you've shown me that you aren't fit for it."

Roland spoke with anger in his eyes and in his voice, sounding so much like their father, Gerrard had to forcefully remind himself he was no longer a boy, but a man capable of defending himself if need be.

And this was not his father, but the brother who had gotten everything. "And thus you have it all—title, estate and a beautiful bride—while I have nothing. Very well, brother mine, but I have every right to stay in Dunborough and by God, I will, whether I am the garrison commander or not!"

"Have you listened to me at all, Gerrard?" Roland demanded, frustration spilling into his words. "I am not taking your command from you."

"Not yet."

"Not ever, unless—"

"Unless I humble myself before you? Unless I become as grim and stern as you? Or I turn into a groveling toady like Dalfrid? That will never happen, Roland, so I'll spare us both the wait. I will no longer command the garrison. I give that task back to you—or perhaps you'll give it to your charming wife. I'm sure she's quite capable of giving orders. I have no doubt that she already rules you as much as our father ever did."

"No one rules me!"

"No?" Gerrard charged. "Not even in your bed?"

Roland came around the table just as his wife appeared on the threshold. He stopped as if she'd shouted that order, while she looked from one man to the other with puzzlement before her questioning gaze settled on Roland. "I'm sorry, my lord. Am I interrupting? I can return later."

Gerrard watched as his brother's rage seemed to melt away, while her eyes shone in a way that made Gerrard feel even more lonely.

At first he'd been completely certain their marriage had been made for gain, whether political or financial, but that certainty had been diminishing every time he saw them together. The way they looked at each other, the way she'd rushed to defend Roland, her clever, cutting remarks at Gerrard's expense...

Whatever they felt for each other, nothing gave her the right to force him from Dunborough. "No, I will leave the chamber, my lady," he said, smiling as if their happiness didn't disturb him. "You may think you're winning, but the battle isn't over."

His expression as stern and grim as his brother's, Gerrard marched past Mavis and out of the chamber, slamming the wooden door behind him so hard, he nearly tore the leather hinges from the frame.

* * *

When Gerrard had gone, it was like the calm after a storm, at least for Mavis. But she could see that Roland was still upset and was sorry that she'd intruded. Perhaps she'd even made their quarrel worse by interrupting. "I didn't realize Gerrard was here, or I would have stayed away."

Roland sighed. "It doesn't matter. He would have been angry anyway. He wasn't pleased that I paid his friends to leave Dunborough and he refuses to continue as garrison commander."

"He's leaving Dunborough?" She tried not to sound pleased, but in truth, she would be relieved if he was.

Roland shook his head, then came around the table and gathered her into his arms. "He won't go as long as he thinks I'm trying to force him to leave so I can say he forfeited any claim to the title and estate."

She laid her head against her husband's chest. "I'm sorry, Roland, if my suggestion about his friends made things worse."

He cupped her cheeks so that he could see into her lovely, shining eyes. "It isn't your fault Gerrard is as he is. He is as our father made him."

"Sir Blane was your father, too," she pointed out, "and you're a good and honorable man."

He gave her a little smile. "Which is why I have hope for Gerrard yet."

Mavis said nothing before they shared a kiss, despite her dread that he was wrong about his brother.

"Now, what brings you here?"

"I came to tell you the cloth merchants have come, and since Dalfrid has not yet returned from York, to ask you how much I may spend."

"As much as you think necessary." He ran his gaze over her and gave her a rueful smile. "I must confess, even I am growing weary of that gown."

* * *

When Mavis returned to the hall, she could hardly believe her eyes. The dais looked as if it had been transformed into an exotic bazaar. Bundles and bolts of brightly colored fabric lay upon every chair and table. Caps, scarves, belts and veils were there, too, and slippers in what looked like every color of the rainbow.

A tall, thin man dressed in a long, bright green tunic with a belt of golden links and a stout man in a short scarlet tunic belted over black breeches came hurrying toward her from the dais.

"What a pleasure, my lady!" the thin man cried.

"A delight!" the plump one exclaimed, bowing. He turned to his companion, who had linked his fingers over his slender torso. "She is as beautiful as they said, isn't she, Marmaduke?"

"Lovely!" Marmaduke replied. "Bartholomew, we are indeed honored to offer this lady our merchandise— although it is the finest to be had outside of London."

Bartholomew looked as if he were about to weep. "We have heard of the fire and your misfortune."

"But help has arrived, my lady!" Marmaduke declared, raising a pointed finger heavenward. "We have brought all our finest fabrics and accoutrements for you to choose from, although you make even your current unfortunate attire look wonderful."

Mavis had to smile as she looked at the two beaming merchants standing with their wares. "Thank you."

Bartholomew gestured toward the dais. "This way if you please, my lady," he said as Marmaduke hurried to display a bolt of brilliant red fabric.

Mavis had intended to spend very little, but their offerings were of very fine quality, and she had to have a special gown for the wedding feast, or what would people think? She also needed at least two more gowns for other days, and the slippers were so comfortable, and there were two caps she simply couldn't resist...

Sometime later, Mavis headed to the solar, where she found her husband still sitting at the table. His hair was disheveled as if he'd ruffled it more than once. His brows were wrinkled with consternation until he looked up and saw her, and a smile bloomed upon his face.

She hoped he would still be happy when he found out how much she'd spent. "I'm sorry to bother you, Roland, but—"

He leaped to his feet and hurried around the table. "Never have I been so glad to be interrupted," he said, pulling her into his arms and kissing her with passionate enthusiasm.

The reason for her visit temporarily forgotten, Mavis leaned into his strong body and gave herself up to the pleasure of his embrace—but only for a moment. "You're so busy..."

He glanced at the table and grimaced. "It's like being lost in a maze trying to figure everything out by myself. Unfortunately, my father kept his sons in complete ignorance about the estate's financial affairs. Only he and Dalfrid knew everything." He sighed. "Maybe that's why I dislike the man. He reminds me of my ignorance daily, if not in words, with his expression. I'm going to dismiss him once I'm familiar with the tithes, taxes and accounts."

"I have to say, Roland, that I don't disagree," Mavis said, not hiding her relief. "There's something about the man I don't like and I can't trust him."

"Then I had better to hurry to understand all this," he replied, making a sweeping gesture that encompassed everything on the table, in the process knocking off a few of the scrolls.

"God help me, just what I need!" he muttered as he bent down to pick them up. She leaned over to help him and their foreheads collided.

"Ouch!" Mavis cried, rubbing hers.

"Did I hurt you?" Roland asked as he helped her up. "I should have given a warning."

"It was an accident," she said, "and no harm done. I won't even have a bruise."

"Nevertheless, perhaps a kiss will make it better," he said, brushing his lips across her forehead. And then her lips.

"I beg your pardon, my lord!"

At the sound of Dalfrid's startled voice, Mavis and Roland sprang apart.

"I didn't mean to interrupt, my lord," the steward continued with one of his smooth smiles while wringing his hands, although his eyes displayed no real regret.

"Ah, Dalfrid," Roland said. "You're back. Did all go well in York?"

"Indeed it did, my lord. I've secured buyers for all our wool next spring." He gave Mavis a smile. "Good day, my lady. You're looking even lovelier than when I left."

"I'm wearing the same gown, too," she wryly noted, "but not for much longer, I'm happy to say."

"Then I would be right in thinking that was Bartholomew and Marmaduke's wagon I saw leaving?"

"Yes. I was just going to tell Sir Roland how much I spent on new garments. Eight marks for the fabrics, ten shillings for some slippers, five each for two caps and some veils for two more."

Roland's brows lowered and she felt a twinge of guilt for spending so much until he said, "Is that all?"

"*All*, my lord?" Dalfrid exclaimed. "That is a considerable sum for so little!"

"It is small enough considering what she lost in the fire."

Dalfrid sighed. "If you approve, then there is no more to be said, my lord."

"No, there is not."

Lizabet appeared and knocked tentatively on the frame of the door. "Beggin' your pardon, my lady, Florian has a question about the bread for the feast. He says he forgot to tell you that he'll have to send word to the miller about the amount of flour tomorrow."

"She'll be there soon," Roland answered for her.

The maidservant dipped a curtsy and hurried away.

"It is a fine day today," he observed, "and I feel like I've been cooped up here for a month. Will you ride with me after the noon, my lady?"

"Gladly!" she replied. "I, too, would enjoy being out in the fresh air."

Dalfrid didn't look pleased, but she didn't care what he thought when it came to spending time with her husband.

"Meet me in the stables after the noon meal," Roland said, giving her a little smile that delighted her and made her wish it was already past the noon.

After Mavis left the solar, Roland gestured for Dalfrid to sit. "I've been going over the accounts, Dalfrid, and there are still a few things I don't understand."

"I shall make all clear in time, my lord," Dalfrid replied. "Your father's affairs were very complicated."

Roland took a seat across from him. "I should also

tell you that you'll find there is less silver than before you went to York."

"Oh?"

"Sixty marks less."

Dalfrid looked as if he'd swallowed a burning poker. "How…how much, my lord?"

"Sixty marks."

"May I ask what required such an enormous sum?"

"Peace of mind. I paid those three rogues who've been leeching off Gerrard to go." Dalfrid still looked horrified, so he added, "I'm sure they would have cost us more if they'd stayed."

The steward tried to look as if he agreed. "I daresay, my lord."

"Speaking of Gerrard," Roland continued, "he's no longer the commander of the garrison, so you will give him no more money."

"None at all, my lord?"

Roland hesitated a moment. It wasn't easy to cut off his brother so completely, but perhaps the time had come. "Not another farthing."

"As you wish, my lord."

There was something else Roland decided to make clear. "And you will never again complain about what my wife spends in her hearing. If she spends too much, tell me and *I* will speak to her about it."

Dalfrid swallowed hard. "Yes, my lord."

"Now I wish to hear about the merchants who want to buy my wool."

"My lord?" Mavis called out as she entered the dim confines of the stable after the noon meal was over and the tables cleared and taken down. "Are you here, my lord?"

A few of the horses shuffled and whinnied, and Hephaestus tossed his dark head. She went toward his stall, thinking Roland would likely be there.

Instead, he came out of a stall at the far end, leading a lovely light brown horse.

"Is Hephaestus's hoof still too sore for you to ride him?" she asked with concern.

"A little, so I'm taking another."

"That's a very pretty beast," she said, running her hand over the animal's soft muzzle. "What's its name?"

"Icarus."

"That seems a name likely to lead to disaster!"

Roland laughed softly, his eyes crinkling at the corners in a way that few others likely ever saw. "I shall be sure to take care. After all, I have every reason to want to live," he said before he called for a groom to saddle Icarus and Sweetling.

As the groom led Icarus away, Mavis leaned back against a post. "I missed you when I woke up this morning. When did you leave?"

"Early. I didn't want to disturb you. You looked so peaceful."

"I was exhausted," she admitted. "After…last night."

His lips turned down ever so slightly and she hurried on. "Not that I regret it," she said, grabbing hold of his tunic to bring him closer.

"Have a care, my lady," he warned with another little smile playing about his lips that she was glad to see. "I may forget that we are not in our bedchamber."

"I may forget that I'm a lady."

"You can be a very saucy wench," he noted, his voice low and husky, his eyes dark with desire.

"And you can be a very bold man," she replied in

kind, reaching out to stroke his chest, until she saw the groom returning.

They stepped aside to let him and a stable boy lead their horses out into the yard, then followed. Once there, Roland made a sling of his hands to help her mount. As she adjusted her cloak, he swung into the saddle on the light brown gelding.

This time, when they rode through the village, people waved and more than one smiled to see them pass. It was as if a pestilence had threatened them, and never come.

Then she caught sight of Gerrard leaning against the wall of the tavern, his arms crossed and his eyes full of anger, his grim expression making him look much more like Roland.

If Roland saw his brother, he gave no sign, and she didn't point him out. She wanted to enjoy this time alone with her husband on a sunny autumn day.

When they reached the far end of the green, two men were in the process of dismantling one of the three stocks set in the middle of it. It was evident that at one time, there had been even more.

"My father believed in harsh punishments," Roland explained before she asked.

"I'm glad to see that you're going to be more merciful."

"If the law is broken, there must be punishment, but the punishment must suit the crime, not the nature of the judge."

He slid her a sideways glance. "Am I wrong to suspect that your father was sometimes cruel even to you?"

"Not until recently," she replied, determined to be just to her father. "When I was little, he was kind to me, or at least didn't mistreat me. But the more he drank, the more cruel he became."

She hesitated, then voiced something she hadn't shared with anyone, not even Tamsin. "I think he was very disappointed with the course of his life. He wanted to be a powerful man at court and saw his chances fade away. He blamed Tamsin's mother in part, for he and his father had made a marriage contract with a powerful lord and she ran off with another. Thwarted ambition would explain why he was so determined to make an alliance with your family."

"Whereas I was never important to my father, not even as a potential heir," Roland replied. "It was always Broderick who had his favor, no matter how dutiful or obedient I was or how I strived to please him."

"Tamsin tried to win my father's love by managing the household, yet he never seemed to notice her, either. She was determined to try, though, even if it meant that she took my place as chatelaine, and left me with almost nothing to do. I understood how important it was to her, though, so I let her, even if it meant people thought I was lazy or vain or stupid."

"Anyone who thinks you're lazy or vain or stupid is a fool," he said firmly. "I think you see and understand things most others miss." He gave her a sidelong glance, and a wary smile. "Perhaps I should be worried."

She answered him honestly, and seriously. "You should be glad, because I saw something in you the first time I met you that made me certain I should accept you for my husband."

The tips of his ears turned red and he swiftly looked away. "You had best take care, my lady, lest you make me vain."

"It's time someone appreciated your merits, Roland, and I do," she assured him.

By this time, they had reached a prosperous-looking manor at the far side of the village. The stone house and yard were large and tidy, the outbuildings many and in good repair. "Who lives here, my lord?" she asked, thinking it must be a family she should invite to the wedding.

"This is Audrey D'Orleau's manor."

She was indeed rich and well-to-do, then, and no wonder the villagers thought a match with one of the lord's sons likely.

A shutter moved on the upper floor, perhaps from the breeze, or by the unseen hand of someone watching the road.

He spoke before she said another word. "Audrey wants a title more than anything else. She tried for Broderick with no success, and she might have tried for me once I inherited, but she would never have succeeded. I have never liked her."

His shoulders relaxed as they passed Audrey's gate— another sign, should she need one, that she shouldn't be jealous. Otherwise he wouldn't be so at ease this close to a former lover's house with his wife riding beside him.

A powerfully built, broad-shouldered man watched them from the portico over the wide entrance to the house. He wore a boiled leather tunic over a padded gambeson and instead of breeches, the gathered cloth skirt of a Scot. His lower limbs were wrapped with fur over leather boots, and he had a huge broadsword of the sort the Scots called a claymore strapped to his back, the hilt visible over his shoulder. He was an imposing-looking man, and he stared at them with unblinking attention.

"Who is that watching us so closely?" Mavis asked.

"Duncan Mac Heath. He guards Audrey's household, and Audrey, too. Rumor has it there are casks of gold inside her house and Duncan sleeps in the storeroom where they're kept."

"He looks capable of fending off several thieves all by himself."

"That he does and so he probably could," Roland replied. "I once saw him strike a man famed as a bare-knuckle fighter outside the tavern. A single punch and the fellow was out cold."

Mavis gathered her cloak more tightly about her, although she wasn't trembling because of the autumn air. It was the cold-blooded, hostile way Duncan Mac Heath regarded her husband, as if Roland was an enemy he wanted to kill. "Does he have any cause to dislike you?"

Her husband shook his head. "No. He always looks like that, like he'd just as soon hit you as look at you. Keeps thieves away, too, that face of his." He frowned. "If you're cold, we should go back."

A gust of wind rushed down the road, lifting her cloak and biting her cheeks. Now she truly was cold. Clouds were gathering on the horizon, too. "Perhaps we should, my lord."

They swung their horses to return to the castle, the Scot watching them intently all the while.

Chapter Ten

Tamsin hurried ahead of her husband to speak to the two soldiers from Castle DeLac waiting in their hall. She had immediately recognized them as two of the men who'd been part of Mavis's escort.

"I'm so pleased to see you!" she cried. She gestured for them to sit as her husband joined them. "What news of Lady Mavis? They arrived safely at Dunborough, I assume?"

"Aye, my lady," Arnhelm replied. "There was a bit o' trouble on the way, though. We stopped at a manor belonging to a Sir Melvin—"

"You'll meet him at the wedding feast," Verdan added helpfully. He nudged his brother and nodded at his belt.

"Right, I was getting to that," Arnhelm said, pulling the parchment from his belt. "Lady Mavis sent this to you. They're having a wedding feast at Dunborough."

"Well, now, that's unexpected," Sir Rheged remarked as he sat beside his wife.

Tamsin didn't immediately open the letter. "You said you had some trouble?" she asked Arnhelm.

"Aye, my lady, there was a storm when we was at Sir

Melvin's. A tree got struck by lightning and fell onto the stable and caught fire. No one was hurt," he hastened to add, "nor the livestock neither. But the stable and a shed was burned, and so was the wagon with all Lady Mavis's dowry."

"Burnt right to cinders," Verdan said.

Arnhelm ignored his brother. "Sir Melvin, good man that he is, was nigh onto useless. Sir Roland took command, and our lady helped, too, but the wagon was gone just the same."

"Oh, no! Poor Mavis, to lose all her things!" Tamsin cried. "She must have been so upset!"

Arnhelm thought a moment before he shook his head and said, "No, no, can't say she was."

"And Sir Roland?"

"He didn't seem to mind much, either. We got to Dunborough pretty quick after that."

Tamsin sighed with relief. "And how is Lady Mavis? Well, I hope?"

"Seems to be, my lady."

"Do they treat her well at Dunborough?"

"Most of 'em." Arnhelm moved in closer and the others instinctively leaned in, too. "I got to say, my lady, that brother-in-law o' hers is some piece o' work. He's a wastrel and he drinks too much and the fellows he spends time with ain't no better. Sorry to upset you, my lady, but I thought you ought to know."

"Aye, we thought you ought to know," Verdan seconded.

Tamsin regarded the soldiers with dismay. "What about her husband? Does he treat her kindly and with respect?"

Arnhelm nodded. "Aye, my lady. Aye, he does. We weren't expectin' him to treat her so well as he does, considerin' who his father was."

"And they go at it like rabbits," Verdan said with a grin. "Right there in the woods that one time."

Arnhelm shot his brother a critical look while Tamsin blushed and Rheged's eyes widened as if he was both surprised and impressed.

"I think we can assume all is well with your cousin and her husband, then," Rheged said as he assumed a more dignified expression. "Have you any other news?"

"Lord DeLac ain't lookin' so good," Arnhelm replied. "Keeps to his bed most o' the time now. I don't think he'll be going to the feast. Sir Melvin and his wife said they'd go, though." Arnhelm grinned. "You'll like them, my lady."

Verdan, suitably chastised, nodded his agreement.

"If there's nothing else," Rheged said, "you may get yourself some refreshments in the kitchen. You'll stay the night, of course."

"Thank you, my lord, we will," Arnhelm replied, rising. His brother got to his feet, too, and together they headed for the kitchen.

"You've met Gerrard," Tamsin said to her husband when they were alone. "Do you think he'll cause trouble for Mavis?"

Rheged ran his hand over his chin thoughtfully. "He might try. He's jealous of Roland, so he might be even more bitter and angry now that Roland's wed to a woman as lovely as Mavis."

Tamsin started to open the letter. "Perhaps we shouldn't wait for the wedding feast to go to Dunborough. I'm sure Mavis won't mind if we arrive early."

Rheged put his hand on hers. "Aren't you forgetting something, beloved? You're with child, and that's not an easy journey. Let's hear what she has to say before we decide."

Tamsin nodded and began to read.

"Dearest cousin,
"We have arrived safely in Dunborough, although all of my dowry did not. Fortunately, the coin was spared, so I am buying new clothes, including a new gown for my wedding feast. It's to be on November 15, and I hope you and Rheged will come to celebrate with us in my new home. I realize you might not feel up to such a journey at this time of year, so if you choose to stay at Cwm Bron, I'll understand.

"All is going well in Dunborough. I had some trouble with one servant, so I dismissed her, as I was sure you would have. The steward is a bit of a trial, but I suppose I shouldn't fault him for keeping a careful eye on the expenses. Roland is well, and the best husband in the world, although you may not agree, being so enamored of your own."

"As well you should be," Rheged put in, grinning. Tamsin smiled in return before she continued reading.

"I hope to see you both soon. If not, perhaps I can come to Cwm Bron when the traveling will be easier.
"Your blessed and loving cousin,
"Mavis."

"There, you see?" Rheged said, his tone comfortingly triumphant. "You've been losing sleep for nothing. She sounds happy to me."

"Perhaps," Tamsin murmured as she perused the letter again.

"She'd tell you if there was trouble with her husband or anyone else, wouldn't she?"

"At one time, I would have agreed with you without question," Tamsin replied. She tapped the letter with her finger. "But this letter…there's a distance…a restraint… She is not as she was, Rheged."

"She's a married woman now," he replied. "We can't expect her to be exactly the same."

When Tamsin still looked worried, Rheged took her hand. "I think I had best plan a journey to Yorkshire in a sennight's time, or maybe a few days earlier. In the meantime, perhaps Arnhelm and Verdan can take a message to her for us, to let her know we may arrive on her doorstep sooner than expected."

His wife's fervent, passionate kiss was all the confirmation Rheged required that his suggestion met with her approval.

"I wonder how many more days will be fine enough for riding?" Mavis said to her husband as they rode along the top of the hills nearest Dunborough a few days later. Ahead the path led down into a wooded valley where a deep stream ran cold and fast. For once, the wind was no more than a mild breeze, and they could talk at their leisure.

"Not many," Roland replied. "But since my hall is so comfortable these days, I doubt I'll miss this much."

"In the winter, anyway," she agreed, giving him a smile that grew when she thought of her secret hope, something that would unite them even more. But it was too soon to tell Roland what she suspected in case she was wrong. "I doubt I'll be able to leave the castle again until after the feast. Only seven more days! I feel as if there are a thousand things to do. Indeed, I feel almost guilty for taking this time to be with you. Almost," she added with another smile.

"I'm honored," he replied with what appeared to be perfect seriousness, except for the hint of laughter twinkling in his dark eyes. She saw that more and more these days, making it easier to dismiss her concerns about Gerrard and the disturbing stings of jealousy that sometimes still troubled her if she saw Audrey in the village. And if what she thought was true...

"I think I'll dismiss Dalfrid after the wedding feast," Roland said. "I've decided to give him a hundred marks with my thanks, to make his dismissal a little more palatable and stave off any complaints he might make."

Mavis would have preferred to see the steward gone even sooner. Nevertheless, she didn't disagree. After all, the man had served the household for years, and although he carried on as if she was inviting the king and his court to the feast instead of less than twenty... well, surely she could endure him for another seven busy days.

"Have you had a message from your father yet?" Roland asked.

"No, not yet." She sighed and tried not to feel hurt. "It's not a good time of year to travel." She brightened as she thought of who would be attending. "Tamsin and Rheged will be, though, and Sir Melvin and Lady Viola."

"I thought I recognized those two men in the courtyard before we rode out. They brought answers to your invitations?"

"Yes, bless their hearts, for they're starting back today. Although Verdan was willing to wait a day or two, I couldn't convince Arnhelm to stay even one night. It seems that while he's proud and pleased to act as messenger, he doesn't like Yorkshire very much. He doesn't have as good a cause as I do to appreciate the country."

Rheged's brows drew together in a frown. "Just don't sit Sir Melvin too close to me. He's a kind, generous fellow, but he talks too much."

"Tamsin will sit beside you and she'll be quiet."

"I wonder," he mused aloud, his expression openly skeptical. "I can more easily imagine that she'll spend half the night leaning over me to talk to you, and you'll spend the other half leaning over me to talk to her. It would be better if you sat together."

"That would not be proper."

Roland shook his head, and so did Hephaestus, whose hoof had healed. "You see? He doesn't understand the rules of etiquette, either."

"He's a horse, Roland," she said with a laugh.

The wind picked up, lifting her cloak and making her teeth chatter, but she didn't want to go back to Dunborough. Not yet. This might be her last taste of freedom from duty and responsibility until the feast was over and all the guests had gone.

"I'm getting cold, but a good gallop will warm me," she said instead. She punched Sweetling's sides with her heels and slapped the reins against her mare's neck.

"Catch me if you can!" she cried as Sweetling took off at a gallop.

The wind whipped past them as they raced down the road, her horse's hooves throwing up mud. Mavis's heart pounded with excitement, her blood throbbing. Soon they were in the valley, with trees close by on every side, their bare branches reaching upward, and the underbrush thick with holly and golden bracken.

Onward and onward they galloped, through the valley, over another hill and down another valley. She no longer heard Roland's horse behind them and laughed to think they'd outraced him and his fine mount.

Until she saw the large tree blocking the road.

With a gasp, Mavis pulled hard on Sweetling's reins to halt her. As the mare pranced nervously, her panting breaths making little puffs of steam in the chilly air, she patted the horse's sweat-slicked neck.

"Good day, my lady!" a voice called from the woods on the right, and a man stepped out of the trees. His cloak, once a bright scarlet, was now filthy and torn. He had a scraggly excuse of a beard, and his hair was dirty and matted. Even so, she recognized him at once as Gerrard's friend Walter.

"All by yourself, are you?" he said, coming forward.

Two more men came out of the woods on the other side to block the road behind her—James and Frederick. Like Walter, their fine clothing was ruined, as if they'd slept out in the rain, and their hair matted, with some growth of beard upon their young faces.

"What do you want?" she demanded, wrapping her reins more about her hands, dismayed by their unkempt state and their nervous desperation that she could feel more than see.

"We want the toll, my lady," Walter said.

"I believe my husband has already paid you handsomely," she replied, trying to sound calm.

"Come on. Let her go," James said to Walter. "It's your fault we lost the money. If you hadn't played dice—"

"Shut your mouth!" Walter snarled, glaring at him before he turned his hostile gaze back to Mavis.

"I suggest you let me pass, lest you feel the wrath of my husband. He will be here soon."

"Maybe he will, or maybe he got waylaid a ways back," Walter replied with a triumphant smirk. "A cart might have cut him off. Maybe his horse stumbled and he fell. Could be the horse is lamed. Or he is."

"How do you—" She caught herself. "You're lying. If you're here, you couldn't possibly know what's happened farther back along the road."

"If it was only us, you'd be right." Walter whistled, and three more men came out of the woods, men even more dirty and disheveled, their beards longer and more tangled. Their clothing had never been fine; it looked like bits and pieces gathered up from a ditch. They carried swords and pikes and one had a broadax. From their hardened expressions, she could well believe they'd used them.

"So this is the lady, eh?" one of them muttered. He walked up and grabbed Sweetling's bridle as the horse shifted and tried to turn. "Well, you *are* a pretty one— too pretty for that foul bastard."

Mavis pulled her foot from the stirrup, ready to kick the fellow if he got any closer. "Unhand my horse and let me go!"

"Not until you've paid the toll, my lady."

"I have no money and if you take my horse—"

"It's not your horse or your clothes I want—well, I do," the outlaw admitted to the amusement of his comrades, although not Gerrard's three friends. "But first I'll have what your husband took from me." He lifted the long, greasy hair covering his right ear.

Or what would have been his right ear if it had still been there.

She felt sick at the sight of the marred and mottled flesh. Nevertheless, she tried to keep her wits about her. "If you don't let me go, you'll lose more than your ear."

"You've got a weapon hidden somewhere, do you? Or just your eating knife?" Walter said. "We'll have to search you for it and won't that be a—"

She lashed out with her booted foot, catching the earless man on the side of his head. He let go and she pulled hard on the reins, turning Sweetling. As she urged her mare into a gallop, James and Frederick jumped out of the way. The man without an ear and the rest of his companions rushed toward her, but Sweetling knocked aside any man who tried to get in her way.

As soon as she was free of them, Mavis leaned low over her horse's neck. Tears stung her eyes and her cloak flew out behind her as they galloped back along the road until she saw Roland riding toward her. Thank God he wasn't hurt! And Hephaestus wasn't lame!

"God's blood, what's happened?" Roland demanded as they met and reined in. "You're white as snow! Are you ill?"

"There was a tree across the road, so I stopped. And then…there were men. Gerrard's friends and others. Outlaws. They said…they wanted…" Her voice caught and for a moment, she couldn't speak as the fear, previously held at bay by force of will, flooded through her.

"Did they hurt you?"

"No. I…I got away before they could. Where were you? They said they'd blocked the road with a cart, that you'd fallen, that Hephaestus was lame."

"There was a cart in the road with a broken wheel.

I never guessed it was a trick, a trap to keep me there while you..."

He fell silent, choked by his anger, and he looked as if he were planning to go after them at once, by himself.

"You'd be outnumbered, Roland," she protested even though he hadn't voiced any such plan, "and it's getting late. Take me home, and then you can go after them tomorrow with more men. I want to go home, Roland, please."

"You shouldn't have ridden away from me like that," he said sternly. "No one can be completely safe upon the roads, a woman most of all, not even on my land."

"I'm sorry," she said, fighting back tears, sorry that she'd been so heedless, but more upset by his harsh tone. "I only wanted a gallop."

"And now you've had it," he said, turning his horse back toward Dunborough and waiting for her to follow.

When they reached the inner ward of the castle, Roland dismounted and helped his distraught wife from her horse. She didn't have to tell him she was still upset; he could see it in her face.

To think she had been attacked, and on his land—his land that he should have ensured was free from brigands, as he should have ensured that Walter and those others were far away.

He spotted Lizabet and called her to help her mistress while he strode toward the barracks. It might be too late to go after those louts today, but he would make certain all was ready to leave at first light. Then, by God, he would catch them, and they would pay.

Long after the evening meal was over—an uncomfortable evening meal presided over by her grimly silent husband—Mavis paced in their chamber waiting for him to retire. If he intended to. Roland had been so angry, she could believe he would rather march along the wall walk all night waiting for dawn than come to their chamber.

Unsure if she should try to sleep, doubtful that she could, she went to the window and peered into the yard. There was no sign of Roland, only the guards.

"You should sleep."

She turned to find Roland on the threshold. "I wasn't sure I could," she admitted.

He didn't reply to that, but went to the washstand and began to wash his face.

"I'm truly sorry I was so thoughtless, Roland," she said, clasping her hands before her.

Leaning on the washstand, Roland sighed deeply, then turned to face her. "And I'm sorry there were outlaws on my land."

Encouraged by his words and his sigh, she ventured closer. "One of them said you'd cut off his ear."

He frowned. "It was my father's preferred punishment for some offenses. It was often my duty to carry out the sentences."

She stared at him, appalled that any father would ask a son to do such things. "As if you were a common jailer? Did you do executions, too?"

"I oversaw them, yes, if the sentence was justified."

"And if not?" she asked, remembering the cruel and evil man his father was.

"If I thought it unjust and my father wouldn't change his mind, I left the task to the garrison commander."

"Gerrard?"

"No. The old one. He died shortly before my father."

"But you did cut off ears?"

"What would you have me say, Mavis?" he demanded, frustration in his voice and his dark eyes. "I am a hard man who's done hard things. Terrible things. Things I regret every day of my life. Things that have made me even more determined to be just and fair. But if there has been a crime that must be punished, I won't shirk from meting it out. If you wanted a soft and easy man, you should have married someone else. I've been told that handsome, charming men like Gerrard swarmed about you like bees to flowers. You could have married one of them, or did they not have enough wealth and power or come from the north, where your father wanted an ally?"

"Roland!" she cried, aghast and appalled. "I told you there was no other man I wanted. I was prepared to flee rather than marry against my will. It wouldn't have mattered if a suitor was as rich as a king, or as powerful, or ruled from the north to the south.

"And if you're jealous of those unworthy men," she charged, "what am I to think about you? There must have been scores of women who wanted Sir Roland of Dunborough, even if Audrey D'Orleau wasn't one of them."

"Women who wanted the cold, hard son of Sir Blane of Dunborough? There was not a one."

"Until me."

"Yes, until you, and I still can't—"

He fell silent, then marched to the door. "You should rest, Mavis, so I'll leave you in peace," he said before he went out and closed the door behind him.

Mavis went back to the window and looked out at the sky, wondering if she could ever truly know, or understand, the man she'd married.

Roland had barely gone five feet before remorse smote him like a battle ax. Mavis shouldn't have ridden off alone, but neither should he have been so angry with her. After all, it was not her fault there were brigands on his lands. Gerrard should have ensured his estate was safe while he was gone and…

No, the responsibility was his. He shouldn't have left Gerrard in charge, and now Mavis had suffered for it.

Worse, he had sounded like a weak and jealous fool.

He half turned, prepared to go back and tell her he was sorry. He hadn't yet found a way to tell her how she made him feel, how pleased and proud and happy, but for this, he would somehow find the words. He must find the words.

Is the baby going to cry?

Tomorrow, he told himself as he started forward once more. He would speak to her tomorrow, after they had caught the rogues who had dared to threaten his wife.

The next day Mavis paced anxiously in the hall, awaiting Roland's return, wondering what he'd do when he caught the outlaws, and those young men who'd been Gerrard's friends. And what would happen the next time she was alone with her husband.

The door to the hall opened and she swiftly turned to see who it was, although surely Roland and his men would have made more noise on their return. Instead, Audrey D'Orleau, wrapped in her fine cloak, sauntered into the hall. Her fearsome bodyguard came in behind her and stood by the door, feet planted, arms crossed.

As Roland seemed to find it difficult to believe that she had married him because she wished to, she found it hard to accept that any woman of intelligence wouldn't want Roland, even if she could believe that Roland himself had done nothing to encourage her. Unfortunately,

Audrey D'Orleau was likely the sort of vain woman who would require very little encouragement.

She was also the last person Mavis wanted to see. Nevertheless, she was bound by the rules of hospitality to greet her. "Good day, Audrey," she said, gesturing for the woman to sit beside her near the hearth.

"I heard that Marmaduke and Bartholomew were here, so I've sent for my dressmaker," Audrey said as she swept back her skirts and sank into the chair. "Now that you've chosen the fabric, Dominique can make the gowns for you. She'll do a marvelous job, I assure you."

"Given the excellent workmanship of your own clothes, I'm sure she will," Mavis agreed with a polite smile.

"I'm sure Roland's been most generous."

"He's a kind husband."

"Indeed?" Audrey replied as she adjusted her skirts to show off the quality of the embroidery about the hem. "Then all is well between you?"

"Quite well," Mavis lied. The state of her marriage was none of this woman's business, and she didn't doubt Audrey was the sort to spread rumors based on very little evidence.

"I was concerned you'd had an argument. I saw Roland ride out today with some of his men and he looked as angry as I've ever seen him."

"You could see that from your upper window?" Mavis calmly inquired.

"You forget how well I know Roland," Audrey replied, not the least nonplussed. "It made me fear all is not well between you and your husband."

"He and his men have gone after a band of outlaws on his land."

"Outlaws!" Audrey exclaimed with genuine shock.

"Yes. They stopped me on the road. Fortunately, I got away and Roland brought me home."

"You got away? By yourself? Where was Roland?"

"I had ridden ahead and some of their band had pushed an empty cart into the road to delay him."

"You rode ahead alone? That was a foolish thing to do!"

"I know that now," Mavis replied.

"Well, you're safe now. As for those outlaws, I wouldn't be in their boots for all the gold in England. The men of Dunborough are like rabid dogs when it comes to protecting their possessions."

Mavis didn't appreciate being called a possession. Nevertheless, she said, "If they've broken the law, they must be punished."

"Of course," Audrey agreed. "I'm sure Roland will ensure that the punishment is harsh enough that other brigands will think twice about attacking anyone on his land. It often fell to Roland to do such things. He's always been…efficient."

Audrey made it sound as if Roland felt nothing when he had to exact punishments; that to him, it was simply a duty to be efficiently done. Here was proof that no matter what Audrey or Gerrard implied, Audrey didn't really know Roland at all.

"No doubt he will do what he considers necessary and just," Mavis replied.

"I thank you for offering me the services of your dressmaker," she went on, hoping Audrey would take the hint and go.

She did not. "I nearly forgot!" she cried, giving Mavis another false smile. "I also came to tell you that I'll be delighted to attend your wedding feast."

Mavis's response was just as fraudulently pleasant. "I'm so glad!"

"I suppose you aren't expecting Gerrard to attend."

In truth, Mavis wasn't sure what Gerrard would do. As long as he was still in Dunborough, there was a chance he would come and disrupt the evening. "I don't know. We haven't seen him."

"Poor fellow! He spends most of his time wandering about the village, I hear, or in…well, a rather unsavory establishment, although rumor has it he only drinks there." Audrey sighed heavily. "He was so angry when he learned Roland was the heir! I feared there'd be murder done before the day was out."

"You were there?" Mavis asked with surprise.

Audrey flushed. "Oh, no. But of course I heard. Dalfrid said Roland barely batted an eye, while Gerrard raved like a…well, like a man robbed of his birthright."

"Except that he wasn't," Mavis pointed out. And if Dalfrid was telling people such things, that was another reason for him to go.

Audrey adjusted her skirts again and didn't look directly at Mavis when she replied. "Gerrard could contest the will."

"On what grounds? There is no one who can dispute Roland's right as the firstborn son and their own father named him heir."

"Their own father was a cruel, vindictive villain who lied the way other men breathe," Audrey returned with unexpected vigor before she quickly resumed her more genial manner. "And there's Eua. She claims Gerrard was born first and she was in the household then."

"She's only a servant and it's well known Gerrard is her favorite."

"You've heard that, have you? Still, Gerrard can try.

Who can say what evidence the courts may decide is more valid?"

Mavis's stomach twisted. If Gerrard managed to speak to John, who was said to take bribes… But Gerrard had no money of his own, so how could he possibly get enough to bribe the king? "If he wishes to lose, he's welcome to try."

Finally Audrey rose. "I suppose I should be on my way, so I shall leave you to wait for Roland, my lady."

Mavis did not invite her to linger.

Audrey started for the door, then turned back. "You may think Gerrard will not win a suit against his brother, but I wouldn't be so confident if it comes before the king."

Mavis stood and regarded her with defiant majesty. "I trust you won't encourage him. To sway the king requires power and money. Roland has both, Gerrard has neither."

"For now, my lady, but a man like Gerrard will surely find a way to obtain them," Audrey replied before she swept out of the hall with her faithful bodyguard behind her.

Mavis sank slowly back onto the chair. Audrey had money…but no title. Gerrard came from a powerful family…but he would be casting himself out of it if he brought suit against Roland.

Most of all, though, to take the matter to the king would require action and determination, and she took comfort from the fact that Gerrard seemed more willing to complain and protest and argue than actually do something that would further his cause.

The rogues had fled on horseback, and although they'd tried to disguise their trail, they hadn't gone far enough or been clever enough to elude Roland and his men. It took them little less than half a day to catch them in a wood near a narrow gorge.

Despite the beards and ragged clothing, Roland immediately recognized Walter, James and Frederick, and he silently thanked God that Gerrard wasn't with them.

He recognized someone else, and for a different reason—Bern, the defiler of women, whose ear he'd cut off as punishment last year. Perhaps Mavis wouldn't be so horrified by the loss of an ear when she learned what Bern had done. As for those other hasty things he'd said…he hoped she could forgive him those, as well.

"Throw down your weapons and dismount," Roland ordered as he swung down from his horse.

James and Frederick instantly obeyed, tossing away their swords as if they'd burst into flames, then just as quickly getting off their horses. The others hesitated until Roland's men drew their circle about them closer. Even the scowling Bern, who had to know there was but one outcome for him now, did as he was told.

"Where's Gerrard?" Walter demanded, his eyes darting about like a trapped rat.

"Not here," Roland replied. "I doubt you'll see him in Dunborough, either, while you await judgment in the dungeon."

"But he's the commander of your garrison!" Frederick cried.

"Not anymore, and even if he were, he wouldn't have been allowed to give you any special treatment after what you've done."

"We just wanted to scare her a little," Frederick whined. "We didn't know that lout wanted to cut off her ear."

"That's right," James fervently agreed, desperation

in his voice and eyes. "We were just going to scare her a little, that's all. No harm in that and no harm done to her, eh, Roland?"

"I am *Sir* Roland to you, and you will be returning to Dunborough to face judgment, the same as any lawbreaker."

"Lawbreaker?" James gasped, finally seeming to grasp that his situation was dire. "We've broken no laws!"

"You waylaid and threatened my wife."

"It was Bern who wanted to hurt her," James charged.

"He hates you, my lord," Frederick added.

"So he was going to have vengeance on me by harming my wife, and you were going to help him."

"No, no!" James protested. "We didn't know it would be your wife who—" He stopped and flushed, while Walter glared at him as if he'd like to slit his throat.

"So you simply wanted to rob whoever was on the road," Roland said, "and in spite of the silver I gave you."

James and Frederick pointed at Walter. "He lost it all gambling!"

"It was a pittance to begin with," Walter sneered. "Hardly enough for men of quality to live on."

"I see no men of quality here," Roland replied.

"So high and mighty, so proud, when you've got nothing to be proud of, not with *your* family. What have we done compared to them? Compared to what Gerrard's done?" Walter demanded.

Roland wasn't sure which one of Gerrard's transgressions, or perhaps several, Walter was referring to, and he didn't want his men or the rest of the outlaws to hear any accusations Walter might make. He went up to the scowling Walter and spoke quietly so that the nearby soldiers couldn't hear. "Whatever Gerrard's done in the past, he wasn't with you when you accosted my wife."

"Not then, but what about the night that girl was raped?"

"She herself said there was only one man and it was Bern."

"But nobody thought to ask her what she was doing in the woods that night, did they? That was your brother's doing." Walter's eyes glowed with malicious triumph. "Arrest me and everyone will hear that your brother asked her to meet him there—and not for a few kisses and not only with him. All four of us were going to have a little sport. But he was too much of a coward to follow through with his own plan and he never came. We went to find him before she went back home. Then Bern came upon her."

This was both bad, and good.

"Bern was guilty of the crime of which he was accused, however she came to be there, and was punished accordingly. As for my brother's part in it, if what you say is true, why didn't you speak until now?"

"Because we were his friends," Walter replied. "I gather friendship is something you know nothing about, or so Gerrard says."

For once, Roland felt no sting at such a comment, true though it was. "If you are what pass for friends, I'm glad I've had none."

As for these three, they had had their chance. "You could have been far away by now and living in comfort with the money I gave you. Instead, you decided to stay and turn outlaw."

"We'll go now!" James cried.

"We'll go and never come back!" Frederick agreed, shrill in his panic.

"Perhaps, for your families' sakes, I ought to let you go, provided you promise never to return," Roland said.

"I promise, my lord," James immediately replied. "I'll never come here again!"

Frederick eagerly concurred. "Nor I!"

"You fools!" Walter snarled, glaring at them. He jabbed his finger at Roland. "Are you forgetting who this is? Whose son and brother he is? Guilty or not, you think he's going to be merciful and let you go? He's lying! He's going to kill us where we stand! We have to fight—or die!"

Before anyone could react, Walter charged Roland like a madman. Roland had no time to draw his sword before the man was on him and wrestling for his weapon. Roland managed to grab Walter's arm, but Walter pulled free, and when he did, he had Roland's broadsword. Roland rolled to his feet and reached for the small eating knife in his belt.

James and Frederick had started to run toward the gorge. The soldiers gave chase, drawing their weapons as they ran.

Walter charged Roland again, but this time, Roland was ready. He deftly avoided the swinging sword and caught the man's side with his knife, the blade ripping through the soiled clothing to the flesh beneath. With a scream, Walter fell to the ground, writhing in pain.

Roland straightened, panting, and saw James and Frederick at the very edge of the gorge. His soldiers walked slowly toward them while James and Frederick, panic in their eyes, backed up. Before Roland could call out for them to stop, the rock gave way under Frederick and he dropped out of sight. His face full of terror, James teetered for what seemed an age on the edge of the gorge before he, too, fell and was gone.

Chapter Eleven

As soon as Mavis heard the commotion in the yard, she grabbed her cloak and hurried outside.

A group of rough-looking, filthy men, including that frightening man without an ear, stood in the yard surrounded by guards. That was a relief, until she saw the three bodies draped over unfamiliar horses. Two of them dripped water, as if they'd been caught in a downpour although the sky was clear. Her heart in her throat, she recognized the clothes of Gerrard's erstwhile friends.

Surely Roland hadn't… He wouldn't, not without a trial.

Where *was* he?

There, near the stables. He was muddy and unkempt and…was that blood on his tunic?

She broke into a run.

"Where are you wounded?" she cried when she reached him.

His reply eased the worst of her fears. "It's not mine."

"What happened?" She nodded at the bodies. "Is that…?"

"We'll talk inside," he said as he ushered her toward the hall.

"Well done, my lord!" Dalfrid cried, appearing as if by magic from the kitchen corridor after they entered and sat beside the hearth. "Now we can all feel safe in our beds! Outlaws and thieves have been a nuisance ever since you went to DeLac."

Roland regarded his steward coldly. "Why wasn't I told of this when I returned, or at least last night?"

"Your brother—who was, after all, the garrison commander—was sure they'd fled, so I saw no need to mention the outlaws when you returned. Last night, you were planning to pursue them. Since you knew they were on your land, I saw no need to say anything more."

"You should have told me. Such information should never be kept from me."

Dalfrid flushed, nodded and backed away. "Yes, my lord."

"The outlaws we brought back alive will stay in the dungeon until their trial."

That was a relief and yet...

"What happened, Roland?" she asked again. "Why are those three young men dead?"

Lizabet arrived with wine and he took a gulp before answering. "We found the outlaws and those three near the gorge. Walter attacked me and as I was defending myself, the other two tried to escape. I slew Walter, and they fell into the gorge." He ran his hand through his hair. "I gave them more money than most men see in their lives, and it wasn't enough. Walter gambled it all away, and the other two were foolish enough to let him and too foolish to abandon him afterward. God save me, Mavis, what can you do with men like that?"

"There was nothing more you could do," she said, her

heart aching when she saw the anguish in his eyes, and yet she was glad, too, because he had spoken of his dismay to her. That had to be another sign that he wanted to be close to her and more than physically.

Someone shouted outside, followed by what sounded like protests, and then Gerrard charged into the hall, his expression full of rage, his hands clenched into fists. "Murderer!" he cried, storming toward the dais.

"I've done no murder," Roland replied as he got to his feet. "We were going to bring your former friends back to Dunborough for trial when Walter attacked me. I killed him defending myself and the other two drowned while attempting to flee."

Gerrard stared at him with angry disbelief. "Trial? What the devil for?"

"They had joined an outlaw band, one you apparently thought had left my land. They accosted my wife and would have done her harm had she not escaped." Roland's voice rose with fury. "So ends the lives of the men you drank and wenched and gambled with, the men you claimed were your friends. The men you brought into this village and this household!"

"So now it's *my* fault they attacked your wife?"

With an effort, Roland regained his self-control. "As they were your friends and here by your invitation until I sent them away, you bear some responsibility."

"I'm no seer to predict what men may do," Gerrard retorted. "If you hadn't sent them away, they wouldn't have had to go outside the law."

"If a man cannot live for several months on twenty marks, he is indeed a fool—and any man who would defend him is likewise a fool."

"You would no doubt consider any friend of mine a scoundrel."

Roland came down from the dais to stand toe to toe with his brother. "Because, Gerrard, they *always* are."

"You cur!" Gerrard cried. "As if you're a saint!" He pointed at Mavis. "Does she know all that you've done? Or will you claim it was all our father's doing?"

"I did as I was ordered by the lord of Dunborough and to keep the peace."

Gerrard sniffed with scorn. "But does she know that you enjoyed this *keeping of the peace*?"

"I did *not* enjoy it! I did what was necessary and only that," Roland retorted, his hands balling into fists. Once again, they were mirror images of each other, alike in looks and posture and rage. "What of that girl you lured into the woods? Walter told me that you were supposed to meet her and planned to have your friends there, too, for what sordid business I can only guess. But you never arrived, so they left her alone, like a lamb led to the slaughter. Have you already forgotten what happened to her? I never can because *I* had to exact the punishment while you caroused with your cronies who now lie dead in the yard!"

Although his face turned red with shame, Gerrard answered with defiance. "I never thought she'd come. She never said she would and it was me alone she was to meet. If Walter and the others planned to join us, I didn't know."

"You should have. You should have known what kind of men they were if you cared about anything other than your own amusement."

"So you would put all the blame for what happened to her on me, as well? Why not? It's always been easier to blame me for everything that went wrong, whether it was a broken bridle or dented sword or an order not obeyed."

"I never blamed you for those things," Roland growled. "Good God, I stayed silent most of the time when our father accused us of neglect and disobedience. Yet in the next breath you mocked me for that very silence."

"Oh, yes, you were silent. Silent as the grave most of the time, unless you were pointing out my faults to me."

"Would you rather I told our father who was really to blame? Or repeated all your complaints?"

"While you're as pure as an angel?" Scowling, Gerrard addressed Mavis, whose face had turned progressively paler as they argued. "He's got you believing he's the good one, the noble one, the upright and blameless one, while I'm nothing but a wastrel."

Gerrard laughed harshly. "Who suffered more under our father's hand? Who got beaten more? And who stood by while I was beaten?" He glared at his brother. "Who let me take the blame more times than I can count?"

"Because you *were* to blame every time we *both* were beaten and other times besides when I tried to speak in your defense—times you seem to have conveniently forgotten!" Roland cried with exasperation. "You were *always* the instigator and if I didn't follow you, if I tried to warn you and prevent you from getting into trouble, who jeered and sneered at me then, Gerrard? Who called me coward and a hundred other names?"

"You *are* a coward!

"Stop, the both of you!" Mavis cried, unable to remain silent any longer. "Roland, please, as long as Gerrard is in Dunborough, there'll never be peace between you for a host of reasons. Give your brother some money as you did his friends and send him on his way."

Gerrard's eyes widened with surprise, and then that

mocking grin appeared upon his face. "So I was right, Roland, and your wife does want me gone—and now we'll see who truly rules in Dunborough. Will you do as she says, brother, and make me go? How much are you willing to offer for that to happen? More than you offered my friends, I trust." His expression grew grimly serious. "Unfortunately, whatever your wife commands and however much you offer, there isn't enough coin in the castle coffers to make me go."

"Every man has his price," Mavis said, desperate to have him gone before he spewed more hateful words.

"Is that a lesson learned at your father's knee, my lady?" Gerrard asked scornfully. He eyed his brother with disdain. "Perhaps I've been wrong to think Roland bought you. Maybe it was my brother who was purchased. How much did Roland cost, my lady?"

"How many times are you going to insult us?" she demanded.

"As many as I like, as long as I'm here."

"Then again I say, it's time for you to go, and however much we must pay you, it will be worth it."

The steward stepped warily out from behind the servants who were crowding the kitchen entrance. "I fear, my lord," he said to the grimly silent Roland, wringing his hands, "that Gerrard is correct. There's not enough coin in the castle coffers to pay him more than a pittance. Your father and Broderick left debts that had to be repaid, and there are the king's taxes, as well as your wife's new clothes and the wedding feast. Indeed, my lord, there'll be barely enough to pay the household expenses over the winter." Dalfrid swallowed hard and his gaze wandered to Gerrard. "There were a few other things that also took some of your money."

Roland regarded his brother steadily. "How much have you taken?"

"No more than I had a right to," Gerrard defensively replied. "I'm a lord's son, not a pauper, and I shouldn't have to beg my brother for funds."

"How much did you take?"

"There was a debt of honor owing. I paid it."

"The greater portion of the funds went to the king and his tax collector," the steward offered placatingly. "It has ever been thus, my lord, although you didn't know it."

"Yet once again you saw fit to blame me for the loss," Gerrard angrily observed.

"The fact remains, my lord," Dalfrid said, looking from one irate man to the other, "that there simply isn't enough to pay your brother any sizable amount."

"I can forego new clothes and the wedding feast," Mavis offered, fearing the quarrel between the brothers was never going to end, "and we'll find ways to manage over the winter if we are lacking coins. The storerooms are full."

"I won't have my wife dressed in—" Roland began. He fell silent, but she could guess what he was going to say.

"I am hardly wearing rags. I would rather have peace in the household than new gowns or a feast."

"That will not save nearly enough," Dalfrid noted with apparently sincere regret.

"Alas for you, my lady, you cannot force your brother-in-law into exile," Gerrard jeered.

"If you were more like a brother and less like a spoiled brat, you would be welcome here," she snapped.

"If you want peace in Dunborough, tell your husband to give me this estate and take him back to DeLac," Gerrard said, his words no longer heated, but as cold as a stream in spring. "He'll never love you, you know. He'll never love anybody. He doesn't know how."

"And you'll never love anybody except yourself—just like our father!" Roland returned.

Gerrard ran another scornful gaze over his brother. "I thought you'd married DeLac's daughter for money and power, but it was something else, wasn't it? You had to win at marriage, too. You had to bring home a beauty and show me that you could bargain for a better bride. We'll see about that, Roland. Mavis isn't the only beautiful woman in the world."

"Shut that mouth of yours, Gerrard," Roland ordered, "or by God, I'll do it for you!"

"As if you could!"

"Dog!"

"Cur!" Gerrard retorted. "And your wife's a bi—"

With a roar, Roland tackled his brother, sending them both sprawling on the rush-covered floor. Roland punched and pummeled his squirming, thrashing brother, who was hitting back with all the power he possessed.

"Stop, stop!" Mavis cried, trying to get between them. This was more than a quarrel or sibling disagreement. This was years of bitter envy and resentment unleashed, expressed with blows and curses, and it must not go on.

Panting, Roland heeded her cries. He rose, wiping the blood from his chin that trickled from his cut lip. Gerrard also staggered upright. His right eye was swelling shut and his cheek was already purpling with a bruise.

"You are both grown men of noble birth, yet you're fighting like animals!" Mavis declared.

"I was defending myself," Gerrard muttered, glaring

at them both, "although no doubt Roland will claim it was me who started it."

"Roland, please! Make him go!" Mavis desperately persisted, her hands clasped like a supplicant, her patience at its end. "I will *not* bring the child I carry into such turmoil!"

The two men, so alike in feature but so different in every other way, turned to stare at her.

"You're with child?" Roland asked after a moment of stunned silence.

"A miracle, apparently," Gerrard said with another mocking smile even as a yearning, wistful look came to his eyes just like Roland's in her father's solar.

"Are you with child?" her husband asked again.

"I think so. I hope so."

"But you're not sure?"

She went to him and looked at him intently, willing him to listen to her. "If I am—and even if I'm not— things cannot go on this way. Gerrard must leave Dunborough completely if there's to be any peace in our household."

Her husband's stern expression didn't change as he regarded her for what seemed an eternity. "As I have told you before, Mavis, I will not force him out."

Gerrard grinned with triumph while Mavis regarded her husband with dismay. "Roland, please!"

"I will not cast him out," he coldly repeated.

If he could speak to her thus, if he could so blatantly ignore her feelings...

She turned on her heel and left them, heading for the bedchamber, where she could be alone.

"Leave my hall, Gerrard," Roland said with that same stern frigidity after she had gone, "lest I change my mind and exile you from Dunborough forever."

Gerrard did not move.

Roland took a step toward him.

Scowling, his face red, his hands still balled into fists at his sides, Gerrard started for the outer doors.

They opened before he got there and Arnhelm, mud splattered and exhausted, stumbled in.

Fighting a wave of nausea, Mavis sat slowly on the bed. She didn't know if she felt ill from witnessing the hostile quarrel in the hall and Roland's refusal to make his brother leave, or if she was, indeed, with child.

Rising again, she went to the window and, despite the cold breeze that threatened rain, opened the shutter and took in deep breaths. That made her feel a little better.

She leaned her forehead against the cool stones and tried to accept her husband's decision, but were they forever to be subjected to Gerrard's anger and mockery and disrespect?

She had lived her life neglected and ruled by her father, her opinions and feelings ignored. Her position had been usurped by her cousin and although she loved Tamsin, she had felt the scorn from those who assumed she was glad to give up the responsibility to another, or was too stupid to oversee the household.

Now Roland was paying no heed to her opinions, as if she were no more than a servant.

Or just a wife to share his bed and give him children after all. A beautiful wife to make a mean-spirited, mocking brother jealous.

Swift footsteps sounded in the corridor leading to the chamber. Taking another deep breath, she prepared to face her husband, come what may.

Roland entered the room without knocking, a travel-worn Arnhelm right behind him. The soldier pulled a parchment sealed with wax from his belt before she could even greet him.

What had transpired in the hall below was suddenly forgotten, for this could herald nothing good.

"I have a letter for you, my lady, from your father," Arnhelm announced. "I was to put it into your hands alone."

She let her breath out slowly. At least her father wasn't dead, and Tamsin and Rheged were all right.

His brows lowered, Roland stuck out his arm to prevent Arnhelm from handing her the letter. "It can wait. The lady is unwell."

"I'm well enough, especially when he comes in such haste," she said, stepping briskly forward to take the letter. "I need to know what news he brings."

"You can wait for her answer in the hall with Verdan," Roland said, and his words were not a request.

Arnhelm looked at Mavis, who nodded her agreement, then tugged his forelock. "Until later, my lady."

Mavis managed a smile before he left the chamber.

She broke the seal. One glance at the handwriting, spidery and thin, told her that her father was very sick, and his written words confirmed it. "My father is ill and wants me to come home at once," she said as she read.

Roland frowned. "It's not easy to travel at this time of year, especially if you're with child."

"I shouldn't have said anything about that. It's too early to be certain, and my father must be very ill, or he wouldn't have sent a message in such haste. I *must* go to him."

"You would risk bad weather and worse roads, and possibly the health of our unborn child, to tend to the man who had little use for you except as something to bargain with?"

"I can't forget my duty as a daughter. I would never forgive myself if I didn't go back."

"And if I forbid it?"

In spite of what had passed between them, she hadn't expected that. "*Do* you forbid it, my lord?"

"Yes," he replied, his visage stern. Forbidding. Unyielding, with no trace of the gentle lover or that wistful man in her father's solar.

Where had that other Roland gone? Was he refusing to let her return to DeLac to prove to everyone that he alone was the ruler of Dunborough? If so, he should find another way. "Unless you intend to lock me in this chamber, my lord, I'm going to do what I think is right. I shall return to DeLac as my father requests and I intend to leave at first light tomorrow."

She waited, tensed, for Roland to again refuse to let her go or to say he would prevent it.

He did not. Instead, he marched to the door, where he paused, one hand on the frame. "Since you will likely not be back in a sennight, there will be no wedding feast."

Then he was gone.

Mavis sat heavily on the bed, relieved he had accepted her decision even if he hadn't done so graciously. She had made her point and carried the day.

So what of it if her victory felt hollow?

As for the wedding feast, Roland was quite right. She would likely still be in DeLac in seven days' time, and who could say when she would return?

Roland strode to the stable, but not to take Hephaestus or Icarus or any other horse out for a gallop. He wanted to be alone, and there was a place at the far end of the loft, away from where the grooms and stable boys slept, that was also shielded from sight. He had found it years ago when he was just a lad and sought a hiding place from his father's anger, Broderick's blows and Gerrard's mockery.

When he opened the stable door, Hephaestus neighed a greeting and he paused a moment to stroke his horse's soft muzzle—but only a moment, lest someone come in and see him climbing up the ladder.

Bent over to avoid the beams, he made his way to his secret place, where a little louvered window provided some air. He lay down and looked up at the thatched roof that he had stared at so many times before. He asked himself the same questions that he had so many times before, too.

Why did everyone always tell him what to do? Why did everyone try to rule him, even now? Even though he was a grown man and a lord, everyone seemed to think they knew better than he did and always had. His father, Broderick, Gerrard, Dalfrid, Audrey and now Mavis—they all seemed so certain they knew better, or that he was wrong.

He had hoped that things would be different with Mavis. He had believed that she respected his opinion and would listen to him. Instead, she couldn't accept that he was right to let his brother stay. But how could he exile him? Whatever else he was, Gerrard was his brother. And look what had happened when he'd compelled Walter, James and Frederick to go. If Gerrard fell into bad company, or outside the law, if he wound up dead or imprisoned, he would never forgive himself.

Could Mavis not see that even as she felt duty-bound to go to her neglectful, greedy father, he was duty-bound to keep his brother from harm, and her, too, even if she didn't agree with his decision? She was his wife, after all. His beautiful loving wife, who surely could have had her choice of other men, but who had chosen him, or so she claimed.

Was it truly possible that he had been her first and only choice? That nothing except pleasing herself had caused her to make that decision?

How much he wanted to believe it! How desperate he was to think she was sincere.

As for Gerrard's claim that he had married Mavis to make his brother jealous…he couldn't deny there was truth in that. When he had seen Mavis crying that first morning, he'd comforted himself with that very thought.

Even if that had been true then, he couldn't let his brother know that, let alone Mavis. He had already done enough damage to their marriage with his quarrels with Gerrard. He wouldn't risk more.

But neither could he have anyone, especially Gerrard, think she told him what to do.

Yet his feelings for her—whether only desire or more—were so strong, his need to have her respect and admiration so powerful, he couldn't trust himself not to weaken in her presence and let her sway his actions.

Therefore, he had best keep away from her until he could retain his self-control. Better to risk gossip of a quarrel between them than have Gerrard or anyone else think he was her slave.

So he decided that despite the possible danger of a journey, he would let her go back to her father.

Although he could not suppress a sigh.

"He's a monster, I tell you! A selfish, mean-spirited, greedy oaf!" Gerrard cried, striding around the main chamber of Audrey D'Orleau's manor house like a bull on a rampage. "He no more deserves to rule Dunborough than his horse—or his wife!"

Audrey adjusted the long, folded-back cuff of her velvet gown. She had long ago learned it was best to let men in such a humor rant and rave until they grew calmer. Besides, she wasn't really listening. She had also learned long ago that Gerrard would never believe Roland could act in good faith, regardless of any evidence to the contrary, just as Roland believed Gerrard could never be anything but selfish and lazy.

"He goes off to Castle DeLac vowing that there will be no alliance with that arrogant scoundrel DeLac only to come home with the man's daughter as his bride. Now he'll do whatever she says. I swear she's bewitched him!"

Audrey sat up a little straighter on her goose-down cushion and reached for the excellent wine in a silver goblet. It, and the equally expensive carafe, rested on a small oak table with wonderfully carved legs. "She is beautiful, but I find it difficult to believe that he would pay heed to any woman, no matter how lovely," she honestly replied. "After all, this is Roland we are speaking of."

She could see Gerrard hoodwinked by a beautiful woman and a slave to his lust, but not his brother. If it were otherwise, she would have persuaded Roland to marry her as soon as word came that he was the heir. "No doubt he saw merit in the match after all," she observed. "DeLac does have friends at court and he's rather wealthy, too. I'm sure the dowry was considerable."

Mavis also had a title, the one thing, besides a husband, Audrey lacked.

Gerrard made a derisive sniff. "All her dower goods

were destroyed in a fire, or so they say, but the loss of the dowry doesn't seem to trouble Roland in the least. To be sure, she's a beauty, but when has Roland ever cared about a woman's looks?"

"Exactly," Audrey murmured, smoothing down her heavily embroidered skirt and sighing heavily. "But she *is* his wife, and there's nothing to be done about it, although you could go to the law, I suppose, and demand an annulment on your brother's behalf."

"An annulment?" Clearly that thought had never occurred to Gerrard. "On what grounds?"

"The lost dowry. Who is to say whether everything was as valuable as DeLac claimed? Did I not hear that the prize he offered in a tournament recently turned out to be made not of real gold and gems but painted metal and paste? There is no way to be sure what the value of the dower goods were. It could well be that Roland didn't even take the time to examine everything on the wedding day, especially if he was anxious to bed the bride." She delicately cleared her throat. "My attorney in York is very learned in such matters."

Gerrard's eyes gleamed with hope and happiness, only to dim a moment later. "What if Mavis makes trouble? She seems to genuinely like Roland, as difficult as that is to believe."

Audrey got out of the ebony chair and strolled toward him. "How a woman looks, what she says in public and how she feels may be very different things. As we both know, Roland isn't exactly a man of passion. She might be…disappointed, shall we say? And only too willing to help us find a way to free her from an unhappy marriage.

"However, I would say nothing of this to anyone except me and my attorney for the time being. We want no word of this to reach Roland, or he will find a way to thwart you." She was careful to make it sound as if her scheming was all for Gerrard's advantage. "My attorney's name is Magnus Carl and his house is near the minster. Anyone in the market can direct you." She widened her eyes. "Come to think of it, Magnus also knows several of the king's household knights. Perhaps he could help you gain an audience with John himself, so you can also take up the matter of your inheritance."

"You're a clever woman, Audrey," Gerrard replied, obviously much—and rightly—impressed. "If I can get an audience with the king, I can tell him how I was cheated of my inheritance." He smiled, his lips curving up slowly. "Perhaps I should let Roland have his pretty little bride and seek only the estate. After all, Roland will have DeLac once Mavis's father dies, and I doubt John wants too much land and power in any one nobleman's hands. He should be eager to give me Dunborough." His insolent grin broadened and he stroked her cheek. "If I had a rich wife, I could better do battle in the courts and win my proper title as well as my inheritance."

It was possible Gerrard could convince the king that he deserved to be lord of Dunborough. He could be very charming and persuasive, and he was right about John not wanting to have too much land in any one man's hands. "But I have no title," she feebly protested. "I'm only a wool merchant's daughter."

"What care I for titles?" Gerrard replied, his voice low and husky. "You're a very desirable woman, Audrey," he murmured before his lips came down on hers.

No man ever wants what he can get easily. Her unhappily married mother's words echoed in her ears and she immediately pushed Gerrard away. "I'm flattered,

Gerrard, very flattered. But I... We..." She shook her head. "Your proposal has been so sudden, so unexpected! I can hardly breathe or think."

"Why do you need to think?" he replied, pulling her back into his arms. "I want you, Audrey, and you want me. I can feel it in your arms, your lips."

This time, when Gerrard kissed her, she didn't protest. Nor did she stop him when his hand cupped her breast.

Heavy footfalls sounded outside the door and Audrey quickly broke the kiss. "That's Duncan."

"What does it matter?" Gerrard muttered, reaching for her again. "He's only a servant."

That was true, but this interruption was also a timely reminder that she mustn't sell her maidenhead unless she was guaranteed a title. "You had better go, Gerrard. We wouldn't want to give Roland any more excuse to slander you."

"I'll risk it."

She deftly sidestepped him as he tried to embrace her. "Think of my reputation," she pleaded. "I'm a woman without a husband and I can't risk being gossiped about. You're so handsome, women will be quick to assume...well, you know. And my sister surely won't approve."

"There's no need to fear gossip if we wed, and Celeste is in a convent."

"But we aren't wed yet. Until then, I have to take care, and it would surely be only right to tell my sister of our intentions first, even if..."

Gerrard scowled. "Even if she hates me."

"She is my only sibling."

Frowning, Gerrard stared toward the door. "Then I shall leave you with your money and your bodyguard."

"For now!" she cried as if he'd cut her to the quick, cursing herself for speaking of Celeste. "Only for now!"

Mollified, he smiled one of his devilishly attractive smiles. "For now."

She went to the door, opened it for Gerrard and discovered Duncan standing in the corridor just beyond. He made way for Gerrard, who mockingly tugged his forelock as he passed the Scot and breezily said, "Farewell, Audrey. I'm off to York!"

"What the de'il was that rogue doing here?" Duncan asked, not hiding his disdain, when Gerrard had left the house.

"He only wanted a shoulder to cry on," Audrey replied, "and a little advice."

That is all he's going to get until he has a title, she finished in her thoughts, *and I won't mention Celeste again.*

Chapter Twelve

"What a pleasant surprise, my lady!" Sir Melvin cried as Mavis, followed by Arnhelm, Verdan and four other soldiers from Dunborough, entered his yard. This time, she had sent Arnhelm and Verdan on ahead to request a night's lodging. She hadn't simply ridden through the gates and ordered Sir Melvin to accommodate them.

True to her word, she had left at first light the day after getting her father's message. Surprisingly, she had found Sweetling already saddled, and the escort waiting in the yard.

"Sir Roland's orders," Arnhelm had explained.

In spite of that positive sign, Roland hadn't come to bid her farewell, nor had he returned to their chamber the night before. She had waited all night for him, both dreading and wishing he would come. That he would see that she was right about Gerrard needing to leave, or at least concede that she might be. That he would refute Gerrard's claim that he'd married her only to make his brother jealous. That he cared about her and her opinions.

But her worry and her hope proved to be for naught, because she didn't see him. Nor did she ask where he was before they rode out of the gates. If he didn't wish to say goodbye, she would not look for him.

"My wife will be most delighted to see you again!" Sir Melvin exclaimed. "Of course you must stay the night." His smile faded. "Going back to DeLac to see your father, I suppose? We've heard he's not well. Not well at all." He reached up to help her dismount and went on without giving her a chance to reply. "Still, we're happy to have you break your journey here. See how well the repairs to the stable are coming along? They'll be done in no time. And that ox you gave us— marvelous strong fella, I must say. But you look tired, my dear. Perhaps you should stay a day or two."

"Thank you for your kind offer, Sir Melvin," she said when he paused to breathe, "and I appreciate your hospitality once again. However, a single night is all I ask. I must get to DeLac as quickly as possible."

"If you must, you must, I suppose. Ah, here is my good wife!" he cried as Lady Viola appeared in the doorway of their manor. "Look, Viola, here she is, safe and sound!"

When Mavis met her at the door, Lady Viola tucked her arm in hers and led her toward the hearth, where a warm fire crackled merrily. The scent of spiced wine was welcome, too, but not as much as the drink itself when Lady Viola offered her a goblet after she'd handed her cloak to a servant. "My dear, how tired you must be! Such a journey and in this cold weather, too!"

"We've been fortunate, really," Mavis replied, although in truth, the days had been cold, and the roads hard with frost and ice. At least it hadn't rained. Or snowed.

"What a lovely gown!" Lady Viola exclaimed as

Mavis wrapped her hands around the stem of the goblet and sipped the welcome drink.

"Thank you," Mavis replied as her chilled limbs relaxed.

"We shall see that all your men have some mulled wine," Sir Melvin declared, "and we've a hearty meal coming, too, eh, Viola?"

"My cook makes excellent stew and bread," she replied. "Would you like to lie down and rest before the evening meal?"

"Yes, please." Mavis was more tired than she could remember being in her life.

"Come, then, to the chamber. Bring the wine with you, of course," Lady Viola said, rising to lead the way.

Mavis got up slowly and carefully. She had found that lately, if she rose too swiftly, she got dizzy.

"I'll attend to your escort," Sir Melvin called out as the women made their way to the stairs leading to the upper chambers.

When the women were gone, Sir Melvin drew his chair up close to Arnhelm and Verdan, who were seated a little distance from the soldiers of Dunborough. They had little in common with the men from Yorkshire and could barely understand half the things they said.

"Well, now, lads, here we are again, eh?" Sir Melvin said as he refilled their goblets. "We didn't think she'd be coming back this way so soon."

"She's a dutiful daughter," Arnhelm replied.

"More'n the old goat deserves," Verdan muttered.

Arnhelm shot him a look. "He's still our lord, so watch yer tongue."

"Not for long, I don't think."

"He's that sick, is he?" Sir Melvin asked, his eyes wide with curiosity.

Arnhelm nodded. "Aye, he's bad off."

Sir Melvin glanced at the Yorkshiremen, then back at Arnhelm and Verdan. "Not that I'm doubting your ability to protect Lady Mavis, but I would have thought her husband would come with her."

"They had a quarrel," Verdan said. His brother gave him another censorious look. "Well, they did! I had it all from Lizabet. It was about his brother, that Gerrard. S'truth, he's like a thorn in their boots! That's why Sir Roland didn't even come to bid her farewell."

Sir Melvin regarded them with distress. "I'm very sorry to hear that. Granted Sir Roland isn't the most congenial of company, but I would hate to think Lady Mavis is unhappily married."

"Could be worse, I suppose," Verdan mused aloud. "When her father dies, they'll be even richer. Might smooth things out a bit, eh?"

"Are you daft or what?" his brother demanded. "Money ain't goin' to make her happy."

"I didn't say it would! I said it'd smooth things over."

"If you ask me, the only thing that'll smooth things over is for that Gerrard to go away and never come back."

"Is that likely?" Sir Melvin warily inquired.

Arnhelm and Verdan could only shrug.

"Well, whatever happens, chaps, make sure your lady knows she'll always be welcome here," Sir Melvin said from the fullness of his kind and generous heart.

Two days later, Mavis regarded her bedridden father with a mixture of horror and pity. His breathing was short and raspy, and he appeared to have aged a decade and shrunk to half his size in the time she'd been gone.

At least his bedchamber was as comfortable as a sick

chamber could be. Thick tapestries covered the walls, and braziers kept it well heated. One of the shutters was open a little to allow fresh air. A table stood nearby, the usual carafe of wine and silver goblet replaced with various jars and pots of medicines and ointments. Another table on the other side of the large curtained bed held an oil lamp burning brightly. It had always been a comfortable chamber, well suited to a rich man who liked the finer things his wealth could provide, but never before had it smelled of illness and medicine.

As she looked down at her father, whatever remained of Mavis's anger and resentment melted away, leaving only the love of a daughter for a weak and ailing parent.

"Father?" she said softly, wondering if he could hear her.

His eyelids fluttered open, to reveal rheumy, blood-shot eyes.

"Father?" she repeated hopefully, leaning closer.

He turned his head toward her and reached for her hand.

"Mavis? You…are…here?" he asked, blinking as if he wasn't sure he could believe the evidence of his eyes.

"Yes, Father, I'm here. I've come home to take care of you."

He blinked and a single tear rolled down his sunken cheek. "You look so much like your mother," he whispered.

But not with tenderness, despite the tear. It was as if he were simply stating a fact.

Confused and worried, she sank down on the side of the bed.

"I never loved her," he said, his voice getting stronger even as his breathing grew more hoarse. "I wanted her for her beauty and the dowry, and that was all. If

I'd known she was so weak…that she wouldn't give me sons… And she told tales…spread rumors. I couldn't find another wife after that… All her fault. Women… useless except to give a man sons."

Mavis had to turn away, unable to look at the man who was hurting her even as he lay dying.

"I should have had sons!" he cried, struggling to sit up. "I would have been a better father to sons."

"It's all right, Father," she said. She tried to keep him still as he moved to get out of bed. "You must rest, Father, please!"

Whether because he was paying heed to her words or was too weak to succeed, he gave up and lay back, panting, his breathing even more labored. "I think I'm dying!"

"Not yet, Father," she assured him, certain his burst of energy had to be a good sign.

His expression altered, as if he saw the gates of heaven opening before him and Saint Peter ready to pass judgment. "I was a terrible brother to my sister, and a worse uncle to her child. I should beg Tamsin's forgiveness for all the wrongs I've done her—and you, too, my daughter."

He reached for her hand, grasped it tightly and looked at her with frantic appeal. "Can you forgive me?" he gasped.

"I can! I do!" she assured him, meaning every word.

He closed his eyes again, his breathing faster and more shallow, but he seemed quieter and at ease. "I'll find a good husband for you, Mavis," he murmured. "You're so pretty and loving, any man should be glad to have you. I'll give you a fine dowry, too. And money. Lots of money."

Her heart seemed to stop. "Father, I'm already married, to a man you chose for me. A good man, Father, and a kind and generous one."

Most of the time.

Her father's eyelids fluttered open and she saw a flash of his old temper cross his features. "You are wed? Without my permission?"

"You gave your permission. You chose the bridegroom—Sir Roland of Dunborough. It was only a short time ago."

"Where the devil is Dunborough? And who is this Sir Roland?"

"The son of Sir Blane from Yorkshire. You made a marriage contract for Tamsin with Sir Blane, but Tamsin…she went away and I was to take her place, but Sir Blane died and—"

Her father suddenly sat bolt upright and threw off the covers.

"Father, no!" she protested as she tried to restrain him. With unexpected vigor he pushed her away, put his feet on the floor and stood for one brief moment before he crumpled to the cold stone floor. "Father!" she cried as she knelt down and tried to lift him. "Father! Help, oh, please, someone help!"

Arnhelm and Verdan came running into the room, then skittered to a halt. Arnhelm came closer and went down on one knee beside her.

"Help me get him back to bed. Verdan, please go at once for the physician."

"It's too late, my lady," Arnhelm said, his face full of pity. "He's gone."

"Gone?" she repeated, dumbfounded. "But he was awake! He was talking! He stood without my aid!"

Arnhelm shook his head, then stood gravely silent, his head bowed like his brother's. Covering her face,

Mavis sank to her knees and wept for the father she had known.

And the one he might have been.

Gerrard slid onto the bench in the tavern just inside the walls of York and sighed heavily. He'd ridden hard, propelled by the hope that the attorney Audrey had spoken of could help him win his rightful inheritance. He had abandoned any notion of seeking an annulment for his brother's marriage. Whatever Audrey believed, he knew women, and however it had happened, Roland's wife genuinely cared for him. With her father's money and power to back her—and despite her father's state— any effort to bring about an annulment would likely come to naught. It would be better to use his energy, and Audrey's wealth and influence, to get Dunborough.

"Ale!" he called out to a passing serving wench. She wasn't ugly, but her bustling manner and sharp look didn't appeal to him. He liked women who were pretty and placid like Esmeralda, who hadn't had the sense of a goose. Otherwise, she would have left the woods when he didn't arrive by moonrise. Better yet, she would have realized his suggestion wasn't serious.

Just as he should have realized she possessed a spark of boldness and liked him enough to risk a beating from her father. That was all he'd thought she'd risked. If he'd had the slightest inkling that a man like Bern would find her, he would never have proposed that clandestine meeting, and he wouldn't have gotten drunk.

He wondered how the convent life suited her. Better, perhaps, than marriage, at least for Esmeralda. The only other girl he knew who'd chosen the convent was Audrey's sister, Celeste, much to his surprise. She possessed more than a little spark of boldness and a fiery temper, too, as he well remembered. Perhaps the nuns had stamped out those traits, though. Thank God. The world didn't need bold, tempestuous girls who would tackle a boy three years older and a whole head taller and break his collarbone.

"Set up in that big house near the high street," a man said nearby, his voice growing loud enough to interrupt Gerrard's ruminations, his Yorkshire accent thick, but understandable. "He's spent a fortune on the furnishings, and her clothes, too. My wife said she'd be tempted to whoredom for half her gowns. I said, if Dalfrid wants you, go ahead!"

Dalfrid?

Gerrard shifted closer to the two well-dressed middle-aged men, prosperous merchants by the look of them.

"Being the steward of Dunborough pays better than I guessed," his black-bearded companion replied. "Hope *my* wife doesn't get a glimpse of those gowns," he added with a laugh.

Gerrard rose, picked up his ale and approached them. "Greetings, gentlemen," he said. "May I join you? You're natives of Yorkshire, I take it?"

"Aye," the older of the two, the one he'd heard first, replied.

"I'm a stranger here with many questions," Gerrard lied, "and of course, all the ale will be on me."

"If you like," the first one said. "I'm Gordon, from Ripon, and this is Randolph, from Tockwith."

"I'm pleased to make your acquaintance. I'm Martin, from Leeds." He sat down and for a while they spoke of the city, and trade, and finally Gerrard brought the subject around to the sale of wool. "I've come to see about purchasing some wool for my weavers. I've heard the steward from Dunborough comes to York sometimes to make arrangements for the sale of their wool."

"We were just talking about him!" Gordon cried.

"Aye, he *comes* here often," Martin said, chortling.

"Buys more'n he sells, though," Gordon added with a snicker.

Gerrard's apparently innocent gaze went from one man to the other. "Do you think he might be interested in selling some of the Dunborough wool next spring?"

"Oh, aye, and he might be here now. I'll warn you, though, lad, he drives a hard bargain."

"'Cept with women!" Martin said, chuckling again.

"You've got to forgive my friend," Gordon said as he tried to stifle his own laughter. "Taverns make him talk too much."

Gerrard laughed easily. "They have a similar effect on me. But that's how men become friends, isn't it?" He signaled for the serving wench and called out for more ale. "Now, tell me more about this steward, if you will. One tradesman to another, eh?"

Sometime later, Gerrard left the two wool merchants sleeping in the tavern, their heads upon the table, and made his way to a large, two-storied, half-timbered house near the market square.

As he got closer, he spotted an alley that ran alongside and ducked into it. Just as he'd hoped, there was a yard at the back and a door leading to the kitchen. Best of all, the door was open and the kitchen momentarily deserted. He crept into the chamber and to the door leading to what was likely the main room of the house. He opened it a crack and was rewarded with the sight of Dalfrid standing near a brazier that lit his face, so there could be no mistake. A woman sat nearby, dressed in a sumptuous gown the like of which Gerrard had never seen, not even on a noblewoman, and with ropes of pearls about her neck. She was no great beauty, but according to those men in the tavern, she possessed certain talents that cost her lovers dear.

This was all he needed to see to confirm what he'd come to suspect.

Dalfrid had been stealing from the coffers of Dunborough, no doubt for years, while claiming there were always more debts and taxes to be paid. It was the only explanation for the woman, this house, that gown and those jewels. To be sure, there were taxes and some debts had been his, but how much more had Dalfrid taken using that excuse?

"It's not enough," the woman whined, her voice high and thin. "I need more for the candle maker and the butcher. I deserve it, don't I? You don't want me to starve, do you?"

"Of course not, my honey," Dalfrid replied, and never in his life had Gerrard heard the man sound so compliant, not even when his father was alive.

To think that he'd provided Dalfrid some of his excuses to steal, all the while claiming, like this woman, that he deserved whatever money he took because he was his father's son.

He heard a gasp and whirled around. Eua stood just inside the outer door. As she stared at him, dumbfounded, the bucket in her hand slipped and crashed to the floor, water spilling everywhere.

"Hello, Eua," Gerrard said calmly, although he was just as surprised. "I wondered where you went. I should have guessed Dalfrid would help you, given that you always were thick as thieves."

"What's happened?" Dalfrid demanded, opening the inner door. "Damn you, Eua—"

Like Eua, he fell silent and could only stare as Gerrard drew his sword and placed it against Dalfrid's chest. "Speaking of thievery, Dalfrid, please inform your charming mistress I've come to escort you back to Dunborough, whether you wish to go or not."

Eua threw herself onto her knees at Gerrard's feet. "I didn't know what he was up to, Gerrard! I swear on my life! I didn't know!"

"You didn't know that he was robbing my father and then my brother? That he was saying there were debts and pocketing the money himself to keep a mistress? Where did you think he got his money?"

"I thought… I thought he was a canny trader, that's all! Please, Gerrard, let me go! For the love of God, Gerrard, you've been like a son to me!"

Gerrard looked down at the woman who'd offered him comfort and kindness although there'd been a price. "You may stay." His expression hardened as he looked back at Dalfrid. "There will be no such mercy for you, Dalfrid."

"Dalfrid!" a woman's shrill voice called out. "What are you—"

The richly dressed woman appeared behind her lover and blanched.

"Greetings," Gerrard said with a little bow, keeping his sword on Dalfrid's chest. "It seems, my dear, you'll have to find another protector—or someone else's purse to pick."

Two days after her father died, Mavis sat in the hall, alone. She should speak to the priest about another mass for her father, who would need all the help that prayers could provide to get him into heaven. She should order chambers prepared for any who cared to attend the funeral mass. Tamsin and Rheged would surely come.

Would Roland? She had sent word to him, but he still had not arrived.

What if she'd been wrong about him from the very start? She had such faith in her own judgment, but what if his reasons for marrying her *had* been purely mercenary? Or the need to best his brother with a beautiful bride? What if he would always put his brother and his own pride before her happiness or even his own?

"Mavis!"

She raised her head to see a familiar and welcome figure running toward her, her cloak swirling around her ankles.

With a cry of happiness and sorrow combined, Mavis rose and held out her arms. "Oh, Tamsin! I'm so glad to see you!" she cried as she embraced her cousin. "Although…although…"

"I know," Tamsin murmured, holding Mavis close as she started to weep. "I'm sorry about your father."

"Once she received your message, she wouldn't have stayed away, not if the babe was due in a day," a deep voice remarked from somewhere close by.

Tamsin's husband walked toward them, sympathy on his face. Even so, there was always something about Rheged of Cwm Bron that made Mavis think of a savage. Roland was as tall and broad shouldered, had the same long hair as Rheged, but Roland's power seemed civilized, controlled, like a snake coiled, or a lion crouched to spring, whereas Rheged seemed more like a warrior chieftain from a darker age.

Mavis pushed such thoughts from her mind. "Please, you must sit—both of you." She spotted Denly near the kitchen door. "Bring wine," she said as Tamsin sat on a nearby bench, "and cheese and bread for our guests. And please make sure there's a chamber prepared for my cousin and her husband."

"Tamsin's already seen to that," Rheged said, sliding onto the bench beside his wife. "I think she forgot she doesn't run the household of DeLac anymore."

Tamsin flushed, but Mavis hurried to put her at her ease. "I wish she did. Then my father might…" She shook her head. "I'm sorry. I don't mean to imply that you could have prevented his death, although if we'd postponed the wedding…"

"He did this to himself, Mavis," Tamsin said gently, "and we both know the kind of man he was. He wouldn't have listened to you, or me, or anyone, if we'd tried to make him eat or drink less. He would only have ignored us."

Tamsin was right, but Mavis felt guilty nonetheless.

"I think I'll go get some ale. It's more to my taste than wine. If you'll excuse me, my lady." Rheged didn't wait for them to answer before he headed for the kitchen.

"I could have had ale brought for him," Mavis said with some dismay.

"He may want ale, but he's also leaving us alone to talk," Tamsin replied. "I wanted to come sooner, but I feared Uncle Simon would find my presence more of an aggravation than a comfort. I didn't realize the end was so close at hand."

"Neither did I," Mavis said. "He looked ill, but when death came, it was so sudden. He was talking to me and he seemed to be getting stronger."

"I've heard of a sick person having more vitality near

the end, as if the body rallies one last time so they can make their farewells."

"But he didn't say goodbye," Mavis said, regarding Tamsin with burning eyes. "He spoke of my mother. And you. At the end he was sorry for the way he treated us both. And then he said…" Her gaze faltered and her voice cracked. "He was going to make a good marriage for me. He forgot that I was already married. I suppose I should have known then that death was drawing close… or at least suspected…"

Tamsin hugged her. "You were hoping for the best."

"I was. I was hoping…as I have all my life…always hoping…" The tears came then, hot and fast, her shoulders shaking as Tamsin held her in a gentle embrace, letting her cry out her sorrow and dismay.

When Mavis quieted and drew back, wiping her eyes, Tamsin asked, "How are *you*, Mavis?"

"Well enough, considering."

"And your husband?"

"Quite well."

"*Where* is your husband?" Tamsin asked more pointedly.

"At Dunborough, of course," Mavis said, trying not to sound upset by that. Tamsin had her own life, her own husband and soon her own family to concern her; she wouldn't burden her cousin with her troubles, too. "I saw no need for him to come back with me. I had an escort."

"And your new home? How is it in Dunborough?"

"It's a large household, so naturally there are some things that take getting used to, but I'm managing. I think I told you in my letter that I had to dismiss a servant," Mavis replied, her mind racing to think of ways she could talk about Dunborough and the people in it without raising suspicion that all was *not* well there.

She couldn't. Not now, so she got to her feet. "If you'll excuse me, Tamsin, there are things to be done. Another mass to be arranged and food to be prepared. I'll have Denly show you to your chamber. I'm sure you'll want to rest."

"*You* should rest," Tamsin said with the resolve Mavis so well remembered, the determination her cousin had always shown even as a little girl. "I'll find Rheged and together we'll speak with the priest about the mass."

Feeling as if she had grown years older in the few weeks since her marriage, Mavis shook her head. "No, Tamsin. That is my responsibility."

Tamsin's gaze searched her cousin's face a moment, then she nodded. "Very well, but promise me that we'll speak again soon, just the two of us."

Mavis would rather not promise, but she knew that look in Tamsin's eye. It was no use thinking she could avoid that conversation. "Of course," she replied before she hurried away.

Holding a mug of the rich, dark ale he'd commandeered in the kitchen, Rheged stuck his head into the hall and was surprised to see his wife sitting not just alone, but completely still and with her head bowed— a sure sign of dismay or agitation.

"Where's Mavis?" he asked as he approached her.

"Gone to tend to household matters," she replied, raising her head. "Something's wrong."

"Her father's just died."

"It's more than that," Tamsin said with certainty. "Her letter worried me and having seen her, I'm convinced that something isn't right."

"She'd tell you if that were so, wouldn't she? Especially here."

Tamsin didn't look reassured. "I thought so. I hoped so, but now I'm not so certain."

Rheged set down the ale he hadn't finished and gathered his worried wife into his strong arms. "Perhaps we shouldn't expect her to tell you all her secrets first thing. Give her time, Tamsin. Eventually she'll tell you if she's troubled. If she doesn't and you still believe something isn't right, you'll simply have to ask her."

"I have."

"Then wait awhile and ask her again. I won't have you worrying yourself sick." He smiled at the resolute, loving woman he had married. "Since I know you won't really rest until you're sure you know the truth, we'll stay here until you do."

"Thank you, Rheged," his wife replied with a sigh as she rested her head against her husband's shoulder.

A few days after Mavis had gone back to DeLac, Roland rode away from the rest of the patrol. He wanted to be alone, away from his men and the household and all his responsibilities, to think about the short, cold letter that had arrived that morning from DeLac, brought by Arnhelm and Verdan.

Lord Simon was dead. He'd died the day after Mavis had arrived and would already have been buried by the time he received her letter. She would return as soon as she was able, and as weather permitted.

That Simon DeLac was dead came as no surprise. And had he not told her the weather wasn't good for traveling? Nevertheless, he would have gone there, if she wished. If she had asked.

He spotted two riders coming toward him on the road. One was Audrey and beside her was the Scot.

"Sir Roland!" Audrey cried gaily, waving and smiling and riding forward to meet him.

He muttered an impatient curse. He didn't want to talk to her. Unfortunately, she and her companion blocked the road. "Good day, Audrey," he said when she reached him and they pulled their horses to a halt.

"A fine day for riding, is it not? No more outlaws hereabouts, I trust?"

"No. You should be quite safe. Now if you'll excuse me, I should be heading back."

"I was planning to turn back, too," she said. "May I ride with you?"

Roland was sorry he'd lied, but he had, so he had little choice now. "Of course."

"I haven't seen Gerrard for quite some time," Audrey said after she and Duncan had turned their horses. Audrey rode beside him, Duncan a few yards behind. "Rumor has it Gerrard's left Dunborough in high dudgeon. Some say he went to York."

Roland didn't realize Gerrard had gone from the village, but he didn't want to admit his ignorance to Audrey.

"You had another quarrel, I take it?"

Audrey had obviously already heard about it, so there was no point denying that they'd argued again. "Yes."

"Gerrard always was a hothead," she said with a sigh. "I'm sure he'll come back soon. He always does. And no doubt you did all you could to keep the peace. He is not such a gentleman as you, Roland. And his bitterness is boundless, although understandable, perhaps. He'd hoped he was the eldest and found out that he wasn't.

Then you bring home an unexpected wife, so he's not even second in the household anymore."

"He was still the garrison commander."

"Something any common foot soldier could aspire to. It must have seemed as if a stranger had usurped his place."

Roland had never considered Gerrard's position in that light—and he should have.

"Poor Roland! And your poor wife, too," Audrey went on. "I'm sure she was upset by his insolence, so it's no wonder she's gone home to DeLac, although I wouldn't have blamed her if she wanted to stay as far away from there as possible, given the way her father drinks."

Roland drew Hephaestus to a halt and turned to look at her. "What did you say?"

"I meant no harm or insult," Audrey said hastily, blushing, "but it's common knowledge that Lord DeLac had taken to drink even before all that business with her cousin."

Yes, he had. He was like the worst drunk in any village, and it would be no wonder if his daughter sought to escape him by any means she could, even by marrying the first man who offered who met with her father's approval.

Had she not told him, too, how her father treated her like goods to be sold? How he had grown cruel? Who would not want to be free of such a father, as he had yearned, deep in his heart, to be free of his?

As a woman, Mavis would have no escape save through marriage or the church. And then he had come to DeLac, the heir to a vast estate, the choice of her father, too. Under those circumstances, of course she had accepted him and wed him willingly.

Although his mind could accept that reason, he felt as if his heart had turned to stone. Or died. He had so wanted to believe it was because of some quality in him—some worthiness that she had seen—that she had accepted him.

No woman of any worth will ever want a cold stick like you. No woman will ever love you unless she's paid. You have no wit, no charm, nothing to recommend you to anybody except our father's wealth and title.

God help him, Gerrard had been right.

"I'm so sorry, Roland!" Audrey said with a sigh, reminding him that she was still there. You deserve someone to take care of you and see that you need only concern yourself with the business of the estate, not petty domestic squabbles. Someone who knows your past and understands."

In spite of his dismay, he answered honestly. "That would never have been you, Audrey."

She looked as if he'd taken away her best jewels. Then she smiled, a false and brittle smile. "You certainly encouraged me."

That was a lie, and they both knew it. "I did not. Even if you had tried to make me want you, you would never have succeeded."

She gasped and glared at him, her face growing redder. "You think you're so high and mighty—you and that little strumpet daughter of a sot you married. Well, you aren't the only one with money and power, *Sir* Roland, and it may be that your hold on Dunborough is less secure than you think! Perhaps I'll marry Gerrard when *he's* lord of Dunborough. Now I give you good day, *Sir* Roland, and never seek to darken my door again!"

She kicked her horse into a gallop and rode off, followed by the Scot.

Roland didn't even watch them go.

He slipped from the saddle and laid his head against his horse's neck. Here at last and thanks to Audrey, of all people, he could believe that Mavis had chosen him—as a means to escape her father.

And now that her father was dead, she had no reason to return, especially after all the things that Gerrard had said. That explained the coldness in her letter, too.

He had known pain and suffering before. He had rarely felt happiness, until he'd married Mavis. Now he doubted he would ever know true happiness again.

He might never again feel so appreciated and respected, admired and desired.

Or loved.

Of all the things that Mavis had done, she had made him believe he could be loved.

"Oh, God help me, Heffy," he murmured roughly. "It would have been better if I'd never met her."

He would have been content, or at least ignorant of what he lacked. And yet…was that really true? Would he have been better off if he hadn't met her? Mavis had given him a taste of what life could hold. More than a taste.

He thought of all the times they'd been alone, and not just in their bed or making love. He remembered her smiles, her voice, the admiration in her eyes, the respect, the way she'd bristled when Gerrard mocked him. Yes, she was his wife, so some of those things could be expected—but not all. Not the loving looks and tender smiles. Not the passion and kind words.

Surely she wouldn't be so loving and sincere if she'd only married him to get away from her father.

Then, as he raised his head and scanned the autumn sky, another revelation crept into his head and heart.

So what if she'd married him to get away from her father? Theirs had been a successful marriage, at least so far, and in spite of his mistakes. His foolish jealousy. His insistence that Gerrard stay. His fear of Gerrard's mockery.

And if he listened to anyone's opinion, it should be that of the wife he loved. So if that meant Gerrard had to leave Dunborough, so be it. If Gerrard then went to the king, if he tried to get the marriage annulled or take Dunborough…?

Let his brother try. He didn't care what Gerrard did, as long as he had Mavis by his side. Winning her love would be the true road to happiness.

That was worth going to DeLac and asking her to come back to Dunborough, even if he had to go down on his knees and beg, he who would never kneel to any man, not even his father or his brother, regardless of how many times they hit him. He would apologize for his anger, for his quarrels with his brother, his harsh words and grim silences. He would vow to be a better husband, a better man, more open and honest, and hopefully one day worthy of her love.

If she did return with him, he would do all that and more to try to make her happy.

His decision made, his course decided, he mounted swiftly and turned Hephaestus toward home. There were some preparations to be made, but he would leave tomorrow as soon as it was light.

Roland brought Hephaestus to a halt in the courtyard, leaped from the saddle and hurried toward the hall—to find Dalfrid weeping and cowering near the dais, with Gerrard standing over him like an avenging angel intent upon his death.

Chapter Thirteen

"Save me, my lord! Don't let him kill me!" Dalfrid shrieked, writhing on the ground like some sort of wounded snake.

"What is the meaning of this?" Roland demanded as he hurried toward them. He was relieved to see his brother, but baffled by Dalfrid's panicked cries.

"He's been robbing us for years," Gerrard declared. "He's got a huge house in York and a mistress, too. A very costly mistress who wears satins and velvets and more jewels than a queen."

"He's lying, my lord—lying to cover his own crimes!" Dalfrid protested.

Gerrard prodded him with his sword. "Dog! You're the liar!"

"Keep him off! Keep him off!"

"I went to York after our last quarrel and was in a tavern when I heard Dalfrid's name spoken," Gerrard said. "Pretending to be a wool merchant, I joined the conversation. It seems a serving wench had come up in the world by becoming the mistress of the steward of Dunborough—a most expensive mistress. I thought of Dalfrid's claim that the coffers were nearly empty and it occurred to me that we may have been duped. I learned where this woman lived and found Dalfrid there. There's no way under heaven he could have come by that house and those clothes and jewels by honest means, and thus our family's empty coffers are explained."

"I won that money gambling!"

"You?" Gerrard scoffed. "You're the worst man I ever met at a game of chance. You never win, and that *I* would gladly wager on. And are you forgetting the woman herself was all too quick to say you paid for everything and she didn't know where or how you got your money? That I can believe," he added with a smirk, "for I don't think she much cared, as long as you got it."

"She's a friend, my lord, merely a friend!" Dalfrid exclaimed.

"With such friends as these, more men would be bankrupt. Give up, Dalfrid, and confess. You're caught." Gerrard regarded his brother with another of his mocking smiles, but this time, it was as if they shared a joke. "We learned easily the value of confession, eh, Roland? Although punishment followed as night the day, it was not quite so harsh if we admitted our mistakes."

Roland nodded, although he was still trying to get over the surprise of the prodigal Gerrard apparently acting as the instrument of justice.

"I never gave that woman so much as a ha'penny!" Dalfrid whined.

"Eua told me otherwise." Gerrard saw Roland's surprise increase and grinned. "Aye, she was there. I knew Dalfrid sometimes gave her money, but I never knew why until she admitted Dalfrid paid her for information she gleaned about our father, especially his plans. She says she didn't know he was robbing us, and I have to say, I believe her, or she would have told our father hoping for a reward."

"Eua lied!" Dalfrid cried. "It was she who took the money!"

The two men regarding him had identical skeptical looks on their faces.

"She didn't have a key to the money chest, Dalfrid, and you did," Gerrard noted. "I'm sure that like your mistress, she also didn't care where you got your money, but she didn't steal it. That's why I let her go."

Roland reached down and dragged the former steward of Dunborough to his feet. "So you have a house in York, Dalfrid," he said, his tone cold, his eyes colder, "and a mistress who likes expensive clothes and furniture?"

"We are to be married, my lord, as soon as I can afford it."

Gerrard laughed with scorn. "If that were so, you could sell some of her clothes, or the furniture. I've never seen such fine tables and chairs. You can go and see for yourself, Roland, although I suspect the woman might be long gone by the time you get there. She's no fool, even if she did give herself to Dalfrid, and I don't doubt she's taken everything she can carry and headed for new pastures, with Eua complaining all the way.

"That's the problem with whores," he said to Dalfrid. "They tend to care more about the money than the men who give it to them."

Roland gestured for two of his soldiers to come closer. "Pick him up and take him to the dungeon with the other thieves."

"No!" Dalfrid screeched. "You can't put me in with common criminals!"

"Why not? Because you're an uncommon criminal?" Gerrard replied.

"I see only a thief," Roland said, "who should be with other thieves."

"No! No! No, my lord, please! I beg you!" Dalfrid cried, crawling toward Roland on his hands and knees.

Roland only crossed his arms as the soldiers dragged the kicking, crying Dalfrid away, until Gerrard turned to go.

Roland put his hand on his brother's shoulder. "Stay a moment, Gerrard. You have my thanks for this."

His eyes revealing nothing, Gerrard shrugged. "At least now you know I'm not quite the wastrel everyone— including you—believed. And since that's done, I'm going back to York."

"Not yet awhile, if you will."

If he could mend things with his brother before he went to DeLac, he would. "I'd like to speak with you in private first."

For a moment Roland thought his brother would refuse. Then Gerrard nodded once and together they went to the solar.

Gerrard stood in the center of the room, his shoulders tensed as if poised to fight, while Roland closed the door behind him.

"I'm grateful that you brought that miscreant back," Roland said.

"You've already thanked me."

"Nevertheless, I thank you again. I didn't trust the man completely, but I never thought he'd rob us."

Gerrard's lips jerked up in a little smile. "I've loathed him from the day he arrived. It's a wonder I didn't catch him sooner. I might have if I'd been paying more attention to him and less to indulging my own desires."

It was the first time Roland had ever heard Gerrard acknowledge any remorse for anything, and he began to hope that things could be better between them, too. "What were you doing in York?"

Gerrard studied him a moment, more serious than Roland had ever seen him. "I went to meet Audrey's attorney. She's thinks there's a chance your marriage can be annulled."

"What?"

"Given that the dowry was destroyed, who could say if DeLac had given all he promised? He's been known to cheat."

"I don't give a fig how much the dowry was and you have no right to try to end my marriage!" Roland declared, the hope he'd been feeling replaced by anger.

Gerrard's mocking grin appeared. "How does it feel, brother, to have your rights usurped?"

Roland crossed his arms. "I didn't take anything from you, but I suspect you went to York for more than trying to end my marriage. You were going to try to petition the king to give you Dunborough."

The grin slipped away and Gerrard became serious again. "I admit I went with that in my mind, but when I realized what Dalfrid had done after years of being trusted and well paid, and as I stood looking at Dalfrid's mistress with her greedy, gleaming eyes, it occurred to me that not only have I been an ungrateful wretch just as you claimed, but Audrey might not have only my interest at heart. I suspect she has other selfish reasons for helping me, and I will not be any woman's toy."

"Not even for Dunborough?"

"No, not even then." Gerrard regarded his brother with the sort of expression only those who've suffered together can share. "After Broderick and our father, I won't be ruled by anyone."

"Including a brother, however well-meant," Roland said, understanding bursting in on him like a lantern lit in the darkness.

"Including you," Gerrard confirmed.

"I should have guessed that was part of the trouble—but it was only part," Roland replied. "We may never truly know if I was born first or not, and there's no way to prove it either way. However, I agree that it isn't right that only I should inherit. I thought so from the first and planned to give you a portion of the estate when you proved yourself worthy. You've done that, Gerrard—more than done it, if I've the right to judge you, and I see now I don't. Nevertheless, I make this offer to you. If you stay, I'll give you half of the estate and the tithes that go with it."

His brother's eyes narrowed. "And if your wife objects?"

Roland spread his hands wide. "I love her, Gerrard, as difficult as it may be for you to believe. I love her as much as any man ever loved a woman and with her good counsel to guide me, I hope to rule Dunborough wisely and well, as our father never did and no matter how much of it is mine. So I won't see her mocked or treated with disrespect by you, or anyone. We must agree on that, if nothing else."

Gerrard tilted his head as he regarded his twin. "And if I mock and tease *you*?"

"If you're on your own estate, at least you'll have less chance to do it. But Mavis is right to think that how you treat me reflects upon us both."

Gerrard's shoulders relaxed and he laughed softly. "Of course she's right about that. Why else would I have been so angry when she said it? As for your offer, I'll consider it. It might be better if I didn't accept it and stay so close to home. After all, mocking you will be a hard habit to break."

Roland wasn't dissuaded by his brother's apparent levity. "I hope you'll stay, brother. Together we are stronger than apart, just as having Mavis for my wife has made me stronger."

"God's blood, don't remind me! She looks like a weak and feeble woman, but any woman who can get you to say aloud that you love her is a rare woman indeed."

"Will you stay as garrison commander here until you decide what you want to do?"

"Gladly," Gerrard replied with another smile.

"Good!" Roland replied with both happiness and relief. "And now I must prepare to go to DeLac."

Gerrard's eyes widened. "Then it's true, what I heard? She's left you?"

"Her father was ill and has since died."

"Yet you stayed here?"

"That was a mistake and one I'm going to hasten to correct, and I'm going to tell her how much I love and need her, as I should have done before." Roland clapped his hand on his brother's shoulder. "I hope that one day, you'll find a woman who can make you as proud and happy as Mavis makes me."

"I doubt it," Gerrard muttered as he watched his brother go.

Audrey saw Roland ride by from the main room of her house. "Look at him," she sneered to Duncan, who came to stand beside her. "So proud of himself—and for what? He outlived his father and his brother, and he turned out to be the firstborn of twins. Otherwise he's done nothing to deserve Dunborough except follow his father's orders. As for that woman he married, I've met her sort before. Looks sweet and innocent, but she's a scheming temptress."

"Dinna dwell on them," the Scot said, his voice a deep growl. "They're no' worth it."

"You're quite right!" Audrey declared, walking to the slender ebony chair and sitting gracefully. "So it's only fitting that they both lose Dunborough, and I shall take great pleasure in bringing that about."

"How?" the Scot asked warily.

"Much can be accomplished with money and influence," she answered with smug satisfaction.

"You'd waste your money on tha'? Just for revenge?"

"By our Lady, I'm not as silly and shortsighted as that! I'll be doing it for my future husband."

The Scot sucked in his breath and his eyes narrowed. "Gerrard?"

"Who else?"

"The man's not to be trusted. He'll take your money and your influence and ne'er wed thee."

Audrey regarded Duncan with a frown. "You sound very certain of that."

"He's that sort o' man. Don't ye mind that girl in the woods? If he e'er gets a title, he'll be like all the rest o' his family—wantin' a rich bride from a noble family."

His words revived her doubts about Gerrard, but she ignored them. "If Gerrard wants my money and my help, he'll have to marry me to get it."

"What then? He'll have mistresses by the score."

"And I shall have a title."

"There's more important things than tha'. What about

a husband who loves ye and would die for ye? Can ye say Gerrard will do either?"

In truth, she could not—but she would not admit it. She was too close to the prize she had sought since childhood, when a noblewoman in the market had called her a common brat after she accidentally got mud on the hem of her gown. "Gerrard will come to love me." She adjusted the embroidered edge of her bodice, much finer than anything that haughty noblewoman had worn, and raised her chin a little. "I have ways."

"Aye, I'm sure you do, although some may call them wiles," Duncan replied, and there was bitterness in his voice.

"Duncan!" she cried with both surprise and a patronizing smile. "Do you think yourself in love with me?"

"Think? No," he replied, his voice low and rough. "I know."

Audrey cursed herself for not foreseeing this. She was, after all, beautiful and desirable. "Naturally I'm flattered," she said as she got to her feet, "and you're a fine bodyguard and a most trustworthy fellow, Duncan, but—"

"But I'm nay rich nor titled, is that it?"

Audrey was suddenly sorry she'd let all the kitchen servants go to the market. "You're very handsome, though," she said, sidling toward the door leading to the yard. Her maidservant was in the washhouse. That wasn't so far. "Much better looking than Roland."

"I'm no' a fool like those others to be put off with smooth words and smiles and flattery," Duncan returned, closing the distance between them. "Ye've no more interest in me than the fishmonger."

"I do!" she replied, moving away from him. She could call out the window for help.

He grabbed her arm and hauled her close. "I've served ye for years and ye've ne'er thought of me as anything but a hireling, have ye? Instead, ye've set yer eyes on them as don't want ye and think ye're better than me."

"Duncan, please, you're hurting me!"

He cast her off and she fell to her knees. "I'm done with ye, bitch. Find somebody else to watch ye make a fool of yerself."

"Bitch?" she repeated angrily as she got to her feet. "How dare you talk to me that way! How dare you call me names! Leave this house! Go back to your gutter of a country! You're a savage and your countrymen are worse and all the women are whores!"

That was the last thing Audrey D'Orleau ever said.

Audrey's middle-aged maidservant shrieked in horror, then dropped her basket of damp laundry and ran into the yard, her skirts flying. "Help! Oh, help!" she cried, her thin and homely face as white as goose feathers.

The groom, a gray-haired man not known to hurry, heard her and rushed out of the stable to see what was amiss.

The moment the older man was gone, Duncan came out of hiding, grabbed a bridle and put it on Audrey's fastest horse. The gelding whinnied and shied, upset by the scent of fresh blood on his clothes.

Nevertheless, Duncan got it saddled and out of the stable. He was already mounted and galloping away from Dunborough before the groom rushed out of the house and ran toward the village and castle beyond.

Duncan was well away from Dunborough by the time Gerrard, the groom, the reeve and several soldiers and men of the village crowded into the main room of Audrey's manor. The room was in disarray, the delicate furniture smashed and broken, the brazier overturned. She had fought, that much was certain, but now her body lay on the floor, her legs splayed apart, her skirts drawn up and her throat cut so deeply, her neck was nearly sliced through.

Gerrard had seen blood and cruelty and death, but nothing that had ever made him feel as sick and sorry as the sight of poor Audrey's violated, bloody body. The reeve, a goldsmith named Jonas, ran from the room, his face green.

"Oh, Audrey!" Gerrard murmured, pulling down her skirts and covering her face with a cloth from the nearby table. It was all he could think to do to give her back some measure of dignity in death and he silently vowed that he would find whoever did this, and that man would pay.

Father Denzail, followed by Alford, the apothecary, pushed through the stunned and horrified crowd. The priest had to turn away as he made the sign of the cross. He uttered a brief blessing, then also fled the room.

Alford bent over Audrey's body like a worried parent, his dark hair flopping over his pale forehead, his blue eyes intent and searching as he examined her. "This was done with a sword," he said to Gerrard. "A heavy, sharp one, wielded by a strong man."

Only then did Gerrard realize the Scot wasn't there. "Where's Duncan?" he demanded of the onlookers.

A man spoke up from the back of the crowd, and Gerrard recognized Matheus, the beefy, red-faced proprietor of the Cock's Crow. "I seen him goin' down the southern road not long ago. Riding like the wind he was, too."

Or like a guilty man.

"I leave her in your care, and the priest's," he said to the apothecary, "while I go catch her killer."

"Again you have my thanks for your hospitality," Roland said to Sir Melvin as he took his leave after spending the night on his way to DeLac.

"Always happy!" the nobleman replied. "It's unfortunate my wife left to visit her sister before you arrived. I'm sure she would have liked to see you."

Roland was not so certain. He didn't think he'd made a good impression on Lady Viola, and although Mavis apparently hadn't told the man or his wife that they'd quarreled, Sir Melvin—or more likely Lady Viola— had probably guessed all was not well when he hadn't returned with her.

As he should have.

"Are you sure you should travel today?" Sir Melvin asked, looking up at the sky. "It looks like rain in the east. The clouds are building."

"Hephaestus has made this journey quickly before and I should be with my wife," Roland replied.

Sir Melvin sighed and smiled. "I see it's useless to try to stop you, but you must promise me that you and your charming wife will stop here on your way back to Dunborough. Viola will be upset if you don't and a man should always try to keep his wife happy. That's the secret to marital bliss, if you ask me."

Roland hadn't asked him. Nevertheless, he supposed Sir Melvin had his reasons for offering this advice.

"We'll be delighted," Roland answered, hoping Mavis would be returning with him. "Goodbye, Sir Melvin, and thank you again."

"Godspeed, Sir Roland! Have a care on the roads!

Are you quite sure you won't wait for the storm to pass?"

"I'll take shelter if I must, but I would rather ride on while I can."

"Well, then, be off with you now and don't forget to bring your pretty wife back with you!"

Roland nodded and swung into his saddle.

"Roland! Stop, ye bloody bastard!"

Roland pulled Hephaestus to a halt and twisted in the saddle to look behind him.

God's blood, it *was* Duncan—and the man was covered with so much blood, it looked as if he'd been in a battle.

"What's wrong?" he demanded when the man reached him and reined in his exhausted, foam-flecked mount. "Has something happened to Audrey?"

Duncan slipped from his saddle and drew his claymore, the hilt likewise bloody, from the sheath on his back. His horse snorted and limped away, while Hephaestus shook his head like a bare-knuckle fighter about to meet an opponent.

"Get down from your horse, man," Duncan ordered with a feverish gleam in his eyes.

Roland's hand went to the hilt of his sword, but show his distress he would not. "Who do you think you are to order me?" he demanded.

"If ye willna dismount, I'll make ye," the Scot answered, moving as if to grab Hephaestus's bridle.

Roland jumped down from his horse, but before he could draw his sword, the Scot had the blade of his claymore against Roland's chest.

"Leave it!" the Scot commanded.

Roland held his arms wide, as if in surrender. Rain

began to fall, the droplets wetting their hair, their clothes and Duncan's sword. Hephaestus whinnied and moved beneath the nearest tree.

"What do you want, Duncan?" Roland asked, keeping his voice calm and steady because he recognized that look in the Scot's eyes. He'd seen it before, in the eyes of men he was about to punish, or as the hangman slipped the noose around a neck.

"I'm going to kill ye."

That much Roland had guessed, although he didn't know why. It was also obvious, in a terrible way, that the man had already attacked someone. "Where's Audrey?"

"Ye don't give a tinker's damn about her! Neither ye, nor your damn brother. You're de'ils, the pair o' ye, from a family of de'ils. I'm goin' to rid the world o' ye!"

"What's happened? Is she hurt?"

"Hurt, aye—hurt by ye and that whore you brought home! You used her and then you cast her aside to marry another woman not worthy to touch the hem of her gown."

"I never took what Audrey offered. I didn't cast her aside."

The Scot's eyes glowed with hatred and his blade pressed a little harder on Roland's chest. "Liar! You shared her bed!"

"I've never been in Audrey's bed, nor she in mine," Roland truthfully replied, willing the man to believe him. "If she says otherwise—"

"She dinna. She didnae have to. I know! I see things! She wanted ye. It's ye she's wanted for years. Couldn't see naught *but* ye for years."

"You're wrong. It was my older brother she wanted. She rarely even spoke to me."

"Liar! She was always wantin' to be in your hall but

she hardly noticed me, the man who loved and protected her like he was her husband. I lived just to hear her say my name but she wouldnae give me the time o' day."

The pain that had come to the man's eyes changed back to hate and again he pushed his blade into Roland's chest. This time Roland felt the point bite into his flesh and a trickle of blood begin to flow.

"And then ye return wi' a wife and break her heart. And now the poor dim sweetheart thinks that brother o' yours is going to give her what she wants. He ne'er will. He'll use her and cast her aside just like you. I should cut out both your hearts for tha'!"

Should. That meant he hadn't gone after Gerrard. Not yet. And Mavis, thank God, was safe in DeLac. But Audrey... *"What have you done?"*

The man's shoulders slumped and he bowed his head. "I should ha'e seen it was hopeless," he muttered, more than the rain wetting his cheeks. "I should ha'e known she'd ne'er want me. But I hoped...and then she said... I'm a proud man wi' a right t' be, yet she said..."

Roland was about to draw his sword when Duncan abruptly raised his head, that hostile, unreasoning glare back in his eyes. He twisted the blade, tearing the leather of Roland's tunic. "What happened was *her* fault. She shouldna ha'e said what she did. And now she's back there." He gestured with his sword, moving it away from Roland's chest to point back along the road toward Dunborough.

It was the moment Roland had been waiting for. He leaped away and drew his sword, ready to fight a man well trained and in his prime.

Duncan attacked like a man possessed, and he was— possessed of unrequited love and unfulfilled desire, driven by frustration and hate.

Their blades met in a clash of metal on metal. Roland twisted away, seeking better footing on the wet and muddy road. Duncan was after him in an instant, preparing to bring his heavy weapon down on Roland's neck or shoulder. Roland caught the blow with his sword blade, then used all his might and weight to shove the Scot away.

Duncan lost his balance and staggered backward, and Roland moved in to strike. The Scot recovered quickly, turning and slashing out with his claymore, catching Roland's calf, slicing through the leather of his boot into the flesh beneath.

Feeling a sharp bite of pain, Roland parried another blow and paid no heed to the blood running down his leg. He disengaged his sword and struck again, swinging his blade beneath Duncan's raised sword to slice through his tunic, opening a gash of clothing and flesh.

That didn't seem to weaken Duncan. Instead, it only served to make him fiercer and more determined, so that he attacked with near-maniacal rage. As Roland moved back to avoid another blow, his wounded calf gave way and with a cry of pain, he fell to one knee.

Shouting with triumph, Duncan rushed in to strike the mortal blow but he was too blinded by his rage to see Roland raise his sword at the critical moment, the end of the hilt resting on the ground like the spikes of a palisade. He ran right up upon the sword, impaling himself. The Scot dropped his claymore and staggered backward, staring in dumbfounded horror at the gaping wound beneath his right arm. His ankle throbbing, Roland started to rise, prepared to strike again.

Gasping, Duncan clutched at his side as the blood poured forth. His mouth worked, but no sound came out before he fell to his knees, and then slumped forward.

Exhausted and in pain, dragging his sword, Roland made his way to Hephaestus. Only then did he feel the blood in his boot and realize how much he was losing.

Duncan groaned and pulled himself onto his hands and knees.

He wasn't dead?

The Scot heaved himself to his feet and lurched toward his claymore. "I'll kill ye, bastard, and your brother, too," he gasped.

Roland sheathed his sword and climbed onto his horse. "Not today," he said.

Just as he would not fight Duncan anymore. He was losing too much blood. Better to leave the field and get to DeLac and send men from there to capture the Scot. Duncan might not be dead, but he was too seriously injured to get far, even on horseback.

Just as he would surely die if he didn't get help soon.

He lifted the reins and, after one backward glance at his attacker still making his way to his sword, Roland clicked his tongue and set off for DeLac.

Roland woke with a gasp, roused by the sharp pain in his leg. Miraculously, he was still in the saddle. Rain was pouring down, and he was cold and soaking. Worse, his leg felt as if it were on fire, even as he began to shiver and couldn't stop.

He remembered Duncan's attack, the blow. And he'd been bleeding.

It was dark, too. Not night yet, but dusk.

Nor were they on the road. Hephaestus had wandered from the muddy way into the bordering woods and was pulling up grass, chewing slowly.

Roland wiped at the water falling into his eyes and

gratefully licked the rain on his lips, for he was very thirsty.

Where was he? Close to DeLac or with miles to go? He looked around, but couldn't see the road.

His teeth chattering uncontrollably, he wiped his face again. His mind was cloudy, fogged with cold and discomfort and pain.

If he kept going, he might be going farther from the road and getting more lost. The best thing—the only thing—to do was stay where he was until morning. Find some shelter. Try to keep warm. Maybe take his boot off, if his calf wasn't too swollen.

He dismounted carefully, yet let out a cry of pain when he put his injured leg on the ground. He couldn't walk far, not like this.

He had to find shelter, at least for the night.

He spotted what looked like a loose pile of timber. Wiping his eyes again, he peered at it more intently. Yes, there was some kind of roof. Or part of one. It was the ruin of a hut or cottage.

"Come on, Heffy," he murmured.

He went to grab his horse's bridle, but he slipped, snapping a branch as he tried to stop himself from falling. The branch slapped Hephaestus on his neck, startling the poor tired beast and sending him off through the trees at a run while Roland fell heavily to the ground.

"There's something in the water over here!" one of the soldiers from Dunborough cried two days after Audrey's body had been discovered. Gerrard and his men had come miles on horseback, dismounting and searching the verge and underbrush for any sign of a horse or man leaving the road. The eagle-eyed Hedley had recently spotted some broken branches, as if a man or horse had pushed through. They'd found the horse not too far from the road, and then moved toward the river.

Gerrard ran toward Hedley, who was trying to pull something to the bank with his sword.

"It's a body, caught on a log," he said as Gerrard skittered to a halt beside him.

Gerrard recognized the cloth swirling about the lower limbs, and the man's hair. "It's Duncan."

He spoke coldly, without pity, for he would never forgive or forget what this man had done to Audrey.

After some of the other men helped pull the body from the water, Hedley crouched and pulled the Scot's tunic up to reveal a deep wound. "That's what killed him, I'll wager, not drowning."

"Then how did he wind up in the water?" Gerrard asked aloud.

A few yards farther along the bank, another soldier was examining the drier ground beneath a willow tree. "There are footprints here!" he called out.

Gerrard jogged closer and examined the footprints and the riverbank. "Looks like only one man," he noted. "Hedley, bring me one of Duncan's boots!"

It took a few moments to work the boot off the dead man's foot. Once it was done, Gerrard took the sodden boot and fitted it into the footprints that had been protected from the rain by the thickly intertwined, leafless willow branches.

The boot fit.

"He might have been trying to get a drink," Hedley suggested.

"Maybe," Gerrard replied. He looked again at the ground, closer to the water. There were no indentations from a man's knees and there would have been if he'd knelt to take a drink.

Perhaps, severely wounded, Duncan had fallen in before he'd gotten to his knees.

"A horse! Sir Roland's horse!" another soldier shouted.

Only his horse?

His heart thudding with dread, Gerrard raced toward the soldier who'd caught hold of Hephaestus's reins. The beast was clearly tired, and he still wore a saddle.

Roland's saddle.

There was blood on it, and on Hephaestus, too.

Chapter Fourteen

Five days after her father died, Mavis awoke from her uneasy slumber to find Tamsin seated on a stool beside the bed, a smile on her lips and worry in her eyes.

"What's happened?" Mavis demanded, sitting up.

"I only wanted to see how you were this morning, before you get too busy with your household duties. I miss the chats we used to have." Tamsin's frown deepened. "Perhaps you should stay in bed awhile longer. No one will blame you if you do."

"I can't. I have too much to do," Mavis said, rising and fighting the little wave of nausea of the sort she'd been experiencing the past few days. Trying to make light of her cousin's concern, she smiled and said, "You were never one to rest when you were in charge of the household."

"I wasn't with child then," Tamsin replied.

Mavis wanted to deny that she was expecting, to wait until she was more certain, but looking at Tamsin's loving, sympathetic face, she couldn't. Not outright. "It's too early to be completely sure."

"Yet you suspect?"

Mavis nodded.

"And still Roland didn't travel with you?"

"We didn't know how ill my father was, and he has much to do at Dunborough," Mavis replied, heading toward the washstand.

Her cousin followed her. "That is no excuse. There must be others he could leave in charge—the steward and one of his senior soldiers."

Mavis didn't want to confess all her troubles to her cousin, as if she was still a child. "I've been happy with Roland. Very happy. He's quiet, of course, and stern with his men, but my first impression was right. There is a good, kind man behind that cold, grave visage. And when we were alone..." She flushed. "It's been wonderful."

"But something has gone wrong," Tamsin persisted. "You told me of the servant you dismissed. Are there others who are lazy or disrespectful?"

"No."

"I'm glad to hear it!" Tamsin hesitated a moment, then said, "You mentioned the steward."

"Dalfrid. I don't like or trust him. Neither does Roland, and he'll be dismissed as soon as Roland's learned what he needs to know about the estate finances. So you see, Roland wouldn't want to leave him in charge."

Tamsin took her cousin's hands in hers and her worried gaze searched Mavis's face. "I fear something more is wrong between you, Mavis. Something serious. Please, won't you tell me? Won't you share your troubles with me, as you used to do? It's no weakness to share your burdens with someone who loves you."

Mavis had been strong for days, but as Tamsin looked at her with such loving concern, the walls of her defenses began to crumble. "There's a woman in the village, Audrey D'Orleau, the heiress of a wealthy merchant. Apparently everyone in Dunborough thought Roland would marry her, including Audrey."

"And Roland?"

"He denies that was ever in his mind. He says all Audrey wants is a title, not him."

"Do you believe him?"

Mavis looked away and searched her heart, seeking the answer to that question, one that had been troubling her for days and no matter how she tried to ignore it. He was so handsome, so powerful, so confident, how could it be that no other woman had sought him?

Yet as she thought of his firm denials and the look in his dark eyes, as she remembered how he'd made love to her, and all the things he'd said, she realized what the answer was. What it should have been all along, and she wished he was here to tell him so. "Yes, I do."

Tamsin's frown deepened. "Yet there is something more?"

While her pride told her to say she could deal with her husband's brother, her heart demanded honesty, so she answered with all of the frustration that she felt. "His brother."

"Gerrard? Rheged calls him a charming wastrel and he told me that Roland and his brother often argue. They may be twins, but I gather they couldn't be more different. That cannot be easy for you."

"Argue? That's far too tame a word. Gerrard seems to live to enrage Roland and Roland always rises to the bait. Rheged is right—they couldn't be more different. Roland is honorable, respectable, dutiful and generous. Gerrard is a selfish, insolent rogue, and bitter because he didn't inherit Dunborough, although he's not fit to rule anything. He even claimed that Roland married me just to somehow beat him, or make him jealous."

Tamsin's eyes widened. "Do you think that's—"

"I don't want to believe it. I don't want to believe anything Gerrard says. And then the last time that they argued, they came to blows like two wild animals. I made them stop and pleaded with Roland to give Gerrard money so he would leave. Unfortunately, there isn't as much in the coffers as we thought. But even if there was, if Gerrard doesn't choose to go, Roland won't make him, although I told Roland I might be with child and how much I craved a peaceful household. And then we got the letter from my father and Roland refused to let me come back."

"He...what?"

Mavis had gone this far. She would tell Tamsin everything. "As you can see, I came regardless and he didn't actually try to stop me. In spite of what he said, there was an escort waiting to go with me." Mavis sat on the stool in front of the dressing table and regarded her cousin with dismay. "Oh, Tamsin, I'm not sure what to do, what to think. I fear I'll never understand my husband, or know how he really feels. I'm afraid Gerrard spoke truly, and I'll never mean as much to Roland as I believed I would. I'm worried that he'll overlook and ignore me, just like my father did. When I thought—hoped—it would be different with Roland."

She went further still, to a place deep in her heart, and confessed the truth that she had not admitted even to herself. "Most of all, Tamsin, I'm afraid he'll never love me, not as I love him."

Tamsin's expression became even more sympathetic. "You love him?"

Mavis nodded. "I think I've loved him from the first time I saw him in the stable here. I was going to run away and got to the stable, but he was there. He'd just arrived, and he was talking to his horse."

"His *horse*?"

"Hephaestus," she replied, anxious now to tell Tamsin what had happened that first early morning. "He spoke so gently to it, and he made a little joke about not looking like a beggar. As he went to leave, though, he paused a moment and I could see him changing, as if he was putting on a costume. He became the cold, stern man most people believe him to be. But he wasn't like that in the stable, Tamsin, not at all, and when he asked for my hand, I saw that other gentle man again. That was why I agreed to the betrothal, because of that soft voice in the stable and that look in his eyes in the solar. It sounds silly, I suppose, but that was the way I felt. And at first, on our wedding night, he was that gentle man. Then afterward, he was cold again and I feared I'd been mistaken after all. But then he would be so passionate, I was sure..." She flushed, but continued. "Yet at other times, he would be grim and silent. Still, as time went on, I thought he would be the husband I'd hoped for, that I could care for, until we reached Dunborough. Again he seemed loving and kind, except when it came to dealing with his brother. Then he paid no heed to me, and was even...harsh."

"Have you told him that you love him?"

Mavis shook her head. "How could I, when I wasn't sure myself? Yet surely he must know I care for him. I've tried to be a good chatelaine and wife. I've gone to his bed willingly. More than willingly—eagerly."

Tamsin regarded her with grave sympathy. "It's difficult to know the heart of a quiet man, especially one who has never had anyone to confide in. It could be that his changes of mood have nothing to do with you, but with his own private battles. And as you don't know his heart, he may be just as ignorant of yours. He isn't a seer, Mavis. You should tell him how you feel."

Mavis couldn't meet her cousin's steadfast gaze. "And if he doesn't love me? If he married me only for gain? Or to make his brother jealous?"

"If what you say is true, that he's been kind and gentle and loving toward you," Tamsin gently replied, "I think he probably cares for you a great deal. A man like that, though...such words won't come easily to him. And we can't really fault him for being loyal to his brother. Perhaps he pities Gerrard, too."

Mavis had never really considered that pity could play a role in Roland's feelings for his brother.

"Mavis!" a man shouted, followed swiftly by the sound of booted feet pounding up the steps. "Mavis!"

She knew that voice!

"It's Roland!" Mavis cried. "Quick, help me into my gown!"

Tamsin had barely gotten the gown laced before the door crashed open.

But it wasn't Roland standing on the threshold.

"Where's Roland?" Gerrard demanded.

Mavis stared at him in stunned surprise. "What do you mean? He's not here!"

"I see that. Where in the castle?"

"He's not here at all!" Mavis exclaimed. "Gerrard, what's happened? What are you doing here?"

Rheged charged into the chamber. "Why are there fifty men from Dunborough in the yard?"

"We came here seeking Roland."

"This is Gerrard," Mavis quickly explained. *"What has happened?"* she repeated, her fear and panic growing.

"Roland left Dunborough to come here three days

ago," Gerrard said. "Yesterday we found Hephaestus four miles from here, alone, and still wearing Roland's saddle."

Suddenly light-headed, Mavis put her hand to her head. Tamsin hurried to her side and helped her to the stool to sit.

"He must have fallen. He must be hurt!" Mavis cried, looking from Gerrard to Rheged. She started to stand. "We must find him!"

Gerrard ran his hand through his hair, the gesture exactly like Roland's, his features just as grim and stern. "We have been looking, and not just for Roland. The same day Roland left Dunborough, Audrey D'Orleau was found dead in her house."

"Who the devil is Audrey D'Orleau?" Rheged asked.

Tamsin drew him aside. "A wealthy woman in Dunborough," she whispered.

"She'd been…" Gerrard began, then hesitated. "Murdered. Duncan was seen riding hell-bent away from Dunborough along the southern road just before Audrey's maidservant found her."

"Who's Duncan?" Rheged asked.

"He was Audrey's bodyguard," Gerrard said.

"Was?" Mavis gasped.

"We found him dead in the river. He'd been wounded before he went into the water, though. Either he was drowned after he'd been wounded or—"

Mavis leaped to her feet. "He attacked Roland! I'm sure of it! He hated Roland. I saw it in his face. And he took the southern road, you said."

"If Duncan attacked Roland, we'd have found Roland on the road, or near Duncan."

If Roland was dead, they would have found his body, but they had not, and Mavis took heart from that. "Roland might be wounded somewhere, too weak to ride, and we *must* keep searching."

"I've been looking for him all the way from Dunborough," Gerrard said, showing his frustration, "and we've found no sign—"

"So we search again! I have men here to help, and Rheged—"

"I'll summon men from Cwm Bron," the Welshman immediately offered. "We'll find him, Mavis. A man like that doesn't go easily to his death. However badly he's wounded, he'll not give up without a fight. There might be some byre or outbuilding, or even a cave, where he may have taken shelter."

"Good God!" Tamsin cried, her eyes shining with hopeful excitement. "The coal-burner's hut! It's a ruined cottage not far from here, in the woods. Roland may have found it and taken shelter, especially if he was hurt. Remember how it rained?"

Mavis's hopes soared. "Gerrard, you and your men rest here while I summon mine to make a search party."

"My men can rest, but I'll lead your party, my lady, if you'll tell me—"

"You lead the way, Rheged," Mavis commanded. "And I'll ride with you."

Tamsin moved to take her hand. "Do you think that's wise, Mavis, in your condition?"

"I'm a good rider," she resolutely replied. "I cannot sit and wait at home, not when Roland is lost." She sidestepped her cousin and grabbed her cloak. "Now I must summon my men," she said, hurrying to the door with Rheged right behind her.

"Mavis!" Tamsin protested, starting to follow them.

Gerrard held Tamsin back. "It's no use asking her to stay behind, my lady," he said with a wry smile, the hint of the merry gadabout in his exhausted eyes. "Your cousin is a very determined woman, or she would be no fit match for my brother, and I begin to see that they are, indeed, made and meant for each other."

It was a day Mavis never forgot, of dread and dismay and hope, too, as she rode beside Gerrard. Rheged led the search party composed of men of DeLac, including Arnhelm and Verdan, and several from Dunborough who refused to stay behind.

Rheged pulled his horse to a halt on the road in a wooded area a few miles from DeLac. "Here's the path to the hut."

Dismounting, he took hold of his horse's bridle, looped it around a tree branch and entered the woods near some thick underbrush. Gerrard also dismounted and helped Mavis down from Sweetling. The soldiers behind got off their horses and began to follow Rheged along a barely discernible path heading away from the road.

Please, God, let Roland be there! Mavis silently prayed. *Let us find him! Let him be alive!*

Surveying the surrounding brush and bare trees, Rheged halted and held up his hand. A few evergreens stood out, green against the barren browns and grays.

"What is it?" Mavis asked anxiously.

"I see it!" Rheged cried, starting forward again with long, confident strides.

Gathering up her skirts, Mavis ran after him, nearly stumbling over a root. Gerrard caught her arm to steady her, then held her hand as they hurried toward what looked more like a pile of downed limbs than a building.

"Roland!" she shouted. "Roland!"

Rheged reached the ruined building first and disappeared around the side, only to reappear just as quickly.

"He's not here," he said dully, despair in his eyes, his voice, the slump of his broad shoulders.

Gerrard muttered an oath and Mavis fought back tears for a moment before she said, "It was worth the effort. We must keep looking. He might have noticed the path and thought it led to shelter, but didn't reach it."

She would not think, let alone say, what might have prevented him from doing so.

"My brother has the eyes of a hawk," Gerrard said with renewed confidence. "He might very well have seen the path, dismounted and started along it. It's possible something startled his horse and they got separated, so Hephaestus headed for home. We'll search from here to the road, and all the way to DeLac, then back to Dunborough if need be."

"As far and as long as it takes," Rheged agreed.

With Gerrard's help, Rheged detailed the men who would search in the woods, and those who would start back to DeLac, while Mavis looked around the hut, seeking any sign of Roland.

She found none.

"Are you sure you won't rest a bit?" Gerrard asked when she joined the search party that would stay in the immediate vicinity.

"Not until we find my husband."

"But if you're with child, you should be thinking of—"

"I *am* thinking of my child, who will need a father. A fine father, like Roland."

Gerrard nodded and took her hand in his strong one. "And he will be. He was more of a father to me than my own. I've been an ungrateful lout to treat him as I have.

Mavis, I was wrong to say he married you to make me jealous. That was just my own vanity. I'm sure I'm very far from his thoughts when he's with you."

Even in her dismay, she realized how different Gerrard sounded, how remorseful and sincere. Too overwhelmed with emotion to speak, she could only squeeze his hand before they began to peruse the ground around them, moving slowly forward, searching for any sign of Roland.

Mavis spotted the broken limb of the birch a few feet from the path, the flesh of the wood looking ghostly, telling her the break was recent. Hurrying forward, she checked the ground and underbrush, until she found another recently broken branch. And then a boot.

Roland's boot—and he was wearing it, lying facedown among the bushes and fallen leaves.

"Roland!" she gasped, kneeling beside him. She saw his back rise and fall, and shouted with urgent joy, "Come quick! It's Roland and he's alive!"

"Gilbert's a very good physician," Tamsin assured Mavis as she paced outside her chamber in Castle DeLac. Nearby, Rheged leaned against the wall, while Gerrard sat on the floor of the corridor, his arms wrapped around his knees, his head bowed.

"Aye, he is," Rheged agreed. "I've seen men recover from worse. I've had worse myself and here I am."

"But his wound was so deep!" Mavis murmured, her hands clasped as if in prayer. "And he's been lying out in the rain, cold and without food or drink."

A loud groan came from inside the bedchamber and Mavis turned even more pale. Tamsin hurried to put her arm around her cousin.

Gerrard didn't move.

"That'll be the cauterizing," Rheged said matter-of-factly.

Tamsin shot him a chastising look. "Come away, Mavis, to the hall. There's nothing you can do here."

"Aye, go and have something to eat," Rheged agreed. "It won't be long now."

"I'm not leaving here until I see Roland," she replied.

At last Gerrard raised his head. "I should have found him sooner. If I had—"

The chamber door opened and the middle-aged physician appeared, wiping his hands on a piece of linen. Mavis could only stare at him, unable to breathe or think.

He smiled, and she lived again. "The worst is over, my lady. The wound is clean and bound, and your husband is sleeping. I'll come twice every day to change the dressing and see that it isn't infected. Otherwise, he needs to rest. I've given him a sleeping draught, and I'll leave more for you to give him if he's in pain."

"Oh, thank you, Gilbert, thank you!" she cried, starting past him.

He put up a forbidding hand. "He needs rest, my lady, and so do you."

"I'll rest after I've seen him," she replied. "I give you my word."

"Very well," Gilbert relented. "Only for a moment."

Gerrard rose. "I want to see him, too."

"I don't think—"

"Come," Mavis said, holding out her hand to Gerrard, unable to deny the pleading look in her brother-in-law's eyes.

Nevertheless, Gilbert appeared about to protest, until he saw Tamsin shake her head. "Very well, but remember what I said."

"I will," Gerrard replied before he followed Mavis into the chamber, which smelled of ointment and burnt flesh.

None of that mattered to Mavis as she hurried to the bed, where Roland lay, pale and still. "Oh, my love!" she whispered as she knelt down beside him and laid her head against his chest.

Gerrard said nothing. He stood looking at his brother, then turned to go.

"Stay a moment," Mavis said, lifting her head and asking the question that had been haunting her since they'd returned to the castle. "Why you? Why did you lead the search party for Roland?"

She thought, but did not say, that if Roland had died before he'd been found, Gerrard would have been the undisputed lord of Dunborough.

"He's my brother," he replied, "and we've made peace between us. And," he went on with one of his roguish grins, albeit a weak one, "I've realized I've been an ungrateful ass."

He became serious again. "I also discovered Dalfrid's been stealing from us for years, blaming me and others for losses when he's been taking the money. I found him in York and brought him back for justice. More than that, my lady, you've made me see myself as others do, and I didn't like what I saw. I owe Roland more than insolence. I want to prove to him that I can be a better man, and worthy to have an estate, however large or small."

"Then Roland has offered a portion of Dunborough to you?"

"Yes," came the answer, but not from Gerrard.

"Roland!"

His eyes were barely open, but his lips jerked up in a little smile before his eyelids closed again.

Mavis and Gerrard smiled at each other.

"Will you accept?" Mavis asked, now hoping that he would.

"I haven't yet decided," Gerrard replied. "With gifts come obligations, and I'm not sure I'm either ready for that, or deserving of such generosity."

"Your recent actions tell me that you are."

"Perhaps." He made one of his grand, sweeping bows. "Now I leave you with your husband, my lady, and look to see you in the hall for the evening meal."

Mavis smiled and nodded, although—and regardless of any admonitions of a physician—she had no intention of leaving this chamber until Roland was well enough to go with her.

Roland turned and groaned as pain snaked up his leg. Opening his eyes, he discovered he was in a chamber. It was large, like the bed, and there was light coming from candles or an oil lamp somewhere close by. How long had he been here?

He turned his head—and there was Mavis, loving, lovely Mavis, smiling down at him like the very angel of deliverance.

"Roland, my love!" she whispered as she bent down to kiss him.

"Mavis," he croaked, his throat as dry as a stone baked by the summer's sun.

She raised him up and put a metal cup to his lips. It was only water, but it was more than welcome. Beyond her, the room was in shadows, so it must be night.

"You've suffered a serious loss of blood," she explained, "but you should recover, thanks to Gilbert, the physician who tended to you, and especially Gerrard, who came searching for you. Another day and it might have been too late."

"Gerrard...came here? I thought...dreaming."

"He's still here," Mavis replied, gesturing at a corner of the room shrouded by shadow.

His brother stepped out of the darkness. He looked exhausted, as if he hadn't slept in days.

Roland struggled to sit up more, but found that made the pain in his leg worse.

"None of that!" Mavis firmly chided. "Please lie back down. You need to rest and regain your strength."

"Don't be an arrogant fool," Gerrard warned, grinning, although his eyes were grave. "One fool in the family is enough. And now that I'm sure you're going to recover, I'll go back to Dunborough to oversee it until you can return."

Mavis reached out to grasp her brother-in-law's hand. "I'm so glad things are better between you."

Roland could see that she was sincerely pleased, but he also knew her well enough to realize that something still troubled her. "What's...wrong?"

Mavis and Gerrard exchanged glances, then Mavis said, "You were wounded in a fight. Do you remember who it was with?"

The memories rushed back, like a wave crashing against the rocky shore. "Duncan. He attacked me." He frowned, remembering the gleam in the man's eyes, the hostility, the pain. "Audrey?" His gaze flew from one grim face to the other. "Is she...?"

Gerrard nodded. "Dead. We think Duncan killed her."

Roland closed his eyes and said a prayer for poor, beautiful, ambitious Audrey.

"Duncan's body was found not far from here, in the river," Gerrard continued. "We were searching for him, too. He was seen riding fast along the southern road shortly before Audrey's body was found. You met him on the road?"

"Yes, and he attacked me," Roland replied, his speech coming easier now. "He was half-crazed with guilt and trying to justify what he'd done, but he was alive when I left him."

"He must have been weak from his wounds and fell into the river trying to flee," Mavis said.

Roland sighed heavily and closed his eyes.

Mavis put her hand lightly on Gerrard's arm. "That's enough for now. We must let him rest."

Roland opened his eyes again. "Celeste," he said, looking at his brother.

"Audrey has a younger sister. She's at the convent of Saint Agatha," Gerrard explained before Mavis asked. "I've sent the priest to tell her," he said to Roland.

Roland nodded and closed his eyes again.

"Now we *must* let him sleep," Mavis insisted.

Gerrard didn't protest and she walked with him to the door. "I'm leaving for Dunborough at first light," he said before he grinned that devil-may-care grin of his. "I promise not to burn the place down, and we'll speak about Roland's offer regarding the estate when you return."

She embraced him warmly. "It's my offer, too, Gerrard. We'd both be pleased if you accepted."

"I'll remember that, my lady," he said, "and with gratitude."

"God's blood, that's tiring!" Roland said several days later as he made his way into the bedchamber at DeLac, a crutch under his arm to help support his injured leg, and Mavis under the other, although not for support.

"Perhaps you should have waited another day or two to join the household for the evening meal. It's only been a fortnight."

"Gilbert said I could, and truth be told, my lady wife, I am heartily weary of these four walls."

"And your welcome was so warm, it was surely worth it," she added with a pert little smile.

"It *was* gratifying," he agreed. "And that bread was excellent. I don't begrudge your absence to make it."

"You were sleeping, as you should."

She expected him to make some light remark about his naps, or lack thereof. Instead, he set his crutch against the wall and, with one hand on the wall for support, turned toward her with a serious expression. Then he struggled to go down on one knee.

"What are you doing?" she cried, aghast, and hurried to help him up.

He shook his head. "No, not until I've done what I must do, the reason why I set off so swiftly and without an escort from Dunborough—to beg your forgiveness for being a stubborn, pigheaded, blind and arrogant fool."

"Roland!"

"Please, Mavis, let me explain why I've acted as I have. I saw you crying the morning after our wedding and thought that despite your smiles, you'd been forced to marry me."

"That morning? When I was at the window? I was only sad to be leaving Tamsin! You should have said something!"

"I was too full of pride and vanity and, I confess, fear. I was sure you had wed me because your father wanted the alliance and you were to be the means to accomplish it. And deep in my heart, I feared no one would ever want me for myself alone. Then I comforted myself with the notion that my beautiful bride would make Gerrard jealous—so you see, he was right about that. But it was only when I thought you didn't want me that I told myself that lie. And I couldn't admit that I cared for you because I thought to do so would make me weak and vulnerable. When we got to Dunborough, I made things even worse. I selfishly considered only my own needs and my own anger. I built a wall between us, not realizing I was still letting my father and my brothers rule me and guide the course of my life. I am heartily sorry for that, Mavis, and I vow that from now on, your happiness will be my first concern. My second will be to be worthy of you. Your opinion will be the one I value above all others. I can only hope that you'll forgive my vain selfishness and stubborn pride, and give me the chance to win your love, as you have won mine."

"Oh, Roland," she said, taking hold of his hands, pulling him to his feet and into her arms. "You love me?"

"I've loved you from the first moment I saw you in your father's solar," he said softly.

"As I've loved you from the morning I saw you in my father's stable," she said, joy filling her heart as she kissed him passionately. She soon drew back and regarded him gravely, for there were things she, too, must say. "I've made mistakes, as well. I was jealous of Audrey and should have told you sooner how I felt about Gerrard, instead of bottling everything up until it burst out like a lightning bolt. I should have realized that as I hoped you would love and be loyal to me, you must love and be loyal to your brother. There are things beyond blood you've shared with Gerrard, suffering you've both endured, that's made a bond between you. I'll never try to come between the two of you again. I will do all *I* can to ensure that our children have a happy and peaceful home."

He held her close. "I'll try to be a better father than my own, although I have no other model."

"You'll be a wonderful father," she assured him, giving him another kiss. "Look how you protected Gerrard all those years, and the generous offer you've made him."

"Which he has yet to accept."

Roland moved to sit on the bed, where she joined him. "I have another offer to make to him, if you agree," he said, taking her hand and kissing it lightly. "Since you are now the heiress of DeLac, I'm thinking I should let Gerrard have Dunborough, and we could stay here. If we do, you'll be closer to your cousin, in a household you know well. Gerrard will have what he deserves, and I will have what I most want—your happiness."

He had caught her completely off guard. "You would stay here? Although Dunborough is rightfully yours?"

"Yes."

Still she couldn't quite believe him. "I thought you said you liked the cold."

"At that time, I would have said the sky was green if you'd said that it was blue," he murmured, pulling her close for another kiss.

Laughing, she gently pulled away. "As glad as I am to be in your arms again, you must do what the physician says."

"For your sake, I will obey," he gravely replied. Then

he smiled a glorious smile. "And I will be just as willing to obey any orders you have to give, now or ever."

"I don't give orders," Mavis replied, her eyes dancing. "I only give suggestions and occasionally my opinion. For instance, I suggest that you try to sleep. It's late."

"By myself?"

She tilted her head, a little smile playing about her lips. "As you are well aware, the cot I've been using is not here tonight. Gilbert said we could share a bed again, although he warned me that you should not overtax your strength. I think we both can guess what he meant by that."

"At least we can share the bed," he said. He took off his shirt and tunic, and she pulled off his boots. He grimaced when she pulled off the one from his wounded leg, then grinned when she helped him remove his breeches.

He got into the bed and patted the place beside him. Fully clothed, she lay down next to him.

"Are you planning to sleep in your clothes?"

"I think that might be best."

"Best for whom?"

"Best for the one who needs to rest. Neither of us seems able to resist temptation when we're naked."

"I give you my word that I won't touch you…although I might accidentally brush my hand against your soft and lovely breasts."

"Then I'd best keep my clothes on."

He sighed heavily. "If you wish."

"I don't wish, but it would be better," she said, nestling against him. "After all, I want you to get well quickly."

Mavis slipped her hand beneath the covers.

"What are you doing?" he gasped.

"Trying not to overtax your strength."

"If you keep doing that, I'm going to overtax us both," he warned.

She withdrew her hand.

"I'm delighted to know that you still desire me, even in my decrepit state."

"You will never be decrepit, my lord. I thought that the first time I saw you. I may become a burden, though, when I'm near my time."

"You could never be a burden, Mavis. I knew that the first time I saw you, too, as I wanted you the first time I saw you." He held her close and sighed. "I never dreamed I would ever be this happy and content."

"Nor I," she whispered.

"I love you, Mavis of Dunborough," he murmured sleepily.

"And I love you, Sir Roland of DeLac," she replied as, smiling, she put her hand upon his chest, the better to feel the steady beat of his strong and loyal heart as he drifted off to sleep.

* * * * *

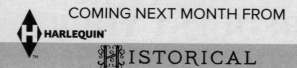

COMING NEXT MONTH FROM

HARLEQUIN®

HISTORICAL

Available January 20, 2015

SALVATION IN THE SHERIFF'S KISS
by Kelly Boyce
(Western)

Meredith Connolly is back in Salvation Falls to prove her father's innocence. But she's not prepared for Sheriff Hunter Donovan...or the way he still makes her feel!

BREAKING THE RAKE'S RULES
Rakes of the Caribbean
by Bronwyn Scott
(1830s)

Kitt Sherard will help Miss Bryn Rutherford—as long as she agrees to his no-touching policy! But trapped aboard his ship, how long can they resist breaking the rules?

THE LOST GENTLEMAN
Gentlemen of Disrepute
by Margaret McPhee
(Regency)

Captain North has sworn to leave his past behind. But everything changes when he confronts pirate Kate Medhurst. Suddenly he must break his vow in order to save the woman he loves...

TAMING HIS VIKING WOMAN
by Michelle Styles
(Viking)

Shield maiden Sayrid Avildottar meets her match in powerful sea-king Hrolf Eymundsson. He may have won her lands—and body—but can Sayrid welcome a stranger to her bed?

**YOU CAN FIND MORE INFORMATION
ON UPCOMING HARLEQUIN® TITLES,
FREE EXCERPTS AND MORE AT
WWW.HARLEQUIN.COM.**

HHCNM0115

REQUEST YOUR FREE BOOKS!

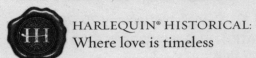

HARLEQUIN® HISTORICAL:
Where love is timeless

2 FREE NOVELS PLUS 2 FREE GIFTS!

YES! Please send me 2 FREE Harlequin® Historical novels and my 2 FREE gifts (gifts are worth about $10). After receiving them, if I don't wish to receive any more books, I can return the shipping statement marked "cancel." If I don't cancel, I will receive 6 brand-new novels every month and be billed just $5.44 per book in the U.S. or $5.74 per book in Canada. That's a savings of at least 16% off the cover price! It's quite a bargain! Shipping and handling is just 50¢ per book in the U.S. and 75¢ per book in Canada.* I understand that accepting the 2 free books and gifts places me under no obligation to buy anything. I can always return a shipment and cancel at any time. Even if I never buy another book, the two free books and gifts are mine to keep forever.

246/349 HDN F4ZY

Name	(PLEASE PRINT)	
Address		Apt. #
City	State/Prov.	Zip/Postal Code

Signature (if under 18, a parent or guardian must sign)

Mail to the **Harlequin® Reader Service:**
IN U.S.A.: P.O. Box 1867, Buffalo, NY 14240-1867
IN CANADA: P.O. Box 609, Fort Erie, Ontario L2A 5X3
Want to try two free books from another line?
Call 1-800-873-8635 or visit www.ReaderService.com.

* Terms and prices subject to change without notice. Prices do not include applicable taxes. Sales tax applicable in N.Y. Canadian residents will be charged applicable taxes. Offer not valid in Quebec. This offer is limited to one order per household. Not valid for current subscribers to Harlequin Historical books. All orders subject to credit approval. Credit or debit balances in a customer's account(s) may be offset by any other outstanding balance owed by or to the customer. Please allow 4 to 6 weeks for delivery. Offer available while quantities last.

Your Privacy—The Harlequin® Reader Service is committed to protecting your privacy. Our Privacy Policy is available online at www.ReaderService.com or upon request from the Harlequin Reader Service.

We make a portion of our mailing list available to reputable third parties that offer products we believe may interest you. If you prefer that we not exchange your name with third parties, or if you wish to clarify or modify your communication preferences, please visit us at www.ReaderService.com/consumerschoice or write to us at Harlequin Reader Service Preference Service, P.O. Box 9062, Buffalo, NY 14269. Include your complete name and address.

HH13R

The men were fast and willing to give chase. They were closing on him. Kitt spied a house with lights on. That would do. He tore through the little gate separating the house from the street and streaked through the garden. He needed to get up and in. Ah, a trellis! A balcony! Perfect.

Kitt planted his foot on the bottom rung of the trellis and climbed upward, feeling the trellis bend under the pressure of his weight at every step. He grabbed the railing of the balcony and hauled himself up, his foot kicking the trellis to the ground as a precaution just in case the men were fool enough to try. Kitt threw himself over the railing and drew a breath of relief. He lay on his back, looking up at the sky, and exhaled. It had been one hell of a day. Maybe he was getting too old for this.

He'd just got to his feet, feeling assured the would-be assassins had given up and ready to think about what to do next, when the balcony door opened. "Who's there?" A woman in a white satin dressing gown stepped outside, her mouth falling open at the sight of him.

Only quick thinking and quicker reflexes prevented a scream from erupting. Kitt grabbed the woman and pulled her to him, his mouth covering hers, swallowing her scream. He'd only meant to silence her, but God, those soft, full breasts of hers felt good against him. She was naked beneath the dressing robe, a fact every curve and plane of her pressed against him made evident.

Maybe it was the adrenaline of the day, but all he wanted to do was fall into her. His intrepid lady didn't seem to mind. She'd not shut her mouth against his invasion, her body had not tried to pull away. It was all the invitation he needed. His lips started to move, his tongue caressing the inside of her mouth, running over her teeth. Ah, his lady had a sweet tooth! She tasted of peppermints and smelled of her bath, all lemon and lavender where he breathed in her skin. She was all womanly heat against him, her tongue answering him with an exploration of its own.

Don't miss
BREAKING THE RAKE'S RULES,
available February 2015 wherever
Harlequin® Historical books and ebooks are sold.

Other books already available in the
***RAKES OF THE CARIBBEAN** miniseries:*
PLAYING THE RAKE'S GAME
CRAVING THE RAKE'S TOUCH (Undone!)

HARLEQUIN®
A *Romance* FOR EVERY MOOD™

Stay up-to-date on all your
romance-reading news with the
Harlequin Shopping Guide,
featuring bestselling authors, exciting new
miniseries, books to watch and more!

The newest issue will be delivered right to you
with our compliments! There are 4 each year.

Signing up is easy.

EMAIL

ShoppingGuide@Harlequin.ca

WRITE TO US

HARLEQUIN BOOKS
Attention: Customer Service Department
P.O. Box 9057, Buffalo, NY 14269-9057

OR PHONE

1-800-873-8635 in the United States
1-888-343-9777 in Canada

Please allow 4-6 weeks for delivery of the first issue by mail.

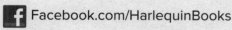
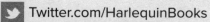

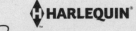